AGENT OF CHAOS

DARK FAE FBI SERIES

ALEX RIVERS

C.N. CRAWFORD

Agent of Chaos

Book 2 of the Dark Fae FBI Series.

Copyright © 2017 by C. N. Crawford and Alex Rivers.

CHAPTER 1

*T*he lone black carrion crow flew above the Thames, languidly flapping its wings. My eyes followed its flight for a few moments. Although the gray city of London spilled in front of me in every direction, it was the crow that caught my eye, its movements so calm and serene. I liked it up here in the crisp air.

On the monument's balcony to my right stood a small group of tourists, listening to a tour guide describe the Great Fire of London. His squeaky voice pierced the air as he tried hard to speak above the wind. I half-listened as he explained about the fire.

Apparently, it had begun in a bakery just below us, before incinerating most of the city and ending at the corner of Pye Lane. Therefore, it stood to reason that the true culprit was the sin of gluttony—that and Catholics. While Salem Puritans were blaming cow pox and wilting crops on witches, seventeenth-century Londoners had the Catholics and sin itself to scapegoat.

I glanced at my phone, wondering if Scarlett had sent anything, but nope. The last message I had from her was the same cryptic text that had been waiting for me when I woke up.

Guess what? Coming to London. Work related, we'll talk when I get there. Meet me at the monument to the great fire at four thirty.

She hadn't answered my replies, or tell me her flight plans. I checked the flights inbound to London, but I wasn't even sure what city she was coming from. The words "Work related, we'll talk when I get there" made no sense. Scarlett was in a covert I'd-tell-you-about-it-but-then-I'd-have-to-kill-you-and-your-cat CIA unit. Normally, she didn't tell me when or where she was flying, let alone why. Why would this time be different? And what was she doing in London?

For that matter, what was *I* doing in London? I'd managed to strike a deal with Gabriel, temporarily renting his guest room for a hundred pounds a week. Much cheaper than a hotel, and we both liked the company.

And yet obviously, I *should* be on my way back to the states. We'd concluded the investigation of the "Terrorist Ripper." In fact, I'd killed the murderer myself.

I had been shot, and had spent three days in the hospital. The trauma I'd mentioned to my chief wasn't total bullshit. That said, the doctors had been quite amazed at the speed with which I recovered once they got the bullet out. Clearly, they hadn't been used to treating pixies.

Still, I wasn't ready to go back home yet. Not until I knew more.

The tour guide shouted over the wind. "So the actual number of bodies recorded may not reflect the true number of hideously charred remains."

A little girl, four or five years old, tried to pull away from her mother's hand to get to the iron mesh surrounding the balcony, but her mother held her tight. The girl noticed me looking at her and grinned, showing a large gap between her front teeth. I smiled back, sympathizing. Never mind the carnage—no five-year-old should be subjected to a history lesson, especially not on vacation.

My phone buzzed, and I pulled it from my pocket. The caller name simply said *Russell*—the third time he'd called in two days.

Moving away from the crowd of tourists, I answered the call. "Hello?"

"Agent Liddell," the familiar gruff voice said.

"Hey, Chief."

"Don't you *hey, chief* me, agent. Why aren't you on a flight yet?"

"Still recuperating, sir. The psychological trauma was quite severe. I think I'm suffering from post—"

"You'll be suffering from unemployment if you don't get back, agent."

"Of course. Just a few more days to recover after being shot, you know? I need time to get over the mental and physical—"

"You've been *recuperating* for eight days, agent. And what's this I've heard from the London attachés about your debriefing interview?"

Oh. That.

During the several days I'd spent debriefing with the FBI's overseas office in London, I'd left out the niggling little details about the killer being a terrifying fae known as the Rix, the right hand man of the Fae High King. I'd left out the parts about how I was a pixie with power of my own, and the part about how I'd traveled to the fae realm. What remained was a story that basically didn't make sense, and unfortunately, the London attachés were smart enough to catch on. At least Gabriel was there to testify that I'd killed the Rix in self-defense, but beyond that, my account of events sounded highly suspect.

I cleared my throat. "You know it's very difficult for people to process memories accurately under severe duress. It's a well-known psychological phenomenon. Of course my story didn't link up perfectly."

"They think you're hiding something." I heard a loud gulp as he took a sip of something. "Let me revise my orders. Return to the London office, clear up your story so it makes sense, and come back to Virginia."

"Sure." I wasn't going back to the FBI offices, but at least this plan would buy me some time. Forget serial killers. They were no longer my singular, obsessive interest. I had a *lot* to learn about the fae, about how I was connected to them. "I'll head back soon."

"I want you on a flight within three days." The line went dead.

I sighed, shoving the phone back in my pocket, and crossed back to the group of tourists, looking out on the Thames again.

The tour guide wore a gleeful expression. "Before the fire, the bubonic plague had claimed half the city. The red crosses on the doors meant people inside were slowly dying of festering and bleeding lymph nodes. So, in a way, the flames were a mercy."

The tourists had gone a bit pale, and the mother covered her little girl's ears as the guide went on to describe the plague doctors in their terrifying, bird-like masks. Surely there was a Disney version of this story he could spin.

As I thought of London's dark and disturbing history—the shadow city, connected to our own—my thoughts turned to Roan. I felt a tiny spark of rage when he entered my mind. He'd manipulated me, had stalked me for years, used me like a pawn for his own personal goals. On the other hand, he'd also saved my life. But I couldn't trust him—not until I knew more.

I glanced at the time. Quarter to five. I'd give it to five, and then I'd find a pub. Scarlett had my phone number—

"*Pink*? Seriously, Cass? Two weeks without me and you dye your hair pink?" the familiar soft voice said behind me.

I turned around, grinning at the sight of her. Scarlett. Sunlight blazed through her auburn hair, and her mouth twisted in mock horror. Still, I could see the amusement twinkling in her green eyes. She was stylishly dressed in leather leggings, a cute black jacket, and a white blouse she'd borrowed from me months ago and never returned.

"Hey," I said, and to my surprise, my voice broke. Tears rising, I rushed to her, hugging her tight, burying my face in her hair as I blinked away the tears. I hadn't realized how much I missed having a familiar, friendly face around me. All the people I had met here, even Gabriel, were still strangers. I couldn't open up to them completely. With Scarlett here, I felt as if I'd regained a piece of myself.

"Hey Cass," she whispered in my ear, hugging me tight.

We held each other for a few seconds, and then she pulled away, and scanned me from top to bottom.

"Well, okay," she said. "Frankly, it looks good on you. Though I don't know what your boss would say. Who's ever heard of an FBI agent with pink hair?"

"I'll dye it before I fly back," I said. I wasn't sure if that would do any good. Roan had changed it with magic. Could peroxide get rid of pink glamour?

Scarlett walked over to the metal grid, threading her fingers through the holes. She stared at the city in awe, and I gave her a moment. Scarlett had a thing for London—especially its ancient history.

"How long are you here for?" I asked.

"I don't know. Until things get sorted out."

"Right." I didn't ask what things. We never asked each other about work.

ALEX RIVERS & C.N. CRAWFORD

She shrugged. "I was hoping you could help us with it."

I blinked in surprise. "Help you? The CIA? How could I—"

She turned to me, lowering her voice to a whisper. "We were hoping for some inter-agency cooperation, Cass. I got cleared to talk to you about it." She nodded at the tourists. "Not here, of course. Somewhere safe."

"But... cooperation about what?"

She looked at me intently. "Trinovantum."

My expression instantly went blank by reflex, revealing nothing. Hearing Scarlett utter the name of the fae city was practically the weirdest thing to happen in weeks. My skin prickled. Scarlett's eyes narrowed, and I knew she could see she had struck a nerve.

"Not here," she said quickly. "We'll go to the embassy. We have—"

A boom interrupted her sentence. A tourist shrieked, pointing. In the distance, a thick cloud of dark smoke billowed into the air, and just beneath it, the flicker of orange and yellow flames.

"An explosion," I breathed.

"Shit," Scarlett muttered. "Oh, shit shit shit. We're too late."

Another boom ripped through the air, and my heart clenched. A towering, glass-fronted building not far from us shuddered, and a cloud of smoke curled from within. Tall, bright flames licked the building's windows.

"The number of the beast," Scarlett muttered. "The idiots had it wrong. It was never about the monument. It was about the fucking fire itself."

"What are you talking about?" I asked.

Boom. Smoke rose from another building, just up the hill. Even closer.

"The Great Fire of London," Scarlett said. "They're

6

repeating it, except with bombs. And the path seems to be in reverse."

"Who's repeating it?"

Her green eyes glinted with rage. "Who do you think? It's *them*, Cassandra."

I swallowed hard. "If the explosions are going in reverse…"

A large explosion thundered, close enough for us to feel the blast and the heat. Screams rose around us as it became clear we were not safe up here in our tower. Frantically, the tourists began shoving each other to get to the stairs. My pulse raced, but I'd have to wait, or we'd all trample each other to death in the narrow stairs.

Boom. The windows and walls blew out of the lower story of a concrete building just below us—the underground station. People in the street scrambled away in panic, screams rending the air. Cars screeched, and the road erupted into a frenzied dance of its own.

"Look," Scarlett said, her voice surprisingly steady.

I instinctively noticed what drew her attention. Two figures strolled from the flaming building—not running like the rest, but moving at a calm pace. Our culprits.

"We have to get to them," she said.

"We're too far. We—"

"Move!" she shouted, racing for the stairs. She thundered down the spiraling steps at a shocking speed, pushing through the crowd at the bottom. I ran after her as best I could, my breath ragged in my throat. When we got to the monument's base, I raced out into the street, just catching sight of those two figures moving up Fish Hill Street, walking past the smoking underground station. Already Scarlett was taking after them on foot, but I had another method of transportation.

My heart thundering, I rummaged in my purse and pulled out one of my many brand new compact mirrors.

I popped it open, then gazed into it, staring at my own blue eyes, my pink hair catching in the wind. I let the reflection becoming part of me, bonding with it, feeling it slide over my body like a second skin. My fae senses searched for another reflection down on the street. *There*. A shop's window, reflecting the running, screaming throng, and the two figures slowly ambling amidst it all. Was it my imagination, or was one of them half the size of the other?

I let the reflections merge, and passed through, feeling the cold magic wash over me. Dizzy, I stumbled onto the street, the heat of flames blazing behind me.

CHAPTER 2

*F*ear.

The emotion vibrated in the air around me, and pulsed through my gut like a bass drum. My body surged with power, making my skin tingle, my heart thrum, my senses sharpen. Fae fed off human feelings, and each of us was tuned to a specific emotion. Some could draw power from rage, others from lust, or happiness.

And my drug was fear. Or, in Roan's charming words, I was a *terror leech*.

Right now, the crowd's terror pulsed through my blood, igniting my powers. With this rush of fear, I felt I could run a thousand miles, or lift a car in the air.

My vision sharpened and I scanned the crowds, searching for two people moving slower than the rest. It took about twenty seconds before I spotted them, strolling through the crowd.

A tall, dark-haired woman and a blond boy. Who would suspect them?

I focused hard on them, trying to see their true forms. For just a moment, their bodies flickered. A pair of fiery wings shimmered on the boy's back, and the woman's feet transformed into strong, brown hooves. Fae, of course.

For a second, I almost dashed after them, pumped up on the hysteria that reverberated between my ribs.

I managed to stop myself in time. My own feelings were far from calm right now. I was a pixie, a half fae. The two full-blooded terrorist fae would easily sense my emotions as soon as I got anywhere near them. Even in this chaos, my pixie emotions would resonate through the air like an alarm. A woman and a child seemed harmless, but I'd learned to ignore appearances. That kid could be a creature from my worst nightmares, for all I knew.

Instead, I needed to follow them from afar, see where they were going, and form a plan. The least I could do was postpone any conflict until we were somewhere less populated. Tucking my head down, I matched my pace to theirs and followed them from a distance of a few dozen yards. I'd bolt after them as soon as they ran.

At the top of the hill, they turned right, disappearing from my view. It took all my self-control not to sprint after them. Instead, I hastened my pace just a bit.

Already, police constables were storming the streets, many of them crouching to help the injured, to bind wounds and staunch the bleeding. When I reached the street corner, I searched frantically through the crowd. Chaos reigned here in the center of the city. Black smoke curled into the sky and sirens blared, nearly drowning out the screaming. Panicking crowds jostled me as they ran from burning buildings. Using my heightened senses, I could still focus on the strange couple as they crossed the street—the only people in London who moved with the casual stride of two humans out for a walk on the beach. I loosed a slow breath, relieved that I hadn't lost them. Still matching their pace, I moved across the street after them, weaving between the panicking crowds.

My phone buzzed, and Scarlett's name shone on the screen. I flicked it open.

"Where are you?" Tension tightened her voice.

I glanced at the street sign. "Eastcheap Street. I'm following them. They're approaching Philpot Lane."

"Don't let them out of your sight." She sounded out of breath. "I'm on my way."

"Right." My gaze was locked on them as they turned left. "They just turned onto Philpot Lane."

"Don't lose them!" she panted into the phone.

"I won't," I snapped. Like she was the only one who knew how to track a perpetrator.

I bit my lip as I turned onto the narrow road. Perhaps I was getting a little *too* close to them if I didn't want to give my game away. I glanced at one of the shop windows, mentally merging with the reflection. The glass morphed to my will, showing a different image on Philpot Lane: The woman and the child walked calmly, their faces now visible. The child smiled, talking excitedly. Anger darkened the woman's eyes, and she didn't answer his prattling.

My pulse raced, and I held my phone to my ear. "I still see them."

Billowing smoke clouded the air, and a fire truck flew by me, sirens blaring. Through the phone, the same siren whined. Scarlett was close.

"Don't engage them yet," Scarlett said. "We'll do it together."

I didn't like the sound of that. I was half-fae and pumped up by terror, but Scarlett was just a human. A trained CIA operative, but still. She'd be no match for the fae. "Scarlett, listen, these two... they're dangerous."

11

"So am I." The line went dead. It was only a few moments before I caught her sprinting across the street. She came to an abrupt stop by my side, breathing heavily. "Where are they?"

I pointed far down the street. "Woman and the little boy."

She squinted. "You're kidding."

"No, that's definitely them."

"Okay. Let's get them. Stay quiet."

Before I could protest, the two fae turned a corner, and Scarlett immediately broke into a sprint.

I followed, easily matching her pace. For a human, she moved shockingly fast. And yet, with all the terror igniting my veins, I was still holding back. "I think you should let me handle this alone."

"What are you talking about?"

I didn't exactly have an explanation for her. I wasn't going to tell her I was a pixie. Not yet. "Never mind."

My heart hammered against my ribs as we ran. Whatever happened, I would keep Scarlett safe. When we rounded the corner, she halted abruptly. Only a few people lingered on this narrow, winding road, and none of them were our culprits.

"Damn it!"

"There!" I pointed further down the road. "Maybe they turned onto the next street. Lime Street."

Scarlett didn't say a word, just sprinted again, nearly knocking over a fleeing businessman. I followed until we took a sharp right.

This time, we found no one on the cramped street except the fae. And they were close—too close. The woman paused, her fingers twitching, head cocked. She glanced back at us, then raced away like a speeding car, her hoofed feet galloping over the pavement. The child's flaming wings fluttered and he rose into the air, soaring away from us.

Immediately, Scarlett and I broke into a sprint, and now I

was certain she was more than just a CIA officer. Her body was a blur of motion beside mine, her crimson hair trailing behind her. We moved like hurricane winds, but the two fae were just as fast, racing for an enormous Victorian hall. The ornate stone sign above the arched entrance read *Leadenhall Market*. Inside, fire raged through the faint shops, and smoke bloomed into the air, black as a cauldron. Soot blackened the remaining windows, and shattered glass littered the ground.

The fae didn't stop, plunging into the smoky hall. As we sprinted after them, I resolved to get Scarlett out of there alive. Nothing else mattered.

Inside the hall, toxic smoke scratched at my throat, burning my eyes. A coughing fit racked my body. I kept running, but I could no longer see Scarlett in the haze. My eyes teared up. Where the hell was she?

A primal scream echoed in the passage. Through the black smoke, the fae child swooped at me, wings blazing in the haze. Quickly, I ducked, staring at the child's dark eyes, his mouth twisted in a horrifying grin. When I rose again, I caught sight of the trail of flames left by his wings. He swooped again, clawing at my face with twisted talons. Pain seared my forehead where he ripped my skin.

I reached into my handbag and pulled out an iron knife— not an ordinary knife. This one burned with malice and anger, yearning for violence. A fragment of the Rix's soul lay trapped in the blade, and it whispered in my skull. When I held the cursed thing, its voice sang in my bones, demanding *blood, blood, blood.*

The fae boy swooped up into the air, then turned mid-flight, plummeting at me, a flurry of burning, screaming rage. I slammed the fae blade up in his direction, striking him between his ribs. He jerked back, shrieking in pain and fear, then fell to the ground, his head smacking on the pavement.

ALEX RIVERS & C.N. CRAWFORD

Yes, the blade hissed in my mind. *More.*

As I stared down at him, a dark smile curled my lips, and battle fury rippled over my skin, making my legs tremble with wrath. The boy was my *enemy*. Enemies deserved no mercy—only pain and death.

Gripping the knife, I stared at the fae child, my lip curling. His dark eyes blazed with terror.

The fae were extraordinarily strong, hard to kill. But iron could kill them easily, poisoning their body, corrupting their magic. All fae feared iron, and this one was no different. Panicking, he scrambled up, then fled. *Chase him*, the knife hummed. *Kill him.*

My body jerked after the flying fae, but I stopped myself. I hadn't come here to murder fae children. Maybe I shouldn't be listening to the evil knife.

I gritted my teeth, thinking of Scarlett, and shoved the toxic thing into the handbag. Still, it screamed in my mind, *Pixie whore!*

The smoke thickened, and the heat of the inferno raged around me. Sweat trickled down my forehead.

"Scarlett!" I shouted, my voice hoarse as the smoke ravaged my throat.

I took three steps before a window shattered just before me, and a burst of flames exploded into the avenue. My heart skipped a beat, and I jumped back, the searing flames too much to bare. Hell itself seemed to blaze all around me. When I glanced behind me, my world tilted. Flames encircled me, blocking every possible escape route.

I stumbled, pulling out one of my compact mirrors. I blinked, trying to see through the smoke. I linked with the reflection, watching it shimmer. From within it, I searched for another reflection, an image of Scarlett. For a moment, I saw nothing but the smoke, until at last a mane of auburn hair appeared. Scarlett was flattening herself against the corner in an archway, a gun in hand. How did *she* get to have a gun in the UK?

The hoofed woman stealthily moved behind Scarlett, her approach masked by the shriek of sirens. She grinned, revealing a row of brown teeth, like rotten fence posts. Just as she lifted a curved blade, a plume of smoke blocked my view.

I let the reflection's gravitational pull draw me in, and I leaped through the reflection, the mirror slipping over my body like liquid mercury. Ignoring the dizziness, I leapt out of a window across from Scarlett, screaming, "Scarlett, behind you!"

The woman swung the knife in a perfect arc. Instead of turning around, Scarlett simply rolled forward, and the blade whistled above her head. It crashed into the nearby window, shattering it to pieces.

Scarlett leapt onto her feet, raising her gun at the fae. She blasted out two deafening shots, leaving behind a high-pitched whine in my ear. The woman jolted back as one of the shots hit her, and she screamed in pain. Her eyes blazed with licks of golden flame, mirroring the inferno.

Scarlett shot again, but the woman dodged. Scarlett let off another shot, missing her again, and the woman bounded forward, slapping the gun out of Scarlett's hand. In a blur of movement, she punched Scarlett in the stomach. Scarlett folded over, gasping, and molten rage burned through my veins.

Okay. Time to get out my psychopathic knife.

I pulled the blade from my bag, and it hissed in satisfaction as it felt my fury. Just as she was raising her deadly hoof above Scarlett's head, I flung it at the woman. The blade found its mark in her side, and as she roared in pain, the knife screamed in my mind for *more, more, more!*

Her flickering eyes snapped wide open, and she fumbled

with the iron knife. She pulled it from her side, then let it fall to the ground. With a final, angry stare, she galloped away.

"After her," Scarlett gasped, thrusting her gun at me. "My gun has… iron bullets, take it. Don't let her get away. Go!"

I hesitated, looking around. Not far from us, another window shattered. I could hardly breathe, and blood trickled from Scarlett's lips. She'd been hurt, bad.

Instead, I crouched down, grabbing her around her waist. "We have to get out of here."

As I helped her to stand, she groaned. "You stupid, sentimental asshole," she muttered, leaning into me. "I'm not important. We needed to grab her."

"You might not be important, but I loaned you that white shirt months ago." I blinked the smoke from my eyes, pulling her along as fast as I could. This place could collapse at any moment. "It's covered in blood and dirt. Last time I lend you anything, Scarlett."

As I pulled her along, she let out a pained laugh. "Sorry." As we neared the exit, she stopped, coughing into the crook of her elbow. "Wait."

"Scarlett!" I shouted. "We need to go."

She yanked her arm from mine and opened her jacket, pulling a small, metallic gadget from her pocket. She limped toward the raging flames that licked the side of the halls.

Idiot. "Scarlett! Fire is bad. Let's go."

"These flames aren't natural." She held her gadget at the fire. "They might have a magical imprint."

The smoke seared my lungs. "A what?"

"We'll talk about this later. Hang on."

She waved the silvery gadget in front of the flames until it emitted a high-pitched beep. Then, she shoved it back in her pocket, tears streaming down her face. "Now we can go."

At last, we stepped out of the inferno into the cooler air, and sirens whined through the streets of London. Through the smoke, I could see armed police with shields rushing along the main road.

Scarlett looked at me askance. "How did you find me in there?"

I swallowed hard. Given the speed at which she'd run, I was almost starting to think Scarlett could be fae, too. At least, maybe I *hoped* she was like me, but I wasn't sure I was ready to delve into this yet.

"Just luck," I said.

"Right." She coughed into her arm. "You should get back to your headquarters, Cass. And I have to get back to the London Station. We both have a billion hours of debriefing ahead of us."

"You want me to debrief the FBI attachés about..." I waved my hand at the building, unwilling to say the word *fae* in front of her. "About what just happened."

"Of course. Get back to your unit, wherever it is. Mine is in the embassy, and yours is... well, it should be in the embassy with the rest of the FBI overseas office, but if that type of unit existed there, I'd know about it. Obviously, you all hoped to remain hidden from the CIA. As if, Cass."

I frowned, my eyes tearing in the smoke. The FBI attachés already thought I was crazy. I wasn't about to run back into their offices and start spewing stories about a child with flaming wings and a woman with hooves. "I'm not part of a..." I cleared my throat, still unsure where Scarlett stood on any of this. "Special unit. I'm just a profiler."

"Right. Of course. Well, I'm sure you have someone to report to. We'll connect again tomorrow." She turned, disappearing into the smoke.

CHAPTER 3

*A*fter a nearly-sleepless night in Gabriel's guest room, I spent the morning obsessively reading the newspapers. The headlines were doing their best to stoke the panic in the city, and at least one paper claimed to have identified the culprits—two human men. Of course the paper didn't say "human;" most people take *that* for granted. They'd been photographed carrying bags while having dark skin, so the evidence was damning.

In the past twelve hours, nationalistic fury had shifted from simmering to incendiary. According to a columnist for *The Sun*, refugees should be greeted with gunships instead of rescue boats. She described them as "cockroaches," and said Britain needed to rid itself of this scourge.

Wonderful. This wouldn't end poorly at all.

Around noon, Scarlett texted me, asking me to meet her at the US embassy late that afternoon. Before leaving Gabriel's to head east, I slipped into a black dress and a pair of comfortable flats. The underground was still shut down, and the streets blocked from traffic. That meant a hell of a long walk through the city.

After almost an hour and a half of walking, I found Scarlett standing outside the embassy, looking nearly as exhausted as I felt. Her eyes were bloodshot, and her auburn hair lay in a tangled mess over her leather jacket—the same clothing she'd been wearing the day before.

Sucking on an oversized coffee, she led me through the various checkpoints to the lower levels. She seemed to have completely shaken off her injuries. The embassy buzzed with frantic activity, and people streamed from room to room. As we walked, I glanced around me furtively, hoping to not run into any of those attachés I'd been avoiding. Scarlett led the way to a small elevator. Once the doors closed behind us, she quickly entered a five-digit code on the keypad, and we began descending slowly.

After the elevator ride to the bowels of the building, I followed Scarlett down a bleak, gray-walled hallway, our heels clacking over the marble floor.

Scarlett rubbed her eyes. "How long did you have to spend debriefing? I swear I had to describe the goddamn hooves four hundred times. They were relentless. *Were they like cow hooves? Horse hooves? Goat hooves?* Like I'm a fucking farm animal expert. I don't know. They were just hooves."

I took a deep breath. Okay. So she'd definitely seen the hooves. How much did she know? "I didn't participate in a debriefing. The FBI doesn't know about the… the hooves." The only interview I'd done had been with Gabriel, who'd been relentless in his questioning about what exactly I'd seen, and how I'd used the knife.

She shot me an irritated look. "Sure, Cass." She took a sip of her coffee. "I probably wouldn't have slept last night anyway. You know what the body count is now? Seventy-three, not to mention the hundreds of people who had their arms and legs blown off. Not feeling great about life today."

I knew her well enough to know she felt guilty about this.

"It's not your fault, Scarlett. You got here as soon as you could, and you didn't have enough information to stop it. Neither did MI5, or Scotland Yard, or the FBI. No one was able to stop it."

"I know," she mumbled, clearly unconvinced.

A lump rose in my throat. I felt more determined than ever to stick it out here in London, to help stop this from happening again. Neither the fae nor terrorist attacks were my area of expertise, but I'd do what I could. "Now we have more information. Maybe the next time, our terrorists will try to recreate another historic disaster. Bubonic plague or something. We'll be more prepared next time."

"True. There was Boudicca's burning of Londinium, several plagues, Bloody Mary's purges... They have a lot to choose from."

At the end of the marble hall, we neared a set of steel doors, and I glanced at my friend. "So, what exactly are we walking into here?"

"The CIA's London branch has two units. One is assigned to the UK humans. The other... well." She shot me a meaningful look. "I think you know what it's assigned to."

I raised my eyebrows, my mind churning. Scarlett had seen the hooves. She had a gun with iron bullets and a wand-like scanner that read magical imprints. She had said the word *Trinovantum* earlier, and seemed to know about the fae. The winged child and hoofed woman with fence-post teeth hadn't fazed her.

I had a general idea of what was going on here. Scarlett's unit was in charge of the fae. Maybe Scarlett was fae herself, given her super-human abilities. Beyond that, I had no clue, and yet I still felt the need to play along. "Right. Of course."

Scarlett pressed her hand to a fingerprint scanner. The doors opened, revealing a white-walled rectangular hall. A bulky blond man walking by stopped dead in his tracks, eyeing me in suspicion.

"Hi, Tim," said Scarlett.

"Who's this?" Tim frowned, his knee jerking. He seemed like he'd imbibed about five coffees too many.

"She's with me," she said. "We have clearance."

Tim glared at me for a minute before nodding. "Okay."

Scarlett led me through a stark marble hall, our footsteps echoing off the ceiling. When she reached a black door, she opened it, motioning for me to enter. As Scarlett closed the door behind me, I stepped in, surveying the space. A white table stood over a rich blue carpet. On one wall hung a map of London, and another sketched map hung on the opposite wall. I crossed to the rough map, staring at it in amazement. I recognized the locations—the palace, the Hawkwood forest, the river that flowed from west to east, mirroring London's own Thames.

"Obviously, you know what that is," said Scarlett.

"Trinovantum," I said quietly.

Scarlett pulled out a chair, taking a seat. "What do you know about it?"

I sat next to her, not entirely ready to answer her questions. In lieu of wine, perhaps a glass of water would be a good start for this discussion. I poured myself a glass, my hand shaking slightly, droplets of water spattering the table.

"Okay, I'll start," Scarlett said. "My unit is in charge of all Seelie and Unseelie operations on the globe—obviously, that's mostly the UK and Ireland. We had reason to believe that the fae were planning an attack on London, but we just didn't know where or what. In an effort to stop the attacks, I've been authorized to negotiate an inter-agency cooperation with your unit." She raked her hand through her auburn hair. "Unfortunately, we were a little late on the Great Fire attack."

"My unit," I repeated. "I'm guessing you don't mean the Behavioral Analysis Unit."

She arched a quizzical eyebrow. "No. Your real unit. Whatever it is you call it. The Federal Unit for Counter-fae Knowledge? Probably not. Unfortunate acronym. What do you call it?"

"The FBI doesn't know about any of this."

"Mmm-hmm." Scarlett tapped her fingertips on the table. "A week ago we received an interesting tip-off. An American case officer apparently killed the Rix, the second-hand man of the Unseelie king. At first we thought it was one of our guys. You know how it is with the CIA—it's hard to keep track of all the operations, especially since almost no one tells anyone anything. Then it turned out that the fae-killer was a federal agent. Agent Cassandra Liddell from the FBI. And I was like, no way. I *know* her. That is a chick who threw birthday parties for her cat until she was twenty-three, and played A Tribe Called Quest in our dorm room nonstop until I wanted to break her laptop. Apparently, she's in a counter-fae FBI unit I never knew existed, and she killed the Rix. Badass."

"Right. But there is no counter-fae unit."

"Listen, Cass, I'm not saying you have to spill everything right now. You have to get clearance. I get that. You feds like your paperwork. Submit form 607/A, *working with the CIA on magic shit*, in triplicates. But just do whatever you need to do, because there's some major stuff going on, and seventy-three people already died. So we need to quit fucking around and get some work done."

"Scarlett." My mind was screaming, trying to keep up. I needed to be cautious with my next question. "How is it that you're able to run as fast as you are?"

Her brow furrowed. "Same as you."

I swallowed hard. *She's a pixie?*

"The CIA has acquired from the fae some capabilities to enhance its operatives," she continued. "Just like the FBI did with you. I saw how fast you could move, too. This is why you're not going to convince me that your unit doesn't exist."

I nodded. Okay. I'd be keeping this particular secret a while longer. "And what do you mean about the Seelie and Unseelie?"

She shook her head. "I honestly don't get why you feds had to bungle into something you know so little about. Okay, let me give you a crash course on this stuff, because we really need to know what you guys do." She took a deep breath. "The fae have two courts, Seelie and Unseelie. Our own folklore actually has a lot of documentation about that. The standard interpretation is that the Seelie court are the faeries of light and sunshine, sparkly-twinkle-shit. And the Unseelie court is like a giant torture dungeon of darkness and murder. But that's just an overly simplistic binary classification, obviously, probably a result of some Seelie propaganda."

Well, I was certainly achieving my goal of learning more about the fae. "And the truth about the Seelie and the Unseelie?"

Scarlett's green eyes sparked fiercely. "The truth is, they're all threats. The only difference is that the Seelie don't have tails and horns, and they're slightly smaller. They look more like very pretty humans. But they're not cute, Cass. They're deadly."

I nodded, trying to take it all in. Roan had horns, so he was definitely Unseelie. What was I? "Surely not all fae are threats. That's just... prejudiced. What if I know—"

"Listen, Cass," she said in a low voice, leaning closer to me. "I don't think this room is bugged, but frankly, I wouldn't be surprised. There might be a bug in the pitcher, in the carpet, in my cleavage... who knows? When in doubt, bug it. That's our motto. Not really—that would suck as a motto. The point is, people here like to *listen*. So before you tell me anything that might get you locked up in isolation, let's just clear up the fact that the only fae you ever met is the Rix, and you killed him, right?" She arched a cautionary eyebrow, widening her eyes meaningfully.

I knew my friend enough to follow her lead. Sticking up for the fae would not make me popular around here. "Of course. Just the Rix, who is dead."

She let out a long breath. "Good."

And yet—what about me? I was half-fae, and I wasn't a monster. Surely no one was born monstrous—not even the fae. Monsters were created, not born. "But I was simply under the impression that not all fae are... evil."

She shrugged. "Let's not worry about evil. Let me put it in CIA terms. We deal with threats. And the fae are, and always will be, a threat to humans. They are stronger than us, have powers we can't predict, and they treat us like slaves. Did you know they feed on our feelings?"

I bristled. I didn't like where she was going with this since, you know, I fed on feelings too. "I'm familiar with the idea."

"And you know what happens when a fae unveils, right?"

Okay, she had me there. "Unveils? No. I have no idea."

She groaned. "Part of our collaboration will be to make a nice dictionary of terms so we're all on the same page. What the CIA call *unveiling* is when a fae loses control. Their glamour is broken, temperature fluctuates around them, and they unveil their true faces. Their bestial side comes out, and they become very violent or crazed with lust or whatever. That fae with the hooves had unveiled."

Roan's image burned in the back of my mind. Whenever he was angry, everything around him became colder, and his eyes turned a deep gold. His horns shimmered into view. And then he usually tore people's hearts out and flung them around like ragdolls. "Okay, I know what you're talking about."

"Good. So forget evil. The fae are dangerous, and we're in charge of ensuring they don't kill us all, okay?"

I swallowed. What would Scarlett say if she knew I was a pixie? Obviously, I couldn't say anything about that *here*, but could I reveal it to her at all? She'd been my best friend since freshman year at college, and we shared almost everything— apart from the details of her work, until now. I wanted to think that if I came out of the pixie closet, it would give her a different impression of the fae, but there was no way I could do it here. Plus, she seemed so damn certain of herself, that all fae were some kind of threat to humanity.

"Okay. Scarlett, I'll tell you guys what I know, but I'm not part of an FBI fae unit, okay? I just stumbled into that stuff by accident."

"Of course you're not." She leaned closer, touching my knee, and whispering. "Why would the FBI hide anything, right? You people are all about transparency, we know that." She leaned back again, frowning. "But if you *were* in such a unit, I would have wanted you to talk to your supervisors and get clearance to talk about it, because all this cloak and dagger stuff is getting us nowhere, and people are going to die."

Irritation flared. "There's no unit, Scarlett!"

"Right." She looked just as pissed off as I felt. "We need to help each other, Cassandra. Because I'm not sure if you noticed, but a lot of people got hurt in those attacks. So do whatever fucking paperwork you need to do to help me stop the next attack."

I heaved a sigh. She was right. We needed to work together, even if I couldn't tell her the complete truth. "Here's what happened. You remember the Resurrected Ripper case? I came here to profile him and help the London police, and it turned out that he wasn't an ordinary psychopath. He was a fae psychopath. Things got kind of intense, and another detective and I managed to take him down. He tried to foment discord in the city by allowing Londoners to think immigrants had committed the crimes, and I'm guessing the hysteria helped fuel his power. Yesterday's attacks probably serve the same purpose. I've seen two tabloids blaming immigrants for the explosions, and one blaming Muslims specifically. The explosions aren't the only threat. London is going to be a tinderbox of panic and scapegoating. More discord, more terror, more power for the fae." It wasn't the whole story, of course. At some point, I'd need to tell her about Trinovantum, but I wasn't ready to say that in front of the CIA bugs.

Scarlett leaned back in her chair, folding her arms, and I suddenly felt like I was being interrogated. "And you just happened to have an iron knife with you? These things are hard to come by."

"My detective friend got it for me. And a Glock with iron bullets. We had to learn fast. I didn't have all the CIA intel about fae."

"Okay. And what about the reports that you disappeared into thin air while the police were interrogating you? What's that about?"

I shifted uncomfortably in my chair. How did I explain that? "They would say that, wouldn't they? Better than admitting how incompetent they were."

Her piercing green eyes locked on me. "Like I said. We need to know the whole story, Cass. Before this blows up to hell."

Maybe the FBI secret unit was a convenient ruse. Unless I told her the truth, there was clearly no other explanation for the things I'd been able to do.

I took a sip of water. "What is this major stuff you were talking about? Is that related to today's attack?"

She downed the last of her coffee. "Our source informed us that we could expect a major Unseelie terrorist attack this week. Our analyst thought it would be in a few days, but he was wrong. We had nothing to go on but that it had to do with the number of the beast."

I blinked. "Six-six-six?"

"Right. Our analysts figured that it was most likely related to the Great Fire of London, which happened in 1666. We just had no idea what they had planned, or that it would happen so soon. It never occurred to us they might actually reenact the London fire. We didn't think they'd do something so... big."

"Why not?"

"The fae are usually not that organized. They don't draw attention to themselves. They normally lurk in shadows, terrorizing a few people on street corners here and there. We really can't explain this new pattern, except that it probably has to do with the Rix, and it definitely has to do with an impending war."

"A war? With humans?"

"No. A war between the Seelie and the Unseelie." Scarlett turned to stare at me. "You ever wonder why I know so much about plague pits? Whenever a fae war breaks out, millions of humans die. That's what's coming for us, Cass."

* * *

SCARLETT LED me down another hall, to a thick iron door. She put her eye to a retinal scanner, and after a second, the door clicked open. We entered a large, white room. Computers lined one wall, and a rack of assault rifles lined another. Three rows of rectangular black tables stood in the center of the room, their surfaces covered with gadgets—digital watches, tablets, phones, and some esoteric contraptions like Scarlett's magic scanner. Behind one of the tables stood a gray-haired, bespectacled man, about to sneeze. After a few seconds, when the sneeze didn't come, I realized that was just the way his face looked.

"Cass," Scarlett said. "This is the guy in charge of our research and development here. His name," she said, gesturing at him dramatically, "is Q."

He sniffed. "My name is Howard." He offered his hand, and I shook it.

I smiled. "Nice to meet you."

"Q," said Scarlett. "Cass here is temporarily joining the good fight, but she isn't really armed for it. She's the agent I told you about with the FBI. You know how they are. Never quite prepared."

"I have a knife," I said defensively.

They both stared at me.

"An iron knife," I clarified.

Scarlett arched an eyebrow. "She needs a gun."

"I have a Glock," I said. "Except I don't have any bullets for it—"

Howard pulled off his glasses, chewing on one end. "If it's a regular Glock, it's also not intended for iron bullets. I assume it's... unpredictable."

"Yeah, it was for close range only."

"Our guns are designed for iron bullets Agent, uh...?"

"Liddell. Just call me Cassandra. Only Scarlett calls me Cass."

"And only Scarlett calls me Q," he murmured, walking over to the gun rack. "It would be nice if she could use people's actual names."

Scarlett leaned on one of the tables. "Q, Cass and I go way back."

Howard returned holding a small handgun and two clips that he carefully slid across the table. "There you go. Already loaded, and each clip has an additional twelve bullets."

"Thanks." I snatched them up and tucked them into my handbag.

Scarlett took a deep breath. "She also needs a magic scanner and a fae detector."

Howard stared at her with an air of hurt pride. "Do you mean an aether sensor and a personal ambience indicator?"

"That depends." Scarlett cocked her hip. "Does the aether sensor scan for magic? Because that's actually what we need."

"It—it..." he stammered. "It identifies imprints of aether within remnants of what you call 'magic.'"

"Right. And the personal ambience indicator... is that the one that detects fae?"

"It reacts when a person gives away a certain wavelength that corresponds with these beings."

"Awesome, Q." She gave him a thumbs-up. "So like I said, Cass needs a magic scanner and a fae detector."

He tutted and inspected the table, pushing his glasses up on his nose as he searched the gadgets. After a moment, he plucked a wand-like scanner just like the one Scarlett had used earlier, and he handed it to me. "It's quite easy to use. You press the red button, and just slide it along the aether remnant... the magic residue. The indicator lights green if it's there."

"Okay." I took the scanner from him, finding it quite light in my palm.

"Once you scan the imprint, you can return here and cross-reference it with our database. Each aether imprint is unique, like a DNA sample or a fingerprint. And we have the names of hundreds of Seelie and Unseelie in the database, so we might have a match. It'll also give us some basic attributes of the scanned imprint, like strength, deterioration, angle from source, temperature…" He probably noticed my eyes glaze, because he stopped listing the attributes.

"Cool, thanks." I traced my fingertips over the scanner.

"As for the personal ambience indicator…" he continued.

Scarlett mouthed *fae detector*.

"I have one left." He rummaged in a drawer below the table. "Ah! There we go."

He handed me something that looked like a silver wristwatch, identical to Scarlett's.

Howard held it up, pointing to a white light on the watch's face. "This indicator will start pulsing in the presence of a fae entity. It will also glow in faint green. Hold out your hand."

Shit. My pulse raced. "There's no need. I'll be with Scarlett most of the time, and I don't like watches."

Howard frowned. "It's really quite comfortable."

I swallowed hard. "I get a skin reaction from metal. A rash. It's very unpleasant."

Scarlett's fae detector didn't warn her against me, probably because my pixie wavelength confused it. But I really didn't want to find out what happened if one touched my skin.

"Just try it." Howard grabbed my hand, then pressed the watch against my skin.

The watch immediately began to judder and glow with a red light.

Howard's forehead creased. "Oh."

Scarlett wrinkled her nose. "What the fuck is wrong with it? It's not supposed to go red."

"No, of course not." Howard pulled it away from me. "Red indicates an error."

Scarlett rubbed her forehead. "The new guy did it, right? Igor?"

"His name is Jeremy. Yes, but I assure you he's quite capable…"

"Capable, my ass! Speaking of asses, did you know I once overheard his theory on women? Apparently, he divides all females into two categories: those who take it up the bum, and those who don't. He's permanently looking out for indicators of how to best classify individual women. Wearing a thong means they're probably good to go, but yoga pants and ponytails are bad signs. So you know, I don't really trust Igor with complex concepts. Or like, making coffee. Or really anything."

Howard frowned. "I suppose, but I assure you, Igor —*Jeremy* is—"

"If Igor can concentrate on his work for a few hours instead of searching for thongs, he might redeem himself with me. Tell him that by tomorrow, I want Cass to have a functioning fae detector."

Howard nodded, and Scarlett smiled, slapping him on the back. "Thanks, Q. You're the best. If there's anything I can do for you—"

"You can call me Howard."

"If there's anything except that, don't hesitate to ask."

CHAPTER 4

hen we left the US embassy two hours later, clouds hid the sun. As we walked, I glanced at the numerous "closed" signs that hung from the cafés and restaurants. After the scale of yesterday's attack, businesses remained shut. We could have eaten at the embassy, but I didn't want to risk running into any FBI agents there.

Specks of ash from yesterday's attacks still floated through the air, mingling with the dull light. Even a day after the attacks, tension still rippled through the city. It was no longer the thrilling panic that sent power blazing through my body, but a vibrant worry that set my teeth on edge and made me jump at every small noise.

"Relax, Cass," said Scarlett. "We'll find them." She dropped her voice to a whisper. "I have some reliable informants. I just need to establish contact when I can."

I rubbed my eyes. "When did our lives get so complicated? It doesn't feel like that long ago we were downing Jell-O shots at costume parties."

"I think we decided we needed more out of life the night that New Jersey guy with the permanent sweatpants boner tried to make out with both of us, then threw up on my shoes."

"That was definitely some kind of low point."

"Hello. My name is Darryl," she said, imitating his New Jersey accent. "Are you girls together? I see you together and I think, maybe they're together. I don't know. Maybe you'd like to get together in my basement without your shirts on and I could photograph you. For art. You know?"

I cracked a smile. Whenever I felt down, it was like Scarlett had a compulsion to make me smile, and her imitations were spot on.

Even so, underneath it all, I knew her mood was somber. When she was stressed, her speech sped up, and she toyed with the ends of her hair, like she was doing now. A line appeared between her eyebrows as the cogs turned in the back of her mind. She hated to let on that she was under pressure, but when the stress got to her, I knew she'd be staying up late and waking through the night with night terrors. Her dietary choices would regress by decades: an ungodly combination of cocktails, comfort foods, and candy. "The holy fucking trinity," she called it.

She was just one of those people who had a hard time turning off her thoughts. She felt permanently compelled to prove herself, as if she could never quite work hard enough or achieve enough.

"How long will you be stationed in London?" I asked, hopeful.

"I might be here for a while, Cass. We're trying to locate portals into... well, you know. But we're preparing for something big."

"Right." It was a measure of how much she trusted me that she was willing to tell me any of this, no matter how vague. "I'm thinking of staying for a while, too."

"Have you been assigned?"

"Not exactly. But maybe we can spend some more time together. We can't work all the time. We need to eat, too."

"No shit." Scarlett's stomach rumbled audibly. "I'm starving."

"Everything's closed," I said. "But I'm sure we'll find something if we keep walking east. We've only been walking for… forty-five minutes."

Scarlett looked down her watch, inspecting the light. "Dammit. Mine is blinking red now too. Fucking Igor."

My throat tightened. *Or maybe it's my pixie magic screwing with your equipment.* "When you said all fae are threats…"

"Shhh."

I leaned closer to her, whispering, "What about half-fae? Like, pixies?"

"Yes," she said quietly. "They're also fae. Therefore, they are threats. They feed off emotions too."

"But what if—"

"Shhh!" She shot me an irritated look, and yet I couldn't quite let it go.

"I'm just saying. Maybe you should expand the way you think. Maybe you can make alliances with friendly ones."

"There are no friendly ones. This is a dead end."

My pulse raced, and I could feel my face flushing. I should just let the topic go, but this was important to me. I *had* to convince Scarlett that not all fae were dangerous, but I couldn't simply tell her about myself. She knew my history. And that meant she'd know that my fae father had murdered my human mother. It wouldn't exactly refute her theories. Once I told her what I was, she'd be wondering how long it would be until I snapped, too.

My heart raced. "You know my theory about evil. I've made my career off this. People aren't born evil. It's created through environmental factors. Neglect, abuse. Head injuries. A combination. It's not something in people's blood."

"I know it's important to you. But you're talking about humans. I'm not. You can't apply your human psychology to… the thing we're talking about."

Her closed-minded attitude was starting to piss me off. But if I couldn't use myself as an example, maybe I could slowly introduce her to some normal, harmless fae. Or at least, as normal as the fae ever got. First, I'd let her get to know them a little. Only after she saw them as nonthreatening would I reveal the truth.

When I looked around the streets, I realized we weren't far from Leroy's. Perfect. We could get food there, and maybe I could slowly introduce her to some of the less lethal fae. "Scarlett, if a fae is glamoured, you don't have the ability to see through the glamour, right?"

"No, we haven't developed that level of enhancement yet. Q is working on it." She glanced behind her. "And that's the last thing I'm going to say in public."

In the embassy, I couldn't talk freely because the CIA operatives might be listening. And now on the streets, we couldn't talk because everyone else might be listening. Classic CIA paranoia.

"Let's talk about your ex," said Scarlett. "The Virginia Stallion. Is he still banging three chicks on the regular?"

I grimaced. "Probably, but I'm not one of them."

"You were always too good for him. The next guy you date needs my approval. A full interview. I may or may not use electrodes."

I guess I wouldn't be telling her about my little make-out session with the muscular fae warrior in his remote cabin. "Fair enough. You get to approve next time. Scarlett, I think I have an idea where we can get some food. An old wine bar not far from here."

"You think it will be open?"

"I'm pretty sure. It's just over here, in Smithfield." We took a right onto a narrow, medieval-looking road.

Scarlett pointed at the sign: *Cock Lane.* "I know this one. Do you know what happened here?"

"I'm gonna guess medieval prostitution."

She nodded. "Yes, but that's not all. Apparently, a ghost haunted the street in the eighteenth century. The Cock Lane ghost, who accused a man of murder. The whole city flew into a panic. Mob rage. Chaos. The whole nine. Ghosts aren't real, of course. So who do you think was behind that?"

"The—"

"Don't say it out loud. But you get my point, right? Those creatures feed off fear." She rubbed her stomach. "And right now, I really want to feed off food. My stomach is rumbling like a tractor."

"We're almost there. The place is called Leroy's." *And the owner is probably fae. As well as most of the patrons.*

She smiled. "Lead the way!"

We moved toward Guildhall, its ivory walls lending it the appearance of a palace of bone, spindly towers looming over the square like ribs. I shivered, thinking of the crimson interior where kings and queens had interrogated the broken bodies of heretics and traitors. A few rays of sunlight pierced the clouds, glinting off the bony spires. Something about this neighborhood made my skin grow cold, but I led Scarlett forward anyway.

Deep in the hollows of my mind, a river rushed over stones, and screams reverberated off the inside of my skull. *Heads under the water, sacrifices to the gods...*

I blinked, trying to clear my thoughts. I had to prove to Scarlett that not all fae were evil, even if I wasn't entirely sure of it myself.

* * *

I DESCENDED the rickety stairs to Leroy's, with my best friend —the professional fae-hater—in tow. My heart pounded hard. I knew I could be making the worst mistake in a long time, but I *needed* to convince Scarlett that not all fae were harmful. Some of them just served you really good drinks.

As I took the final step and surveyed the room, my pulse raced. I hoped to hell Scarlett couldn't see all the weird shit going on in here. From the main room, dark tunnels branched off like spokes from a wheel, and fae lingered in each one, hunched over glasses of wine.

Candlelight and shadows danced over the central chamber. Everyone in the place looked bizarre, at least to me. An angular man sat in a corner, his skin snow-white and his black hair cascading down to his hips. He was playing bone dice with a small, dark woman, every inch of her arms tattooed with runes.

Sitting at a round table near the bar, three nearly identical women whispered to each other, their hair braided with seashells and flowers, silver-flecked eyes glinting wickedly.

In an alcove beneath a cluster of guttering candles sat a bearded man smoking a pipe. Purple smoke pooled around him on the floor, clouding his feet.

And as always, if I moved my head just right, I could penetrate further through their glamour. Whiskers on the man with the pipe, spiked teeth on the raven-haired fellow, the tattooed woman glowing with iridescent light. And the three seashell ladies wore clothing that shimmered, translucent, nothing underneath. Clearly, they were exiles from the court of Trinovantum, where women's bodies were supposed to be covered up. I liked them already.

"This place is awesome." Scarlett took in the atmosphere, apparently oblivious to the magic. "How did you find it?"

"I just happened upon it."

"I love it. How…" She frowned. "What's that smell?"

An acrid scent reached my nostrils—like plastic burning.

Scarlett raised her hand, staring at her watch. The surface had gone completely dark, and a small plume of smoke rose from the face. No wonder. It must have overloaded.

I shook my head. "Fucking Igor."

"I'm going to kill him," she muttered. "These things are expensive." She took it off and thrust it into her bag.

I pointed to the empty chairs at the bar. Leroy was nowhere to be seen. "Shall we sit over there?"

As we moved closer to the bar, I half-feared Scarlett would suddenly pull out her gun, but she seemed completely oblivious to the strange figures surrounding us. As a pixie, I could see beyond the fae glamour, but Scarlett couldn't.

We took two seats at the empty bar, scanning over the menus. As I debated between a cheese plate and lamb, someone pulled out a chair to my right.

Alvin plopped into a chair, grinning at me. Just as I'd expected. His skinny form always haunted the place like a stoned ghost, his scraggly blond hair hanging in his face. He wore a T-shirt that read *What Happens in Area 51 Stays in Area 51*, with a cartoon drawing of an alien.

"Why, hello," he said.

Scarlett raised an eyebrow. "Friend of yours?"

"He happens to be a lovely young man." *Even if he's a fae.*

Alvin smiled at me. "Glad to see you made it out of all that terrorist shit alive. I thought you'd be okay. You're tougher than you look." He jerked his chin at Scarlett. "Who's your friend?"

"Scarlett, this is Alvin," I said. "Alvin, Scarlett."

He lowered his face, looking at Scarlett from under his eyelashes. "Your hair is dope."

"Thanks, kid. I like your shirt. You gonna join us?"

Alvin leaned on his elbows. As usual, his eyes were blood-shot, and a cloud of marijuana smoke hung over him. "Are we getting dinner? I could eat a satyr's legs right now."

Scarlett frowned at the expression, but didn't say anything, "Absolutely." She leaned back in her chair. "And how do you know Cass?"

"She bought me food once or twice. She's a lovely person. Thoughtful." He nodded slowly. "Always pays her debts."

"Debts?" Scarlett asked.

"He means the bill," I cut in.

Alvin stared at me, his eyes flickering with flames. "I need to have a word with you."

"Now?"

He nodded, his eyes blazing hotter, and I instinctively glanced at Scarlett. She looked at us, her eyes wide, but said nothing. She didn't see it.

I stood. "I'll just be a minute. Can you order us dinner from Leroy? And something for Alvin."

"Sure."

Alvin led me toward one of the stone tunnels, nearly empty of patrons. He huddled by the shadowy wall, glaring at me like a disappointed teacher, suddenly looking older than he normally did.

I raised my eyebrows. "What is it, Alvin?"

"You could say I'm a little vexed." For just a moment, fear flickered in his eyes. "Why would you bring a counter-fae CIA officer into this bar?"

God damn it. Alvin, apparently, knew everything. "What makes you think she's an agent?" I bluffed.

"I don't think, man. I *know*."

The air down here felt cold and dank. "She thinks all fae are a threat. I was hoping that if she could meet some nice young gentleman such as yourself, over time, her opinion might change."

He narrowed his eyes. "And why are you so dead-set on convincing her?"

"She needs to know the truth."

He cocked his head. "It's Scarlett who needs to know the truth, is it? You wouldn't, by any chance, be dead-set on trying to convince yourself?"

I folded my arms, matching his stance. "What are you, a fucking fae psychologist?"

"You owe me a favor, remember?"

"I remember," I said quietly. Owing a favor to a fae was like giving them a blank check, and breaking a promise to a fae was a bad idea.

"The CIA has a… thing, yeah? Like a place when they write down all the fae names and what we done?"

"A database?"

He looked at me blankly. "Right. I'm in that database."

I blinked. "And what did you do?"

"That's neither here nor there. But I need you to get my name removed."

"Alvin, I'm not saying I know what you're talking about, but that's not something I can do. I'm not in the CIA. Also, it's probably treason."

"I have faith in you, man. Plus, you have to do it. You owe me." His eyes were heavy-lidded. "I'll help."

"Help?"

He shoved his hand into his pocket and pulled out a small pouch. He handed it to me. Inside was a small pendant inset with a marble-sized blue crystal. "You can use this to get people to do what you want. All you need to do is show it to your friend. Tell her to remove my name. Simple."

I gave him the pouch back. "I'm not going to compel my best friend to do something she doesn't want to do."

"Nah, it's not like that. She'll be *happy* to do it once you show her the pendant."

"That's... that's even worse! I'm not hypnotizing my friend to—"

He thrust the pendant into my bag. "You owe me, Cassandra. If I'm not deleted from that database... I'm as good as gone, innit?"

"What are you talking about?"

"Not all the fae are clueless when it comes to technology. There are fae technomancers. And they found out about the database."

I thought about it. "Fae... hackers?"

"Yeah, man. It's just a matter of time until they... I don't know what's the word. Open it."

"Crack it? Decrypt it?"

"Yeah, whatever."

"Why do you care?" I asked. "There are hundreds of fae in that database."

He scrubbed a hand over his mouth, his eyes wide with fear. "You've just got to trust me."

What was in that database that would freak him out so much? Something he didn't want other fae to know, so...

Then, it hit me. "You're the CIA source," I whispered. "You're the one who tipped them off! You told them about me, and the mark of the beast."

He clamped his hands on my shoulders, gazing into my eyes. "You have to take my name off that thing, Cassandra. You don't even want to know what they'll do to me."

He turned, disappearing into the shadows.

If Alvin was giving up the chance to eat a free meal, it was serious.

* * *

WHEN IT RAINS, it pours, and in my case, it was a fucking

deluge. When I turned back into the main chamber, my heart skipped a beat.

Where Alvin had been sitting, Roan now sat at the bar, drinking amber wine. He lifted his glass to the light, swirling the wine around to watch it, the movement oddly sensual. Hypnotic, almost. Scarlett was clearly eyeing him with interest, as would any woman with a pulse.

Roan wore a black T-shirt and jeans, his tattoos curling over his arms, which were corded with muscle. Candlelight wavered over his golden skin, gilding his hair. If I let my eyes lose focus, I could almost *see* his magic tinging the air around him. Strange and seductive, it almost stained the air around him with gold, yet there was a hint of darkness in it, midnight shadows spilling through the amber like ink through water. I could feel his power rolling over my body, prickling my skin—somehow forbidding and inviting at the same time. He looked infinitely more relaxed than the first time I'd met him here—probably because we'd successfully rescued his best friend from the prison in Trinovantum.

I swallowed hard, suddenly regretting bringing Scarlett here. I wasn't quite ready to introduce her to Roan, the dangerous fae I'd kissed in the Hawkwood Forest, lying bare on his rug, his powerful hands on my skin… For just a moment, when I thought of that kiss, my chest flushed.

Instantly, Roan's head turned to me. His gold-flecked green eyes bored into me. My mouth went dry. Of course. He could sense what I'd been feeling, which only made my cheeks burn hotter.

With a wicked grin, he raked his gaze up and down my body. I gritted my teeth, forcing myself to think of necrotic flesh. That should kill my mood.

With my excitement suitably dampened, I nodded at Roan. He replied by raising his glass to me and taking a sip.

I smoothed out my dress, then returned to my chair and pulled it out.

As I sat, I took a deep breath. "Roan. Imagine meeting you here."

"Cassandra." His eyes lingered on me for longer than normal social interactions allowed. His fingers tightened into fists, and he no longer seemed quite as relaxed. "I was pleased to learn you were unharmed."

I swallowed hard. So, he'd already checked up on me. "And when did you learn that I was unharmed?"

"As soon as I could." He glanced at Scarlett, and he nodded. "Nice to meet you."

"Likewise," Scarlett said.

"Sorry," I blustered. "I forgot to introduce you. Scarlett, this is Roan. He's... he sometimes hangs out here."

Scarlett smiled. "Cass, you seem to know everyone. I'm getting the impression that you're a bit of a barfly here."

"I'm not here that often," I protested. "I only know Alvin and Roan."

Leroy finally shuffled over to us, leaning on the bar. "What would you like to drink, Cassandra? The usual?"

"I don't have a *usual.*" I thought of the claret with its clear, fruity flavor. "But yes, that'll be great, thanks. And one for Scarlett, along with the cheese plates."

"So..." Scarlett was sipping red wine, her expression suddenly serious. "Roan, is it? That's an unusual name."

Roan sipped his wine. "It's been in my family for centuries."

I drummed my fingernails on the table. Of course it had been in Roan's family for centuries, considering he'd been alive for five of them.

Scarlett narrowed her eyes. "Is that so?"

Shit. This was a little too early for the grand fae reveal, and she was starting to become suspicious.

Roan's gaze slid to me, candlelight dancing over the perfect planes of his face. "I'd been hoping to find you."

"Oh?" I asked. Maybe I needed to stop this conversation before it got any worse. "That's interesting, but perhaps we should find another time to talk." I widened my eyes at him, trying to warn him.

He twirled the stem of his wineglass between his fingers. "You shouldn't be in... this sort of bar. It isn't safe."

I frowned. "What are you talking about?"

"You are in danger." He cut a cautious look at Scarlett. "I have heard from several people that you're being targeted."

"By whom?" Scarlett asked sharply.

He shrugged almost imperceptibly. "I can't say."

"Because you don't know?" I asked. "Or because you just really like being cryptic?"

Roan's eyes ran up and down my body, his lip slightly curled as if he were weighing me in the balance and finding me wanting. "Someone like you cannot protect yourself among the sort of people you find in here."

He was trying to warn me without explicitly saying *fae*, but he was treading awfully close. In any case, his assessment of my skills rankled. "Is that so?"

He narrowed his eyes, and I had the sense he was losing patience. "Leave here, and return to your friend's home for now. I can't afford for you to get hurt. I'm going to need your help in a few days."

"My help with what?"

His response was a widening of his eyes, a silent warning to me. He couldn't say any more in front of Scarlett.

Scarlett leaned over me. "How well do you know each other, exactly?" Her green eyes locked on him. "And what makes you think Cass is being targeted by someone?"

Roan arched an eyebrow, unperturbed by her interrogation. "I have my sources."

"Yeah? Care to share them?"

"No."

"Right." I took a deep breath. "I'm not going anywhere, but thank you for the suggestion."

"You're in danger. And you're not capable of surviving without help." Shadows flickered in his eyes, and his wineglass frosted as the room seemed to chill unnaturally. "Perhaps I shouldn't be giving you the choice."

Scarlett, I knew, was already reaching for her gun, and I was pretty sure Roan was about to unveil right in front of her.

I held up my hands, now desperate to calm this situation. "Okay, everyone relax." I met Roan's gaze. "Roan, I will speak to you another time." I gave him my *I'm not fucking around* face.

The air grew colder until my breath misted in front of my face. For just a moment, his horns flickered on his head.

Scarlett jumped to her feet, pulling her gun. "I knew he was too hot to be human." She pointed the gun directly at Roan's chest—he didn't even flinch. "There's a dozen iron bullets in this gun, you fae fuck." The playfulness had long since left her voice. "One wrong move and you're dead."

A deathly silence reigned over the bar, and everyone stared at Scarlett. The word *iron* rang in the air like a death knell. A few of the fae slipped out of the room like shadows; others closed in, their eyes gleaming.

Ignoring the gun, Roan turned to me. "There are many things you don't know, but trust me when I tell you—"

"She's not trusting a word you say, fae!" Scarlett's voice was low and controlled. "Now shut the fuck up or I—"

Roan moved faster than lightning, his hand a blur. She yelped, the gun clattering to the floor. Roan held her wrist firmly as he loomed over her. "I could have snapped your arm in two," he spoke through gritted teeth. "Because you're a friend of Cassandra—"

She swung at him with her wine glass, shattering it against his face. He roared, letting loose, and she rolled to the floor, bounding back, gun in her hand.

I could sense the turmoil in the air as the façades slipped away. Wings, horns, and tails appeared in the crowd as the fae began unveiling around her.

"Jesus," she breathed, swinging her gun left and right, trying to keep everyone at bay. "What is this?"

"Scarlett!" I commanded, my heart slamming against my ribcage. "Listen to me. Calm down, and don't shoot!"

"They're all fae!"

"They're all harmless," I shouted, far from sure. Roan definitely wasn't. "You're the only one in here threatening to kill people. Let's get out of here, and talk about this outside."

I grabbed her by her leather jacket, and dragged her to the doorway. She kept the gun trained on the fae as she backed out of the place, and up the stairs.

Before we left, I cast one last look back. Roan leaned on the bar, anger burning in his golden eyes.

CHAPTER 5

*I*n the narrow alley, Scarlett's cheeks reddened, matching her name, and she holstered her gun out of sight. Shadows from Guildhall's gothic spires crept over the ivory stone, and sunlight lit up her hair like flames. "You did not just take me to an Unseelie bar."

"I was trying to—"

She held up a hand to silence me, then yanked out her phone, pressing it to her ear. "Fulton? Hey, it's Scarlett. Listen, I have identified a location—"

Oh, hell no. I yanked the phone from her hand, and hung up the phone, shoving it into my cleavage.

Her features were etched with fury, and for a moment, I wondered if she was about to pull her gun on me. "What the fuck, Cassandra?"

I flinched. Scarlett *never* called me by my full name. "Listen, Scarlett, you're shooting from the hip. You have absolutely no idea what's going on."

"*I* have no idea what's going on?" She pointed a shaking finger at me. "You're completely naïve if you think you can be friends with the fae. Cass, if it were anyone else, I'd have brought you in by now, you know that, right?"

I took a deep breath. "I do, but it isn't anyone else. It's me, okay? You know me well enough to trust my judgment, right? I'm not an idiot."

"Of course you're not an idiot. That doesn't mean your judgment is always sound. Remember on Saint Patrick's day, when you tried to make out with the guy dressed as a leprechaun on the subway—"

"Okay! I'm not asking you to trust my judgement about mixing drinks. I'm asking you to trust me about this. At least until you get it straight." I crossed my arms. "You have some prejudiced, closed-minded attitudes. Just give me a few minutes to explain."

I had to tell her. I had to explain that I was part fae, and I just had to trust that she knew me well enough to understand I wasn't a threat.

Scarlett took a step closer, still pointing at me. "If the fae escape to tear loose in London—"

"Give me twenty minutes."

"Ten!"

"Okay!" I pulled her phone from my cleavage, handing it back to her. "But first, message that Fulton dude and tell him you made a mistake. Your guys are probably launching choppers to find you right now."

She glared at me for a minute, and I knew she resented having to admit a mistake. Scarlett was a relentless perfectionist. Still, she took the phone from me, muttering as she hammered out a text.

My mind raced as I tried to figure out what I should reveal, and what I needed to keep from her. Maybe it was a strange sense of protectiveness, but I didn't want her to know that I'd kissed Roan. Scarlett already hated him, and I had a feeling she'd go after him, trying to keep me safe. Sure, Roan was dangerous, but he'd also saved my life and helped take down the Rix.

I just needed to tell her about the whole pixie thing, and then I'd have to watch her choose between her best friend and her deepest convictions and loyalty to the human race. Simple. She'd have to trust me.

A chilly breeze rippled over the bone-colored stone of Guildhall square, toying with my pink hair. My heart raced.

I couldn't tell her about me just yet. It was too much at once. When Scarlett met my gaze again, I swallowed hard.

"Yes?" she said.

Might as well just launch into it. "Two things. The first is Roan. He helped with the investigation that led us to the Rix. He saved my life in there, in the church where we captured him. He's on our side." I took a deep breath. "I think."

Her eyes gleamed with intensity. "And the other thing?"

"I've been to Trinovantum."

She barely moved, only the wind ruffling strands of her auburn hair. "You what?" she breathed.

"I can't tell you how I got there, just that I've been there. I don't think all the Unseelie are united. There are power struggles and conflicts in there. We should use this. Make alliances and friends. Do you understand me?"

Scarlett grabbed my hand. "Where is the portal?"

"I'm not telling you that."

She dropped her grip on me. "Because you think I'll send a troop of CIA agents to infiltrate the city."

"Yes." *That, and I can't tell you about it without revealing that I'm fae.* "And I think you need a fae to get you in. Like I said, Roan helped me."

Scarlett stared at me, searching my face. "There's a lot you aren't telling me."

I folded my arms. "Okay. Specifics later. But you get the gist."

"What does your FBI unit think about your little trip to Trinovantum? Surely you haven't hidden the portal's location from them."

I clamped my hands on her shoulders, staring into her eyes. "There is no unit, Scarlett, it's just me."

Her jaw dropped. "Cass... you were serious? You just stumbled into this by chance?"

"I didn't know anything about the fae when I first came to London. There is no FBI counter-fae unit. My debriefing with the overseas FBI office basically made no sense, because I had to leave out all the magic. They now think I'm lying to them. Which, in fact, I am."

A line formed between Scarlett's eyebrows. "You killed the Rix... by accident? Do you know our guys tried to assassinate him four times? *Four* fucking times, Cass. And you found him in a church with a *knife* and just killed him?"

I frowned. "You know, I'm a very good field agent. And like I said, I had help from Roan. Are you getting my point yet? About alliances? There could be fae willing to help us against the greater threats. People like Alvin are not our targets, and if you storm Leroy's, or find the fae portal, you'll just start a war. Fae against humans. Do you know what it would look like if the fae unleashed the full force of their terror on humans, Scarlett? They'd destroy us. You need to keep doing what you always do. Be covert. Be careful. Use them as double agents. For fuck's sake, try to be subtle."

Scarlett chewed her lower lip. "Okay. I'll need to talk to my chief; these aren't calls I can make on my own." She stared into the slanted afternoon light, thinking about what I'd said. "You make a good case."

I let out a breath, but it caught in my throat as shouts

rang out from the main road, off the pedestrianized square. My pulse began to race.

"What the hell is that noise?" I began moving for the street, and Scarlett followed behind me.

As we moved closer to Gresham Street, the shouts grew louder.

"Sounds like a lot of angry people." Scarlett reached for her gun, and I shot her a cautionary look. Londoners *really* weren't used to seeing guns, especially carried by people in plainclothes.

As we turned the corner to Gresham Street, my heart skipped a beat. A small mob had formed just outside an old stone church with towering glass windows. Two men gripped improvised weapons—a piece of wood, and a strip of metal.

I pushed into the edge of the crowd, shouting, "What's going on?"

A middle-aged woman pointed at the armed men. "These two gentlemen think those are the two lads from the papers. The bag men. I don't think they are, but no one listens to me. Someone called the cops."

Two young men stood flat against the wall, clearly terrified. Apart from their skin color and age, they looked nothing like the men in the papers. The mob's excitement and fear whispered through my blood, filling me with power. Some of them were after blood. Others were scared of it, their bodies buzzing with panic.

"What makes you think it was us?" one of them shouted defiantly.

One of the vigilantes gripped his stick. "You just wait there until the police get here, and we'll let them sort this out."

Another man shouted from the crowd, "Just let them go. It's not them."

The second captive scowled. "This is bullshit, man. I'm not sticking around for this." He started to walk away, but one of the thugs shoved him back into the wall. The man retaliated with a vicious right hook. In the next moment, fists—and sticks—were flying. Half the crowd seemed to be defending the so-called "bag men," and the others were trying to attack them.

The terror ignited my power. Scarlett reached for her gun, but I gripped her arm. "No guns. When the cops arrive, they're not going to know who you are, and they might attack you."

"Fists, then," she said.

"Fine." *You use fists, and I'll use magic.*

We pushed through to the center of the crowd. From the corner of my eye, I watched Scarlett deftly disarm one of them. An elbow slammed into my back, but the crowd's fear sang in my blood, spurring me on. Shielding my head from the blows that rained around me, I looked up at the enormous church windows, feeling for a bond with their reflections. When it clicked into place, I envisioned fire raging in the hollows of my mind. Then I let the reflections erupt with flame. I created a raging inferno, the glass roaring with illusionary fire.

Then, I pointed to it. "Fire!" I shouted. "The church is going to explode!"

Screams erupted, and the crowd began to scatter. The two captives took off on foot, sprinting down Gresham street, and I took a deep breath.

In the dispersing crowd, I searched for Scarlett, but I couldn't see her vibrant auburn hair anywhere. What the hell? She'd been right next to me, hadn't she?

"Scarlett?" I shouted, crossing back toward Guildhall. The street was now completely empty. It wasn't like Scarlett to abandon me in the middle of danger like that. She was the kind of friend who would drag you to safety first, then worry about herself.

I pulled my phone out of my pocket, frantically dialing her number. But her phone didn't ring. Instead, the line simply went dead.

CHAPTER 6

It was another two hours by the time I got back to Gabriel's house, and the summer sun had already set. On the walk, I could hardly think straight, my mind churning over the question of what had happened to Scarlett. I'd spent twenty minutes searching for her around Guildhall and on Gresham Street. The cops had arrived just after everyone had fled, and I gave them a description of Scarlett. They had not been even remotely interested. I called the CIA office to report what had happened—they'd been a little more interested, at least, and gave me a number I could call if I had any more information.

I continued to try Scarlett's number, hearing only silence on the other end of the line. I didn't think Scarlett would just *leave* me there without explaining, but she obviously knew how to look after herself. Maybe she had run off to chase down someone, and didn't have time to give me all the details. And there was every chance the shitty reception was a result of yesterday's attack, and an overload of the mobile network.

I climbed the stairs to Gabriel's apartment, and slipped

the key into the lock, clicking it open. This place was almost starting to feel like home.

"Cassandra?" Gabriel's deep voice called from the living room.

"It's me." I followed his white-walled hall into his warmly lit living room. Gleaming wood floors, books stacked on oak shelves, a soft blanket neatly folded on the sofa: This place was a welcome refuge from the city's chaos. Too bad I hadn't been able to bring Scarlett with me.

Gabriel sat on one of the sofas, resting his elbows on his knees, his expression grim as he stared at the TV. The news station was playing a clip of yesterday's attacks—a stone building, with flames roaring from its windows.

"Everything okay?" he asked. The sight of him soothed my raging mind. He wore a blue T-shirt, the color striking against his dark skin and muscled arms.

I plopped down onto the sofa. "Scarlett and I ran into a bit of a lynch mob. A couple of men with sticks believed they had found the 'bag men.' And in the chaos, I lost track of Scarlett."

His brow furrowed. "Are you worried about her?"

"Kind of. I've also seen how she can fight and how she can run."

His hazel eyes met mine, then he frowned at my dress. In the chaos of the street brawl, it had torn, and dirt smudged the black fabric. "You all right?"

"Yeah. I'm fine." At this point, Gabriel knew more than anyone else about me. He knew that I was a pixie, and about Roan. He'd been there when I had killed the Rix. If there was anyone I could easily open up to, it was him.

The problem was, what I had learned today about the CIA was highly confidential. Revealing their counter-fae unit to anyone was tantamount to treason.

I decided to follow a path I'd been relying on a lot lately:

telling as much of the truth as I could, while cloaking the details I needed to hide.

"I think the fae are trying to create strife amongst the humans. If we tear ourselves apart with terror and anger, someone's gonna feed off it."

Gabriel held my gaze, and we let the unspoken thought hang in the air: *just like I do.*

He took a sip of his tea. "You said that fae feed on fear that's nearby, right? Can they feed off fear that's happening all over the city?"

"I don't know. DCI Wood—the Rix—he was definitely trying to create chaos."

A new face appeared on the TV screen—a white woman with gray hair, standing before flashing lights and a cluster of microphones. It took me a moment to recognize her as the mayor of London, Alice Jansen. Her tidy, gray bob framed her face. She wore a neat black suit and seemed composed in all the chaos.

Gabriel picked up the remote, turning up the volume to hear her speak.

"... attacking our homes and spreading fear. They seek to disrupt our life, to endanger what we hold dear, but I promise you this! This carnage is not something we will dismiss. We will find the people responsible for these... terrorist acts, and they'll learn the full force of our impact. I urge the citizens, if you know of anyone who might consort... with those who harm us, do not hesitate to report! Immediately inform the—"

Gabriel flicked off the television. "Wonderful, Mayor Jansen. Now we'll be swarmed with calls about every dark-skinned person in the city. She should be trying to calm things down and letting us do our jobs, but of course, this is wonderful for her career. She looks like she's hard line, taking action against injustices."

"People don't want to be calmed. They want someone they can blame. Anger is the perfect antidote to fear." I pulled out my phone, disappointed to find that Scarlett still hadn't returned my call.

"Yeah, you're right about that." His brow creased. "What is it? Your mind is somewhere else."

"I guess I'm pretty worried about Scarlett. She still hasn't gotten back to me."

"Phones still aren't working properly, right? And you said she knows how to look after herself."

"Yeah." I thought of her easily disarming the thug, and at Leroy's, holding more than two dozen angry fae at gunpoint. She was one of the few people in the city actually armed with a gun.

"Good. She probably went to her hotel, and you can reconnect tomorrow. Where is she staying?"

"She didn't say."

He met my gaze. "You look knackered. Get some sleep, okay? The phone network will probably get back on its feet by tomorrow morning, and you'll be able to get hold of her."

My stomach rumbled, the sound embarrassingly loud. I'd basically been walking all day, and I hadn't managed to eat anything before the shit storm had erupted in Leroy's.

Gabriel smiled. "Tell you what. Go shower, and I'll fix you something to eat, okay?"

I smiled gratefully. "Thanks. You're amazing."

I rose, making my way to the guest room. While the rest of Gabriel's flat was spotless, I had, unfortunately, transformed this room. After just a few days, I'd managed to drag it down to the state of havoc that normally surrounded me. It was doubly impressive, since I didn't have that many belongings to begin with. Somehow, all my clothing, both dirty and clean, lay scattered on the bed and the floor around it. Numerous shopping bags littered the rooms—remnants of my shopping spree a week ago, a result of my extended stay. A bra hung from the doorknob, a fact I couldn't even explain. Underneath I could still see Gabriel's own tidy style trying to break free, but the Cassandra Liddell storm of bedlam overwhelmed it all. Tomorrow. I'd clean it all up tomorrow.

I headed for the bathroom and turned on the shower just the way I liked it—hot enough to turn my skin bright pink. As steam filled the room, I stripped off my dress and underwear. I stepped into the scalding stream of water, feeling it pour over my bare skin. I shampooed my hair with apple-scented shampoo and scrubbed my body, working up a lather over my reddening skin.

Please be okay, Scarlett.

When my body could no longer take the heat, I turned off the water and stepped out, wrapping myself in a clean towel. I toweled off my hair, squeezing out the water. When I glanced at myself in the mirror, a thought struck me. Of course! Why hadn't I thought of it already? I could search for Scarlett through a reflection. I took a deep breath, feeling the reflection wash over my skin like cool water. I tried searching for Scarlett, feeling for her presence, a vision of her auburn hair.

I found nothing; just my own face staring back at me, my eyes tired, cheeks pink. It wasn't surprising, I supposed. My magic would only work if she were both nearby and in the presence of a reflection.

I stepped out of the steaming bathroom, back into the bedroom. From the pile of clothes on the bed, I grabbed a pair of black skinny jeans, pink underwear, and a striped T-shirt with a collar.

With my wet hair dampening my shirt, I joined Gabriel in his cozy kitchen. The air smelled of garlic and onions. Tears stung my eyes—possibly from the onions, but more likely at the care this man showed me.

I sat at the small table, overlooking the street. "Gabriel, you are too good to me. This smells amazing."

He scooped spaghetti onto a plate for me, then ladled the steaming tomato sauce onto the top. "Someday, you'll cook for me."

"If you're some sort of masochist, we can make that happen whenever you want."

He laid the plate before me, along with a fork and spoon. My mouth watered, and I picked up the cutlery, twirling the pasta onto my fork. One mouthful reconfirmed to me that Gabriel was a godsend: heavy on the garlic, just a hint of chili, and a ripe tomato flavor. I swallowed, practically ready to confess my love for Gabriel. Instead, I said, "Damn. You are a hell of a cook."

Gabriel smiled, flicking on the kettle for tea.

"So, I didn't ask you about your day," I said, sounding very much like a wife. I nearly added *how was it, dear*, but I bit my tongue. Gabriel's wife had died several years ago, and I doubted he would find it amusing.

He shook his head. "I went to four of the sites. We're trying to find evidence linking this attack to a specific group. The *mayor* wants names."

"Well, that would prove a bit tricky, considering the fae are the culprits."

"Honestly, I have no idea how to handle this." He dropped two teabags into mugs, and filled them with hot water. "I can't tell anyone the truth."

"How do you think you might handle it?"

After I'd killed the Rix, who had also been the Detective Chief Inspector of the City of London Police, Gabriel had been appointed temporary DCI. Now Gabriel was stuck. He had to catch the guilty party, knowing very well he couldn't.

"I don't know." He slid a cup of tea over to me, and joined me at the table. "I might have to catch some fae and 'prove' that they did it, while counting on them to stay glamoured. Which, I... uh... was hoping you could help with."

I swallowed another mouthful of pasta. "Of course I'll help." I wondered if the CIA's counter-fae unit would be interested in working with Gabriel, someone within the London police force who knew the fae existed. As soon as I found Scarlett, I'd ask her about it.

"For now," Gabriel said, "the police need to focus on preventing the public from killing each other."

"Good luck with that," I mumbled.

* * *

DARKNESS SURROUNDED ME, the gap under the bed just high enough for me to lie on my stomach. Fear raked its claws through my heart. I wasn't quite sure what had prompted me to hide under the bed in the first place, except that I'd known in my gut something terrible was about to happen in my parents' bedroom.

I could hear my mother crying, begging, her words unclear. Her fear rippled through the walls, sharpening my senses, both energizing and horrifying me at the same time. My father was yelling, rage lacing his voice. I'd never heard him so furious before, and the panic nearly stole my breath. Somehow, my own fear was coursing through me like a drug.

And then a sharp noise: my mother's scream. "Horace, don't!"

Then, a sound I'll never forget. People don't scream when their lungs are punctured. They wheeze, and gurgle.

I whimpered under the bed. I couldn't scream either. Or move, really. Fear paralyzed me, my mind trying to piece together what my father had done to my mother. I sobbed and closed my eyes, waiting for my mother to come get me, waiting for those comforting arms to envelop me.

They never did.

It must have been an hour later when I heard that gruff voice, and a stranger's face appeared under the bed.

"There's a girl here!" he called back, and then said to me, "Don't be scared, come out. You're safe now."

I crawled from under the bed, trembling, and rose on shaky legs.

He looked at me over the rims of his glasses, and I tried to focus on his blue eyes. "What's your name?"

"Cassandra," I stammered. "I heard everything. What happened? I wasn't sure if I should come out... Is my mom okay?"

"We'll get to that in a second. Cassandra, how old are you?"

"Thirteen."

"Okay, Cassandra, we're going to walk out, so I want you to take my hand... and I want you to close your eyes, okay? Just until we get out and talk for a bit."

With all the fear burning through my system, my senses were on overdrive, but I did as I was told. This man seemed like he was in control, and I needed someone to be in charge right now.

I closed my eyes, letting him lead the way. But in the hall next to my room, a strange metallic smell—copper, maybe—wafted from behind my parents' bedroom door. The scent was uncanny, like an ancient memory, resurfacing. Something that had once fueled me, thrilled me...

The scent overpowered me, and I *had* to know what it was. I broke away from the cop, opening the door to my parents' room. When I did, it took me a moment to register what I was looking at. The maroon stain on the floor, the red covering the bedsheets. My mother, her eyes open, but vacant. I could have sworn she was staring at me, blaming me.

It was my fault. I wasn't a little girl; I was thirteen. I should have crawled from under the bed and stopped my father from doing this… And why had my mother's fear rushed through me like that? There was something *wrong* with me.

The cop yanked me from the room, but when I turned, two new figures had appeared with the cop: Roan and Gabriel. The three of them towered over me.

Roan turned to the cop. "Is that her?"

"That's her." The cop's lip curled with disgust. "She didn't even try to help."

"A coward," Gabriel said.

"And corrupt," Roan said darkly. "She's a terror leech. I bet she enjoyed her mother's fear."

I tried to say I didn't enjoy it. I wanted to scream that I was sorry, but the sound that came out of my mouth was neither words nor a scream. It was that horrible noise; the one I'd never forget.

A wheeze, and a gurgle.

I sat up in bed, clutching the sheets, tears streaming down my face. As my eyes adjusted to the dark, I recognized I was in Gabriel's guest room. The bedclothes had twisted off me, and I'd knocked the pillow to the floor. I licked my lips, a bitter taste in my mouth.

The door burst open and Gabriel barged in, his gun in hand, wearing nothing but boxer briefs and a white T-shirt.

He scanned the room quickly. "Are you okay? I heard you scream."

"Yeah, sorry." My voice croaked. "Just a nightmare."

Lowering the gun, he frowned at me, then quickly looked away. I was wearing nothing but a skimpy tank top, my lower half bare, apart from my underwear. I pulled the sheets over my legs.

Once I'd covered myself, he said, "You're shaking."

I let out a small, forced laugh. "It was a particularly bad dream. I get them every once in a while."

He nodded. "Me too."

"Yeah? What do you dream about?" I didn't want him to leave.

"My wife," he said. "The day she… died."

"Oh." Somehow, I wasn't surprised. "When was it?"

He crossed into the room, hesitated for a moment, then took a seat on the edge of the bed. "Two years ago."

"What happened?"

He looked at me, and I saw understanding in his eyes. "We were walking down the street. She wanted to buy me a birthday present." His voice sounded hollow. "A shirt. I was always so picky about the shirts I wear… still am. So it took much longer than it should have. And maybe I didn't want that morning to end. Just a nice, simple morning with my wife, away from work. It was a sunny day.

"And then, in the fourth shop, a man approached us… and for a moment there was this strange look in his eyes. He pulled a knife and plunged it into her stomach. So fast—you wouldn't believe how fast. He was muttering to himself, but it was complete gibberish, like a made-up language." A shaft of moonlight from the window illuminated half of his face in silver light.

My throat tightened. So this was why Gabriel had been ready to believe in the fae.

"He looked at me, and his eyes flickered," Gabriel continued. "For a second, they were red, and empty. And then they flickered back. He let go of the knife, and ran out of the store. I was too busy trying to help my wife… I never even tried to stop him."

A lump had risen in my throat, and I swallowed hard. "Did they catch him?"

"They found his body in an alley, not far away. His head

was a pulp of bone and blood. He'd bashed his own head over and over into a wall. At least, that's the official conclusion."

"You don't believe that?"

He shrugged. "I don't know."

"And your wife?"

"She died right there in the store. Blood loss. The killer had ripped right through her organs…" His voice broke, and he let the sentence trail off.

A heavy silence fell over the room, and I let out a shuddering breath. "When I dream, it's always about my mother's death. My parents' deaths, really. It was a murder-suicide. My father killed my mother, and then killed himself. I was in the next room when it happened, bravely hiding under the bed. I didn't do anything to help. I didn't even call the cops." A tear rolled down my cheek. "In my nightmares, there's always someone there to accuse me. And you know, with the fear…"

At this point, my thoughts became incoherent, and I stopped. I couldn't tell Gabriel how fear was a drug to me— even as my mother had been murdered. *That* was more than even Gabriel could handle.

"How old were you?" he asked softly.

"Thirteen."

He wiped a tear off my cheek. "You were just a child."

"If I'd just gotten to the phone and picked it up, or if I'd gone into the room…"

"You were thirteen," Gabriel said. "You were just a girl."

I sniffed. "Yeah." He didn't understand. I *could* have stopped it. I knew I could have. My father had always had a soft spot for me, even near the end, when he'd begun to behave erratically. And yet, I'd just hidden under the bed and let it happen.

Still, Gabriel's soothing presence made me feel better. He was sitting so close I could see the stubble on his chin, and he

ALEX RIVERS & C.N. CRAWFORD

smelled amazing. His sad eyes drew me in. What would he do if I crawled into his lap and started to kiss him, felt his heart beat under my hand?

"That's a hell of a nightmare, Cassandra."

"I always see my mom, dead at the end. I always hear her death rattle."

"In my dreams, I manage to move fast and save her." He looked out the window. "The nightmare starts when I wake up."

CHAPTER 7

*I*n the morning, I stood before the bathroom sink, brushing my teeth. I'd dressed casually in black jeans and a sky-blue T-shirt. Milky morning light streamed in from the bathroom mirror, illuminating my pink hair.

And yet, something felt amiss, and the hair rose on the back of my neck. I spat into the sink and rinsed off my brush. When I looked at myself in the mirror again, I realized what the problem was.

I couldn't feel the reflection.

Unease crept over my heart as I searched for the reflection, trying to connect to it. Nothing. What had happened to my magic?

I rushed into the bedroom, where a full-sized mirror hung on the wall. I could easily feel its reflection.

Okay, so there was something wrong with the bathroom mirror. I returned to it. This time, to my relief, I could sense it again. Maybe it was a magical hiccup. I grabbed for my makeup bag and smoothed tinted moisturizer over my skin, then a hint of glossy blush. As I stood before the mirror, the reflection's presence disappeared again.

Frowning, I touched the glass, trying to figure out what was wrong. To my horror, pain pulsed through my fingertips as I touched it. I pulled my hand away quickly, staring.

The reflection flickered, but I wasn't the one doing it.

The mirror grew darker as I watched, starting at the top left corner and spreading like pooling ink. It was reflecting a different, dark room—bare walls, almost no light. When the center of the other reflection shimmered into visibility, my breath caught in my throat.

Scarlett sat in the dimly lit room. She'd been tied to a chair, her arms pulled behind her back, a rag taped in her mouth. A red gash marked her forehead, and a purple bruise darkened one of her eyes. Crimson stained her shirt. I tried reaching into the reflection, but I had no control over it. It wasn't mine to command. I couldn't leap through it, either.

Rage blazed through my bones, and I had an overwhelming desire to hurt whoever was doing this.

As quickly as it had come, the image disappeared. I stared at my own horrified face for just a moment, until maroon blotches appeared at the top of the mirror, slowly forming letters. Words, written in blood, stained the mirror, forming faster now, smeared and thick, as if they had been drawn with a finger. Finally, an entire message lay scrawled on the glass.

> *Lucy Locket lost her pocket*
> *Dear old Grendel found it.*
> *Winchester Geese kept it safe,*
> *Tied a ribbon 'round it.*
>
> *At one o'clock, at Sheerness Dock,*
> *Dear Lucy must arrive*
> *Fail to get her there on time,*
> *And Scarlett burns alive.*

At the message, dread tightened its bony fingers around my heart, and I scrambled to try to find Scarlett again, to connect with the reflection. Nothing.

A moment later, a small parchment materialized, slipping thorough the reflection, right onto the counter by the sink. I held my breath, waiting to see if something else would happen. I could feel the reflection again, but when I tried to search for Scarlett, I felt nothing. Whoever had abducted Scarlett could perform reflection magic—that much was clear.

I grabbed the parchment. One side was blank, while runes covered the other. I dropped it back on the counter, not sure what to do with it.

Two blood-streaked words trickled down the mirror: *burns alive.* I suppressed a shudder. I wanted to scream, to smash the mirror. I wanted to storm out of the house and find my friend, to eviscerate the person who'd taken her, but I had no idea where to start. How was I supposed to make sense of that message?

I gripped the edge of the sink, forcing myself to slow my breathing until I could think clearly. The abductor had been watching me through the mirror. That's why I hadn't felt the reflection—it had been in someone else's control. He knew who I was, though not necessarily *where* I was. To find someone with reflection magic, you only needed the person's image in your mind.

The message scrawled across Gabriel's mirror was a ransom letter. Scarlett had been beaten—either to get information from her, or to deliver a message for me. As a CIA officer, she'd be trained to resist torture, but everyone had a breaking point.

Unless...

What if it wasn't real?

I'd created fabricated reflections in mirrors—just yesterday, in fact, at the church. As adrenaline blazed through my veins, I ran to the bedroom and stared at the mirror, searching. I stared at my pale face, my body shaking, but I couldn't link to Scarlett.

Either she was too far for my abilities to locate, or the fae who'd captured her had covered up the reflections to sever the line.

Trembling, I ran to my phone and dialed the number the CIA officer had given me. After three rings, a man answered.

"This is Fulton."

"Hi." A hot tear rolled down my cheek. "This is Special Agent Cassandra Liddell. I was given this number—"

"Yes, Agent. Your phone isn't secure, so please keep it simple."

I tried to keep my voice steady, but the tears were streaming now. I *knew* something was wrong, that it hadn't just been an illusion. "Did anyone manage to locate Scarlett?"

A moment of silence. "No."

I gripped the phone tighter, pressing it to my ear. "Are you sure?" I asked, frantic. "She might be in her hotel or—"

"She is currently unavailable."

"I might have some information about her whereabouts." I wiped another tear from my cheek. "But I'll need your help."

Fulton took a deep breath. "Come to the embassy." The line went dead.

I shoved the phone in my pocket.

Scarlett meant the world to me, and that was exactly what the abductor wanted. Complete and utter leverage, to control me through fear. He wanted me to immediately jump and act on his demands. And yet, I had to put those feelings aside, think of it as a professional. If I had been called to assist on this kidnapping case, what would I have done?

Slowly, I exhaled. First, I'd demand proof of life. I had just seen Scarlett, but I couldn't be certain it had been reality and not an illusion. If wanted to demand something, I first needed to establish a line of communication. In this case, I had the mirror, and since I couldn't bond with it, the abductor was probably still watching me.

I rushed into the bedroom, flinging clothes around until I found my bag. Frantically, I rummaged around it until I found a pen and an old receipt. Bending over the bed, I scribbled a short note: *I need proof that Scarlett is alive. What is her favorite food?*

Then, I hurried back into the bathroom, thrusting it at the mirror, a bead of sweat trickling down my temple. I tried to maintain a fixed, cold posture as I held it up, tried to calm the shaking in my hands. If the abductor saw terror etched over my features, he'd consider it a victory. I had to show him I was in control.

Stony-faced, I held it up as a minute went by. Then another.

Was he watching me? I was sure he was. Watching, searching for weakness. Control, it was all about control.

Another minute. Maybe he didn't really have her, or perhaps he wasn't into two-way communication. He'd be communicating on his terms only.

After five minutes, I slowly lowered the paper. The CIA might be able to help establish a line of communication, and maybe they could trace—

Shit!

My heart thrumming, I dashed back to my handbag, rifling through it until I found the magic scanner. Racing back to the bathroom, I pointed the wand at the mirror.

Nothing.

If there had been remnants of magic there, they had dispersed. Damn it! The CIA could have used that information.

I gritted my teeth. Whatever the message meant, the time limit was quite clear. Scarlett's seconds were ticking away, and if I failed, she would burn.

* * *

GABRIEL STOOD BEHIND ME, frowning at the bloodied mirror. I had filled him in quickly, dragging him to the bathroom to look at the note.

"Any idea?" I asked. "We have to take someone named Lucy to Sheerness Dock?"

He took a deep breath. "Some of it's familiar. Not sure what it all means together."

My pulse was racing. "Give me what you have."

"Hang on." He had pulled out his phone. "To start with, Sheerness Dock is nowhere bloody near here. It's in Kent. And not the close part of Kent."

"How far is the drive?"

"Looks like an hour and a half, assuming there's no traffic."

"Wonderful."

I checked my phone for the time—just before nine. "Okay, well, we have time. I just don't know who Lucy is. Is it just me or does Lucy Locket not sound like a real name?"

"It's an old nursery rhyme, and this is a variation on it. After the first line, it all changes. She was a prostitute, or a courtesan or something. The pocket... I don't know, but I always just assumed that was her..." He cleared his throat. "You know, her pocket."

I stared at him. "Okay."

"There's another link to prostitutes there. The Winchester Geese. Medieval prostitutes, licensed to operate by London's Bishop of Winchester. Called the geese because they beckoned men to their rooms with long, white gloves."

74

This made no sense. "Scarlett isn't a prostitute, so I don't get the connection. I don't understand how this all adds up."

Gabriel's eyebrows drew together. "What are the chances that the Rix and this new person both independently communicate through bloody nursery rhymes? That it's just a coincidence?"

I shook my head. "Maybe that's how the fae speak to each other. I don't understand the whole prostitute thing, though."

"What did you tell me about the attitude towards women in Trinovantum?"

My pulse was cracking out of control. "They have some very old-fashioned views about women's virtue."

He nodded slowly. "Maybe whoever is doing this is suggesting that you're morally corrupt or something."

"So they're coming after me for some reason." I took a shuddering breath, no longer able to convince myself this had all been a ruse. "And we need to get a Lucy Locket to Kent by one, or, supposedly, they'll burn Scarlett alive."

Gabriel raked his fingers through his hair. "It's an eighteenth-century rhyme. If Lucy had ever been real, she'd be dead by now."

"Fae live for centuries. She's probably a fae, and we just have to find her. Maybe she's a sex fae, like Roan. Where were the Winchester Geese? Did they have a particular brothel?"

"Southwark."

"Do you have any specifics?"

"Winchester Palace had connection to the Winchester Geese. The palace ruins are still there. That's all I have to go on."

I wrung my hands together. "Okay." Whenever I walked in the ancient parts of the city, I felt a surge of energy. "I've been getting the feeling that fae like to stick around all these old buildings. Maybe Lucy Locket hangs out by

Winchester Palace. We just need to find her, and get her to Kent."

Gabriel picked up the parchment. "What's this?"

I'd almost forgotten about it. "It came through the mirror."

Gabriel carefully examined both sides.

I pulled it from his grasp. "I don't suppose you know what it says?"

"Nope."

"Maybe this is something we need to give to Lucy so that she'll come with us."

"Maybe." Gabriel scrubbed a hand over his mouth. "I have a question for you. Is this person targeting Scarlett just to get to you? Or could it be about Scarlett?"

I swallowed hard. "Scarlett's CIA unit handles fae activity. I found that out yesterday. It's highly confidential; that's why I didn't tell you earlier."

He stared at me. "Okay."

"Before I head to Winchester Palace, I'm meeting one of the CIA officers in the embassy. Maybe they'll have a better clue than we do about what the hell this parchment means, and the nursery rhyme. They could bring in the big guns, maybe locate Scarlett with their gadgets. They have analysts that can work on the message, and translate the writing on this paper, and all sorts of devices that can—"

"Okay, I get it. They're the best," Gabriel said.

I took a picture of the bloodied mirror with my phone to show the CIA. "I'll go talk to them, while you go sniff around those ruins and see what you can find. Maybe Lucy is lurking nearby…"

"But we've got very little time. Don't you think it's better if we go looking for this Lucy together?"

"The CIA can probably get us a chartered helicopter to fly us to Kent."

"Good point.

"I'll join you in Southwark once I'm done."

"I'll drop you off at the tube station, and I'll drive to Southwark. We'll have the car there to drive to Kent in case we can't get a helicopter on time." He arched an eyebrow. "Did you say Roan was a *sex fae*?"

I cleared my throat. "It's not important."

"Right." He shook his head, as if trying to clear the image. "Anyway, if we don't get ourselves a helicopter, we've got two and a half hours to find Lucy."

"If you find Lucy before I get there, don't let her out of your sight." I yanked my bag off the floor and pulled out the gun with the iron bullets, handing it to him. "If she tries something, use this."

He took the gun from me carefully and checked it. Satisfied, he looked at me. "Cassandra. We're going to get Scarlett back."

"Sure," I said without conviction. "See you there."

CHAPTER 8

*A*fter a quick underground ride, I strode through the grassy Grosvenor Square toward the embassy. My thoughts churned in my mind. Hadn't Roan said I was in danger? So how, exactly, did he know? I was being targeted, and he'd predicted it. If only five-hundred-year-old fae warriors carried cell phones, I might be able to clear this up.

When I got closer, I took out my phone and looked at it. Quarter to ten. I called Fulton again.

"Agent Liddell," he said.

"Yeah." I answered. "Listen, we don't have much time. I'm almost there."

"Good. I'll wait for you outside to bring you into our London Station."

"No, wait, Fulton. We have no time to—"

The line went dead.

"Asshole." Fulton really needed to improve his phone manners.

In front of the embassy stood a balding man in a suit, his cold blue eyes fixed right on me.

I flashed my FBI badge at him as I approached. "Fulton?"

He nodded.

"Agent Liddell."

He pulled open the door. "Come in, we'll talk inside."

"No. There's no time. Scarlett has been abducted, and whoever took her will kill her by one o'clock if I don't get something to Kent on time. And not the close part of Kent. We can talk on the way."

"I must insist that we talk inside." Fulton looked over my shoulder. "These matters can't be discussed out here, it's not—"

"Listen, Fulton. We have very little time. Here, let me show you." I shoved my hand into my bag, intending to take out my phone and show him the picture of the message in the mirror.

His reaction was instantaneous. His hand flew to his side and drew his gun, aiming it at my chest. I stared at him, stunned.

"Don't move, Liddell. Don't even think about moving."

"I was just reaching for my phone." My jaw clenched, anger surging. "Are you insane?"

"Am I insane? Let's review. You show up here yesterday, and the moment we get a fae detector on you, it acts up. Sure, we thought it just malfunctioned. But then a case officer called us to tell us she was with you, when suddenly the line went dead. We checked her locator, and realized it was offline. We haven't seen her since. So what would you think?"

My heart pounded. This had gone very wrong. "You have it all mixed up. I got a message this morning. Scarlett has been—"

"I've got it mixed up? That's easy enough to test." He kept one hand on the gun, and with the other, he reached behind his back, pulling out a long, black wand. "A fae detector. Very sensitive. I assure you, it doesn't malfunction. Let me just scan you, and get this misunderstanding behind us, shall we?"

"Listen." I took a step back.

"Don't fucking move!" he barked. He aimed the device at me and pressed something.

It instantly began to emit a high-pitched whine.

"How surprising, Liddell," Fulton snarled. "You know what it says here? Let me give you a hint. It doesn't say *human*."

"For fuck's sake—"

"Are you really Agent Liddell? Or did you kill her and take her place? Don't move, fae, and don't get any ideas. The gun is full of iron bullets."

I held my hands above my head, staring at him in frustration. I *had* to get him to help me. If I could just reach into my bag, I could pull out that pendant Alvin had given me. If Fulton looked into it, he'd do whatever I wanted.

"Let me just show you one thing." Slowly, I reached down for my bag. "I'm going to pull it out of my bag. It's not a weapon, it's—"

"I don't think so!" He shouted. "Put the bag on the ground. Now!"

Shit. I knelt and slid my bag off my shoulder onto the ground.

"Kick it over here."

I did as he said. He bent and picked it up, never taking his eyes off me, his gun still pointed at my chest. He hoisted the bag on his shoulder and opened it with his free hand. Then he glanced inside and raised his eyes, smiling mockingly. "Not fae, huh?" he asked. He pulled the rune-scrawled paper from the bag. "I suppose this is written in English?"

I held out my hands, as if trying to calm a wild animal. "You don't understand—"

"No more talking!" He put the paper in his pocket, and

then took another look into the bag. I considered rushing him, but I was too far away. "And, as I expected, a weapon." He stuck his hand in his bag, pulling out the iron knife.

Instantly, his mouth slackened, his eyes widening as the knife began screaming for blood in his mind.

I lunged forward, shoving his hand with the gun up in the air. His gun arm had gone limp, and the weapon clattered to the floor. But his other arm swung for me fast, the corrupted knife in his grip. My own fear spurred me on with wild energy, and adrenaline burned through my nerve endings.

I blocked his arm, the blade slicing through my shirt and cutting my side. The cut wasn't deep, but the blade was iron, and I could hear the evil thing whispering gleefully with my blood on its tip. Fulton's eyes were unfocused, but his lips were moving, whispering the knife's threats and curses, his voice guttural and angry. Behind him, I glimpsed three suited men rushing out, pulling out guns. I twisted Fulton's hand, and he screamed in pain, loosening the knife. I snatched the blade from his hand, tore my bag from his shoulder, and bolted, sprinting for St. Audley Street.

"Stop!" someone screamed behind me. Praying that they wouldn't shoot in a street full of civilians, I dashed onto the sidewalk.

I sprinted, my breath ragged in my throat. At an intersection, a black cab screeched to a halt, the hood blocking my way. I leapt onto it, rolling over the hood, landing hard on the other side. From under the cab, I could see four sets of feet pounding toward me—Fulton and the three other agents.

The cab driver was getting out of the car, yelling something at me. Time for me to lose the spooks for good.

Inching up, I glanced at the rearview mirror of the cab, feeling the reflection, searching for a different one, far away…

Then, I froze.

I couldn't leave without the damn fae runes. Whatever they meant, I might need them to get Scarlett back.

Slowly, I lifted my head, peering through the cab window, and one of the agents raised his gun. I dove just as he shot, and the bullet shattered the glass, whistling inches from my head.

To my left was a street full of shops, and civilians milled around the sidewalks. At the sound of gunshots, they began screaming, trying to run. I sprinted for them, followed close behind by the agents. They wouldn't shoot at me in the crowd.

Looking over my shoulder, I saw two of the agents behind me, jostling people out of their way.

My lungs burned, and screams pierced the air. And then thirty feet in front of me: Fulton's face, red with rage. He and another spook had run ahead and cut off my escape route.

I had less than a second to decide what to do. I nearly ran back into the road, but police sirens were winding through the air now. Soon, I'd have the cops to deal with too. My heart slammed against my ribs. If I didn't get out of this, Scarlett would burn alive.

Frantic, I glanced to my left: a boutique clothing shop. I lunged, yanking open the door and scrambled into the shop. A sleek-haired sales assistant gaped at me as I looked around frantically, searching for a way out through the back.

There was none.

But there were dozens of mirrors.

It was time to stop thinking like prey, and to start thinking like a hunter.

CHAPTER 9

I dashed through a doorway to the changing booths, and a quick scan told me each one was occupied, with feet below the curtains. There was no time for niceties. I pulled open one of the curtains, revealing a young man in his underwear and a T-shirt, clutching a pair of jeans.

"Those look great on you." I grabbed him, pulling him out and throwing his shoes after him.

I yanked the curtain closed, ignoring the man's confused protests. Outside, I could hear Fulton screaming at the sales assistant.

I blocked that out, and focused on forming a bond with the mirror, letting my mind click with its reflection, until I felt a coolness spreading in my skull. From the reflection, I searched for a different mirror that showed me the entire shop, scanning through the possibilities until I found the right one. Fulton and his pals were standing in the middle of the shop, guns in hand. Panicking shoppers ran for the door.

"Where is the back door?" Fulton barked at the woman behind the counter, using a British accent.

"There… there is no back door," the woman said.

Fulton exchanged looks with one of the men, and said something in a low voice. I watched as his lips formed the words. *She's in here.*

"Ladies and gentlemen, please leave the store!" Fulton shouted in his fake accent. "This is police business!"

To my surprise, he flipped a badge—a local police badge. Maybe all the CIA operatives here had fake police badges for moments such as this. "Please leave the shop!" he shouted. "There is a dangerous criminal in here!"

I watched as the young man from the changing booth, now wearing pants that were far too small for him, walked over to Fulton. He pointed behind him, though I couldn't hear what he was saying. I had no doubt he was pointing Fulton to my changing booth, and my pulse raced. Fulton nodded at one of his men, who crept forward.

I felt for the other reflections in the store, linking to one in the empty storage room, and quickly moved there, sliding through the mirror, its surface rushing over my skin like water.

A second later I heard a spook shouting, "Clear!" from one of the other changing rooms.

Siren screams pierced the air.

I stared at the mirror, using it to monitor the store's other reflections. An officer was pulling one curtain after another, yelling, "Clear," each time, except for one instance, when an indignant sixty-year-old woman in a skirt and bra shouted at him. He apologized, closing the curtain.

By now nearly everyone had left the store, and Fulton and his men spread out, searching for me.

I needed to get Fulton alone. But I was exhausted, and my thoughts were racing. What I needed was more fear to energize my body.

On the wall in the storage room hung an electricity box. *Perfect.*

I yanked it open, shutting down the switches, plunging the shop into semi-darkness. Only the faint afternoon light from the front windows lit the place.

With his gun drawn, Fulton was getting close to the storage room. I searched the mirrors, looking for an obscured reflection in the shop. I found one behind a rack of coats, and I took a step into the glass, letting it wash over my skin. My heart racing, I stepped out again behind the coats. Then, feeling for all the reflections in the store, I imagined them clouding, their surfaces covered in steam.

A man's voice called out, "What the…"

I concentrated, forming letters on the mirrors, as if drawn by an invisible finger.

Can you see me?

"Sir…?"

"Shut up, she's listening to us."

Can you hear me?

A man came close to the rack of coats that obscured me, and I jumped through the reflection back into one of the changing booths, using the mirror to keep careful tabs on the four men. One of them began to pulse in fear, and I felt the delicious tendrils of energy emanating from him, curling around my body.

I let the mirror steam up again, then wrote, *I can see you.*

"Perhaps we should get backup…"

"She's just playing with your mind. She's one woman, dammit!"

More steam, then, *You should run.*

"Ignore those damn mirrors!" Fulton yelled, no longer bothering with the British accent.

RUN.

I let out a small laugh, a creepy giggle, and two of the men whirled, their guns pointed. One of them shook visibly. I was the bogeyman, the ghost in the haunted house, the thing that went bump in the night.

"There!" Fulton shouted, dashing for my changing room, but when he pulled the curtain aside, I'd already slipped through the glass, now laughing in a different part of the store. I pushed a small rack of clothing down, letting it smash to the floor, then jumped through the reflection again, always moving, always out of sight.

These men were *terrified*. And they should be. With their fear blazing through my body, I was stronger than any of them, faster than any of them. The fear that made them jittery and unfocused sharpened my thoughts to a fine-point needle.

I focused on the mirrors again, clouding them with dark mist. In the mist, I imagined strange figures slithering, never completely in sight.

A shot rang out, shattering glass. One of the men had shot a mirror. The surface fragmented, and I focused on that mirror, letting the figures in it grow closer, angry red eyes glaring in the murk.

An officer stood by a changing room. When he turned his back to me, I shimmered into that room and grabbed him from behind, blocking his mouth and nose. He pulled at my hand, desperate to breathe.

Too bad for him. I was much stronger than him now. At last, his body went lax, unconscious. I gently laid him on the floor, pulling the gun from him, shoving it in my bag. Then, I linked to the mirror behind me, imagining his terrified face in a mirror in the main room, the smoke enveloping his body as he screamed soundlessly, dark figures closing in around him.

"They have Curtis!" someone shrieked.

I heard the bell ding as the front door barged open, one of them fleeing.

"Scan the mirrors," Fulton shouted. "I want the magic print of this bitch."

The other officer moved closer to one of the mirrors, his face milky white. Through my bond with the mirror, I shifted the reflection, and imagined him appearing in it, eyes wide, hand trembling as he moved the scanner. Then, I created a slender, gray-skinned woman with gaping eye cavities. She stepped up behind him, her mouth wide, reaching for his throat. Screaming, he whirled around, looking for the illusionary woman.

Smiling, I slid my hand through the mirror, stroking his neck. I yanked my hand back as he whirled again.

"I'm calling backup," he shrieked, then ran for the door.

Only Fulton was left.

He was scared, but not as much as the others. I couldn't make a mistake with him. If he saw me, even for a second, he would shoot. And he wouldn't miss.

"Fulton…" I purred, then shifted back to the changing rooms. Through the mirror, I watched him turn, his gun waving left and right as he searched for me.

"Fulton…" I giggled again, the same creepy giggle. He whirled, shooting twice at the air.

I stepped back into the mirror, letting its magic rush over my skin, and emerged not ten feet from him, crouching below a rack of clothes.

"Fulton!" I whispered.

He jumped, letting out another shot. He backed up—directly into a mirror. And that was just what I needed.

When he turned around, I leaped through the mirror behind him, grabbing him around the neck and mouth, pressing hard to cut off his air.

He was stronger. Instead of trying to pull my hands away,

he elbowed me in my stomach. I gasped but forced myself to keep hold of him, my body surging with power. Fulton tried to point his gun at me, and I whirled him to the mirror, smashing his body against the glass, hard enough to stun him. His gun clattered to the floor. Still, I kept my hands over his nose and mouth.

He was fumbling now, fighting for his life, and his raw panic only made me stronger.

At last, he slumped in my arms. I waited for another second, not putting it past him to fake unconsciousness, but I couldn't feel his fear anymore. He was out. Laying him on the floor, I checked his pulse, relieved to feel it thump weakly beneath his skin. Then I fished through his back pocket, pulling out my parchment. I shoved it into my bra. I wouldn't let it get away from me a second time. I took his fake police badge as well, shoving it quickly into my bag.

I glanced toward the door. A CIA officer stood outside, talking to a group of cops.

Okay. Time to get the hell out of here.

I linked with the mirror behind me, searching for a reflection far from here, to the east, in the direction of Winchester Palace, finding one in a narrow street. I slid through the glass, feeling the reflection's magic rush over my skin like cool water.

CHAPTER 10

I moved along a narrow, cobbled alley beneath a brick archway. Constantly using and manipulating reflections took a bit of a toll, and the journey through the glass had left me feeling slightly queasy.

Gabriel was not far away, searching for Lucy. But before I found him, I had another little task to complete. I pulled out my phone, searching for a cell phone shop. The nearest one was about five minutes away, by London Bridge Station.

I tucked my head down, moving swiftly along the sidewalk.

The exhilaration of the escape quickly wore off, and a dark cloud of hopelessness began to pool in the back of my mind. The CIA should have helped me establish communication with the abductor. They could also decipher the runes, and help me figure out who the hell Lucy was. They could have chartered a helicopter for us, to save time. But they were on the wrong track, assuming that I had something to do with Scarlett's disappearance. And now, after I'd displayed my magical powers in the clothing shop, I was sure that they were certain of it. Once again, I was a fugitive.

By the station, I spotted the T-Mobile shop, and dropped another hundred for a cell phone. Before switching SIM cards, I made sure I still remembered Gabriel's number. As soon as I stepped out of the shop, I scanned the sidewalk for the most oblivious-looking person I could find. A woman with an oversized bag was heading for the train station, chatting into her phone. When she walked past, I dropped my old phone into her bag. That should throw off the CIA at least a little.

As fast as I could, I crossed the road. While I jogged back to Clink Street, I called Gabriel from my new phone.

"Hello?"

"Gabriel, it's me."

"Whose phone are you calling from?" His voice sounded tired.

"I just got it. The CIA was a bust. They think I had something to do with Scarlett's disappearance. Things got... messy."

"Bloody hell, Cassandra."

"Any idea who Lucy is?"

"Not yet. There's not much around here, to be honest. The palace is a ruin. There's an old jail across the street, a museum now. I don't see anyone who looks fae. I'm still looking. A few detectives in the station are helping out—"

My pulse raced. "You told them about this?"

"Chill. I didn't tell them anything significant. I just said she's a person of interest, probably a code name, and they're looking."

"Okay." I checked my new phone's display. Twenty minutes past ten. By eleven thirty, we should be on our way with Lucy to Kent, and I still had no idea who the hell Lucy was. Panic tightened its grip on my heart. If Gabriel had no idea where to find Lucy, maybe I needed to find someone who did.

"I'll be there in twenty minutes. I'm going to check out one more lead. Let me know if you find anything."

"Sure." He hung up.

I shoved my new phone back in my bag.

I had to get help, and I knew who could offer it. I'm sure there would be a price, but for Scarlett, I would do anything. I just needed to find him.

I stepped into an alley, where no one could see me, and pulled a compact mirror from my bag. Immediately, I felt my mind bond with the reflection, and its cool magic filled the inside of my skull. The glass pulled me closer, sucking me in, and as it did, I searched for Roan, envisioning his perfect form. To my relief, the reflection shimmered, giving me a glimpse of his powerful, sun-kissed body.

He was lying on a bed in a hotel room, shirtless, his eyes shut. My pulse raced, and I let the reflection pull me in deeper.

Dizzy, I stumbled into his room.

Roan sat bolt upright, and he reached for the sword by the side of his bed.

My heart raced, and I held out my hands. "It's just me."

He stared at me, his fingers on his sword's hilt, then he relaxed again. "Did you come to have your friend threaten me with iron bullets again?" The ice in his voice seemed to chill the room by ten degrees.

"No." I swallowed hard. "Sorry about that. I didn't know she'd react that way."

"Perhaps you don't know your friends very well."

I took a deep breath. How was I going to convince him to help the woman who'd wanted to shoot him? "I need your help," I said simply.

"Fascinating."

"My friend... the one you met yesterday—"

"The one who wanted to kill me."

93

"Right. She's been abducted."

He raised his eyebrow. "Why?"

"I don't know. I think she was taken by a fae. Maybe it's someone who was pissed that I killed the Rix. I got a sort of... ransom letter. In rhymes, like the Rix wrote. The letter said I should go find the Winchester Geese and find a girl called Lucy Locket, who is related somehow to a guy called Grendel. I need to take Lucy to Sheerness Dock, and it must be before one o'clock, or something terrible will happen."

"Something terrible will happen to your friend," he clarified.

My stomach was churning. I was running out of time, and yet, pushing Roan too far would backfire. "Right."

"The one who tried to kill me."

I cleared my throat. "In her defense, she *didn't* kill you. And the abductor is threatening to burn her to death. And by the way—how did you know I was going to be targeted?"

He rose from the bed. "I told you to get home and stay safe, didn't I? I know people, I hear things. Your name came up more than once in the past few days. I don't know why you'd be targeted in this way. The Callach says that you're important to restoring Trinovantum to its former glory. Perhaps someone else knows your significance and wants to keep things as they are." His emerald eyes burned into me. "It was only a matter of time. You should have heeded my warning."

I shivered. "What significance? The thing about me being the key? What the hell is that about?"

He shrugged almost imperceptibly. "It doesn't seem like you have time for a lesson on centuries of fae politics."

"Right." My fingers tightened into fists. "What about Lucy Locket?"

"Achieving what you ask is more difficult than you'd imagine, and would come with a great personal risk. Why would I risk my own safety to help a stranger who wants to kill me?"

When he put it that way, I didn't have much of a case, but I had to make one anyway. I cocked my hip. "If you recall, I helped you save Elrine. I broke into the prison, and helped free her. I believe you owe me."

"I owe you nothing." His words were full of confidence, but doubt flickered across his emerald eyes. This bothered him.

I was desperate, and out of ideas. "Scarlett is my best friend." It sounded like a pointless plea, even to me, and tears stung my eyes. "Fine. I'll figure it out on my own. I'm running out of time."

I turned to find a mirror, but Roan's voice stopped me. "Wait."

As I looked at him, I tried to keep the hope from my eyes.

"You'll never achieve this on your own. It's absurd. Tell me. After we get Lucy to Sheerness Dock, will you come with me? I have to keep you safe until the council gathering."

"What council?"

"I will explain later. Do you *promise*?"

"No." I shook my head. This wasn't good enough. "I will go with you, but only after I free Scarlett completely. I need to be sure that she is safe, and I still don't know what happens after I bring this Lucy chick into Kent." My heart began to slam against my ribs. I was quickly running out of time. "I won't go anywhere until Scarlett is safe, back at home. Think of Elrine. It's the same."

Roan stared down at me, his muscled body glowing with a pale, golden light. "Fine."

I took a deep breath. "Okay." I pulled out the paper from my bra. "Whoever abducted Scarlett sent this to me through the mirror. It has something to do with Lucy. Can you tell me what it says?"

He took the paper from my hand, scanning it. "It's a ticket."

"A what?"

"It's just as I thought. Lucy Locket is in Grendel's Den. It's a fae club of sorts. It's connected to the ruins of Winchester Palace, and this ticket is how you'll get in."

"Connected to the ruins?" I asked. "Through magic?"

"Of course. But you can't go wearing… whatever it is you're currently wearing."

"Why? The magical bouncer won't let me in?"

"That's exactly right."

"So what should I wear? Am I going for prudish fae event, like at the ball, or fun fae like at the afterparty?"

"These fae are exiles from Trinovantum. Hedonists, who couldn't abide the king's prohibitions."

"So what you're saying is, wear something low cut."

"I don't know anything about human fashion. Just wear something better than this." He brushed the back of his knuckles down my abdomen, just over my T-shirt. Even through the fabric, his touch sent a rush of electricity through my body.

My pulse raced. "How am I supposed to know what exactly to wear?"

"Look, it's easy. You humans have a foolish ceremony. I believe you call it the Festival of Oscar."

"We have nothing like that."

"I saw it on your television. They worship a golden god."

I blinked, trying to make sense of this. "You mean the Oscars?"

"I think so. The sort of dresses they wear would fit this."

"Right." I checked the time. Half past ten. We had one hour. "I'll meet you in the entrance to Winchester Palace in twenty minutes. I'll be wearing something better than a T-shirt."

CHAPTER 11

$\mathcal{I}$ didn't have time to go to some kind of haute couture shop and purchase a fancy gown. I wasn't even sure where you found those kinds of shops. Instead, I walked into the first place I saw in the street—a place called *Oasis*, and I scanned the mannequins. Most of them wore casual sun dresses, cocktail dresses, jeans, and T-shirts. At last, near the back, I spotted the closest thing I could get to Oscar's glamour: a cream maxi dress. It was a Grecian style, with an empire waist, neckline that plunged to the waist, and a backless halter. When I pulled it off the rack, I saw that it also included a slit way up the thigh. I had a feeling Roan would like this one, but I'd need some accessories to dress it up.

I grabbed my size off the rack, and crossed the shop toward the changing booths, snatching a gold-plated necklace along the way, and some matching hoop earrings.

I hurried into one of the changing rooms, my mind vaguely connecting to the reflection by my side. As fast as I could, I stripped off my jeans and shirt, pulling off my bra and shoving everything into the bottom of my bag. My pulse raced, and I tried not to think about the ticking clock. I could only hope that Roan wasn't fucking with me, and that all this was an important part of getting into Grendel's Den.

I slipped the dress over my head, and the soft fabric slid over my bare thighs. I tied the halter behind the back of my neck.

How much time did I have left to find Lucy? My hands shaking, I snatched the necklace, clasping the ropes of fake gold around the back of my neck. Next, I looped the hoop earrings through my ears.

I rifled through my bag for a moment. As fast as I could, I smudged some lipstick onto my pale cheeks, giving them a rosy sheen, then filled in my lips. I rifled through my bag a minute, pulling out a pen. I twisted my hair around the pen in an approximation of a messy updo, and appraised my appearance in the mirror.

Okay, so it wasn't quite Oscar material, but it would have to do.

I snatched my bag from the ground, and stared into the mirror. Handy thing about changing rooms. If I continued to be a fugitive for the rest of my life, I could avoid using credit cards by just taking clothes out through the reflections.

I let my mind form a bond with the mirror, and as the reflection shimmered, I felt myself falling into its gravitational pull. I searched for Gabriel, until I saw a glimpse of him walking past a parked car on Clink Street. When I'd found him, I let myself fall into the mirror, and its cold magic washed over my skin in a thrilling rush.

I slid from the car into Clink Street, eliciting a panicked shriek from a nearby middle-aged man.

By the side of the narrow road, Gabriel was standing by the ruins of an old palace, its remaining walls over grown with ivy.

As I approached, he turned, his eyes widening. "Where

did you come from?" His gaze slid to my dress. "Where did you get that outfit?"

"I'm here. I…"

A sudden dizziness spell caught me, and as I started to lose my balance, Gabriel caught my elbow, steadying me. I leaned into him, breathing in his clean, soapy smell. For just a moment, I closed my eyes, battling the nausea rising in me.

"Are you okay?" he asked softly.

"Yeah. Just give me a second. I think the mirror-traveling is disorienting."

"I'd imagine so." He wrapped an arm around my back.

I took a deep breath, trying to marshal my strength, but I felt drained. Maybe I was overtaxing my powers. Once I got Scarlett away from her abductor, I'd sleep for a week.

"Are you sure you're all right?" asked Gabriel.

"I'm fine." I opened my eyes, stepping away from him.

Gabriel frowned, and I had the distinct impression he was mentally working overtime to keep his eyes on my face and not on my plunging neckline. "I'm a bit perplexed about your attire."

"I found out where we need to go. It's a fae club called Grendel's Den, and apparently, they like their women to dress fancy."

Gabriel arched an eyebrow. "'Lucy Locket lost her pocket, dear old Grendel found it.' And do you know where it is?"

"I'm not sure. It's connected to Winchester Palace, but…" I pointed at the overgrown ruins. Arched windows remained in two walls, but that was about it. An herb garden grew in the center of it, with bluebells and primrose growing among the foxglove. "Is this Winchester Palace?"

"That's it. There's nothing connected to it."

"We'll have help, I think. We just need to wait a bit." I pulled my phone from my bag, checking the time. "Roan should be here in about five minutes."

ALEX RIVERS & C.N. CRAWFORD

Gabriel crossed his arms, and I could see him visibly tensing. "Roan? Are you kidding me?"

"We need his help, Gabriel. Neither of us have any idea how to get into Grendel's Den, or who Lucy is. We can't do this without a fae. A proper fae, not like me."

"If Roan is so helpful, why couldn't he just tell you how to get inside? Why did he need to accompany you? Let me guess. He wanted something in return."

My fingers tightened around the strap of my bag. We had just under thirty minutes to find Lucy and get her into Gabriel's car, and I didn't have the time or the energy for arguments. "Why don't we discuss strategy at a later time? Right now, I care about one thing, and one thing only. And that's getting Scarlett back. Anyway, if I go within ten yards of a fae club, there'll be chaos. They'll sense my pixie aura and leap all over it. Roan can hide it. Like it or not, we need someone who knows the fae world."

Gabriel glared at me. "I don't trust him."

"I don't either. But he did save your life and mine. And he knows the fae culture a hell of a lot better than we do."

"What happened to working with the CIA? How did we get Roan involved?"

"The CIA thing is a bit complicated." My sentence trailed off as I sensed unease in the nearby crowds.

When I looked further down the cobbled road, I saw what it was that had unsettled the humans around me. Roan was walking toward us, towering over nearly everyone around him. The only one who could match him in height was Gabriel, but it was more than just Roan's height that set him apart. He didn't look quite human, and despite his casual clothing—a simple black T-shirt that showed off his powerful arms—he didn't blend in remotely. Maybe it was the intoxicating whorls of lethal-looking tattoos covering the golden skin of his muscled arms. Or perhaps it was the

100

way his hair seemed to gleam in the sun, or the severe black lines of his brows. The deep, emerald gaze locked on me, a green you didn't find in human eyes. He looked like an ancient god, one capable of stunning displays of divine wrath. And despite the effect he had on everyone around him, he walked with a casual saunter, his hands in his pockets, as if he didn't notice the hearts fluttering around him. Even *I* felt the excitement and nervousness rippling over the women he passed. And he felt it much more keenly than I did. He was tuned to lust—it energized him, made him stronger.

As he approached, the look he gave me—a slow, lingering gaze up and down my body—seemed designed to remind me that he'd once seen me naked, and that he'd caught me having a very dirty dream about him in his cabin.

On top of the excitement in the crowds around me, I could see Gabriel's body tense, as if ready to fight. He *hated* Roan, and I had a feeling this was about to get messy. I needed to keep them both focused so we didn't waste any more precious time, when we should be saving Scarlett.

Roan completely ignored Gabriel as he walked up to us. Instead, his eyes took in every inch of my body. "The dress isn't bad."

"Glad you approve," I said. "Should we get going?"

Without so much as glancing at Gabriel, he said, "Your human should stay outside."

Gabriel folded his arms, widening his stance. "I'm not *her human*, and I'm coming with her. Clearly, she is safer with me than with you."

"Don't be a fool." Roan finally slid his gaze to Gabriel. "Cassandra needs me to hide her aura and help her find the club. You'll just get in the way."

Gabriel's lip curled. "I'm not leaving Cassandra alone with you, demon."

I sighed. Gabriel still called fae "demons," and I wasn't able to break him of that habit. "Gabriel, I just need to go."

Roan took a step closer to him, his eyes glowing a pale gold. "I am not shepherding you around, human. You will stay outside."

Gabriel's body was tensing, his jaw tightening, and he pointed a finger at Roan. "Listen, you arrogant cun—"

"Shut the fuck up, both of you!" I was about to completely lose it. "*Cassandra* can speak for herself perfectly well. Roan, Gabriel is coming with us; deal with it. Gabriel, don't antagonize him until we get to Lucy. This testosterone display is a waste of time. We have—" I checked my watch "—a bit less than twenty minutes to find Lucy and convince her to come with us. You can compare dick sizes later."

Roan peered down at me. At last, he said, "Very well, but your friend won't be able to enter the inner court of Grendel's Den."

"And we need to get into the inner court, I take it? Who is this Lucy? Do you know?"

"I've never met her, and I don't know what she looks like, but I believe she is one of Grendel's concubines. That parchment will get you in, but not him."

I pulled the paper with runes from my bag. "Do you have a ticket?"

Roan's hands were in his pockets, as if he didn't have a care in the world. "I don't need one." The smug tone was unmistakable.

"Fine, I won't go into the inner court." Gabriel managed to inject a sense of disgust into the last two words.

"Another thing." Roan pointed to my handbag. "You can't go inside with that."

I shook my head. "I need it. I know it looks stupid with the dress, but—"

"It does look stupid with the dress, but that's not the

point. The fae guarding Grendel's den don't allow bags in. You'll have to leave it at the entrance."

The bag held my knife, wallet, new cell phone, the last of my cash, and—most importantly—my mirrors. "I can't leave it behind."

Gabriel nodded at his black sedan. "You can leave it in my car."

I stared down at the tiny strips of fabric masquerading as a dress. "I can't carry anything in this dress. I'll be defenseless."

"You won't be defenseless," said Roan. "I'll be with you."

Gabriel's hazel eyes met mine. "Are you all right with this, Cassandra?"

"I don't feel like I have a lot of choice," I said. "He's right. He can mask my aura, and I don't fancy our chances of finding Lucy on our own."

"Fine." He held out his hand. "Give me your bag."

I pulled the parchment from my bag, then handed it to him. He crossed to his car.

For just a moment, I thought I saw golden horns glimmer above Roan's head. "You'll have to stay close," he murmured. "If you want me to hide your aura."

"Is there anything else I need to know?"

"Don't get into any fights, or the guards will close in."

"Yeah, I'm not the one who randomly rips people's hearts out, so I think I'll be good. How do we get in?"

He pointed to an arched doorway in the old ruin, which seemed to be a dead end. Another building stood directly on the other side of it. "Through there."

"There's nothing there." But even as I said the words, the glamour shimmered for a moment, revealing a deep hall lit by twinkling lights, and the faint pulse of a rhythmic music.

* * *

ROAN LED us through the wildflower garden. I glanced back at the street. Clearly, we were trespassing, and yet no one seemed to notice. Part of the glamour? Or just English politeness gone too far?

He led us through the stone doorway, and what had appeared to be a brick building on the other side gave way to a hall of high, peaked arches—hemlock boughs intertwined with gold—and among the leaves hung tiny, glowing lights.

At the end of the hall, before an ornately-carved wooden door, stood two guards, their ginger hair flowing over green, velvety uniforms. While the soldiers in Trinovantum had been wearing heraldic emblems of skulls under water, these two men wore a stag insignia—not unlike the stag pin I'd seen Roan wearing. As soon as they saw Roan, they nodded at him, and stepped out of the way. Before it opened, I caught a glimpse of the door's carvings—it looked like three tall, thin crones, and a man with a stag's head.

The door opened into an enormous hall, crammed with a throng of colorfully dressed guests, their bodies caressing, grasping, licking. Under stone walls carved with gargoyles, the fae writhed against each other, dressed in the most stunning fabrics I'd ever seen—sheer dandelion yellows, sage greens, and chicory blue. A deep, melodic music pulsed through my core, the rhythms strange and hypnotic, haunting tones that blended together in otherworldly combinations.

The hall was nearly as stunning as the guests. Shimmering white vines climbed the walls, reaching up to the high ceiling—a starry sky that seemed to shimmer between phantom branches high above, as if we were both inside and outside at the same time. And from the vines, a riot of wildflowers grew, in colors that dazzled my eyes. Their delicate scents, blended with the smell of medicinal herbs, filled the air.

Here, the fae had shed their glamours, and a man with satyr's legs pushed past me, smelling faintly of goat fur. I glanced at Gabriel, whose gaze had locked on a tiny brunette dressed in a tiny blue corset, red panties, and sheer white thigh-highs. She was dancing on her own, stroking her fingers up and down a pearly necklace. Her arms shimmered with iridescent scales.

I squeezed Gabriel's arm. "Stay focused."

His wide eyes met mine. "How is this place in London?"

"Magic," I whispered.

In the humidity of the place, his deep copper skin had taken on a faint sheen, and I found myself wondering what it would feel like to kiss his neck. What was wrong with me? The waves of lust in this place were getting to me. And that meant there were humans among the fae in here, too.

Roan turned to look at me, his deep green eyes burning into me. Here, where my senses seemed to be heightened, I could see the gold flecks in his eyes.

He beckoned me closer. "Stay close, Cassandra."

I nodded, keeping within a foot of him. As we moved through the crowd, we passed a stone dais to my left. On its mossy surface stood a cluster of musicians playing stringed instruments and some sort of hand drums, their voices blending together. In peaked alcoves around the room, the fae writhed, some of them with humans.

Roan turned to me, grabbing my hand, his eyes now completely gold. He hadn't shed his glamour, or unveiled, but by the tension in his body, I had the sense that he was restraining himself.

"I'll take you to the inner court." He pointed at another carved wooden door on the far side of the hall. It was enormous and featured a naked woman, wrapped in her long hair and ivy. "Let's go."

I turned to Gabriel, who stood staring at one of the beautiful singers—a siren, I thought—with dark skin, silver hair, and a crown of black thorns, her eyes pale as starlight. Platinum bird wings curved behind her back. "Will you be all right here?"

He stared down at me, a flicker of fear in his eyes. "I'll be fine. But if we get separated... Just make sure I don't get stuck in here."

I reached up, touching his cheek. "I won't leave you behind."

Roan's grip tightened on my other hand, and he began tugging me away. I held Roan's hand as we slipped deeper into the crowd, bodies brushing against my skin, some of them nearly naked. My new dress slid over my skin, and without a bra, I felt practically naked myself.

As we passed another alcove, I took in the scene. Twenty feet away, a shirtless male sat on a large chair. Straddling him with her arms around his neck was a tall, beautiful fae woman, her raven hair tumbling down her back. She turned, her eyes locking on me. Avelina. Last time I'd seen her, I'd left her unconscious body naked in a castle hall after stealing her dress. As bad first impressions went, that was probably at the top of the list.

I was certain she was about to run for me in a stormwind of fury, but instead, she simply returned her stare to her male companion. I lowered my eyes, taking a lot of care to be as invisible as possible.

I pulled Roan close to me, whispering into his ear. "I saw Avelina."

Roan turned to me, his eyes deep as amber. His gaze slid over my body, and at the look he was giving me, my pulse raced. For just a moment, he reached for me before curling his fingers into a tight fist. I wasn't entirely sure what it meant when his eyes changed color, but I thought I had an idea.

"Everything okay?" I asked. "Are we on our way to find Lucy?"

"This place," he rasped. "It's overwhelming."

I nodded, knowing what it felt like to be overwhelmed with human emotion. Roan was the type of fae who tuned in to sexual excitement, and this place was a hurricane of lust.

I squeezed his hand, conscious of the ticking clock. "Let's go."

He nodded. "Right."

He turned, but from behind, a deep voice interrupted us, "Roan Taranis."

The voice was sharp, full of disdain and mockery, and I could see Roan tense as he heard it.

We turned to face the speaker. A tall, broad-shouldered fae loomed over me, his eyes black marbles, his hair as white as snow. He sipped a glass of wine. "Imagine seeing you here, after all those years. I heard you were out of prison, but I couldn't believe it."

"Kellen," Roan spat. "I'm surprised you can still use your tongue after all the years it spent lodged up the king's arse."

"Treasonous words." Kellen's lip curled, and he took a step closer. "Talking about our king like that. And what are you doing in this... den of debauchery? The king might be annoyed to hear you were seen here. It would only confirm what everyone knows about your family."

"I could ask you the same question."

"My position gives me certain leeway, Taranis, while you are always standing at the edge of the precipice." He turned to me, mockery in his eyes. "And who is your woman? Aren't you a lovely sight... and your eyes are so..." He reached for my face.

"Stay away from her," Roan growled, smacking his hand away.

"I'll take what I want, Taranis." Kellen stepped toward me.

Oh *hell* no. I really regretted not having access to my weapons right now. My heart was slamming against my ribs. This was not a good situation.

Roan growled, and I touched his arm, hoping to calm him down. If he attacked Kellen now, we'd never get to Lucy.

"Roan. Let's go," I hissed at him. "I can take care of myself."

"Sure you can." Kellen grabbed my face, pressing my cheeks as he examined me like a prized cow. I slapped his hand away, and he smiled, and grabbed it again. "Taranis," he breathed out in wonder. "Those deep blue eyes, the flecks of green... They are unmistakable."

"You're dead, Kellen," Roan snarled, stepping closer.

I stared as his ears lengthened into points. Antlers gleamed from his head, and his tattoos began to glow, metallic copper now instead of black. His hair paled, from deep gold to nearly white that draped over his shoulders, and his eyes burned, a fiery amber. White claws grew from his fingertips, and he growled, the deep, animalistic sound sending a primal pulse of fear through my gut. I couldn't explain exactly why—maybe it was because he no longer looked quite human—but the sight of him unveiling sent a sharp spike of fear through the ancient part of my brain, the part that told me to run when I was about to die. I managed to stand my ground, my legs shaking, but if he'd cast a look in my direction, I would have fled the club and not looked back.

The look he was giving to Kellen conveyed something like *I'm going to rip out your lungs.* And if that happened, I'd never get to Lucy. I also had the disturbing feeling that once he gave in to his violent side, he wouldn't be able to stop.

I grabbed his arm. "Roan, don't!"

Kellen smiled, sharp teeth shining in the dark hall. "I've been wanting to slaughter you for a long time."

"Don't move, demon." Gabriel moved up behind him, holding the gun I'd given him that morning, pointing it directly at Kellen's back. "Ever heard of a *gun*, demon? This one's full of iron bullets."

My heart thumping, I looked around us. So far, everyone around us was too busy writhing on each other to notice. I prayed this would last.

Kellen turned to Gabriel. "I know what a gun is. Their bullets are all made of useless lead."

He stepped toward Gabriel, reaching for the gun. Gabriel took a step back and shifted the slide quickly, letting a bullet pop out to the floor.

"See for yourself." Gabriel smiled calmly. "But move slowly. If you shout or move too quickly, you'll get an iron bullet in your skull." He kicked the bullet toward Kellen.

The fae stared at him, and I caught the faint tremble in Kellen's hands. Slowly, he bent and touched the bullet, and hissed in horror. He rose too fast, and Gabriel raised the gun just a bit higher, his eyebrow quirking in a silent warning.

"You dare bring an iron weapon to this hall?" Kellen growled.

"Shut up." Ferocity burned in Gabriel's eyes. "You and me, we're taking a little walk. If you do anything to startle me, I'll shoot. I'll empty the fucking magazine in your ribs. It has twelve bullets, all iron. Believe me, I've been itching to do some demon-killing for years. What do you think? Will you survive it?"

My stomach churned, and I suddenly regretted dragging Gabriel into this. If anything happened to him, I'd never get over the guilt.

"This is what it's come to, Taranis?" Kellen growled. "Slumming it with humans who carry iron?"

"Move," Gabriel barked, taking a step closer. "Now."

Kellen's eyes narrowed, but the two of them walked

slowly into the crowds, Gabriel's gun now hidden under the flap of his jacket. I stared after them, my heart in my throat. At the first opportunity, Kellen would tear Gabriel's head off. I could only hope Gabriel wouldn't give him the chance.

"Come on." Roan touched my arm. "Your friend has done well. But this encounter was ill-timed. Let's get Lucy, and get out of here. Fast."

His features had returned to normal, his tattoos black again, his hair a deep honey.

I quickly bent to pick up the discarded iron bullet, and palmed it before a random fae dancer stepped on it. We moved closer to the door with the naked chick, glowing with a golden light. Two guards stood before it, and at the sight of Roan, they shifted slightly.

One of them, a fae with dark hair, stared at me. "Sir, you are always welcome, but the girl can't enter."

Reaching into my dress, I pulled out the parchment and handed it over. The guard glanced at it, then moved away from the door. The door swung open, revealing a spiral stone stairwell, overgrown with ivy. Roan grasped my hand, leading me down.

* * *

WE WALKED THROUGH A DOMED HALL, its walls half-claimed by plants. Among the vines and flowers, the walls glittered with gems and gilt bas relief sculptures, depicting stag hunts and ancient trees. It was an immense display of wealth, and I could now understand why they were so particular about not allowing bags in the club.

Underneath the sweet perfume of wildflowers, the scent of something dark and rotting hung in the air. The club's music now seemed faraway, hardly penetrating these walls.

We crossed through a tall, arched threshold into another

room—an octagonal shape with a domed ceiling formed from hemlock vines that glittered with lights. In leafy alcoves around the room, fae sat at wooden tables. Candlelight from chandeliers cast dancing light over the room, and the shadows seemed to writhe around us. A gilt-framed mirror hung on one of the walls. Always good to know where the reflections were in any given situation.

On the far side of the room, before a dark alcove, stood four of the largest fae I had ever seen—nearly seven feet tall—holding curved swords with nasty-looking blades. Their silver eyes were alert to their surroundings in a way I easily recognized. They were bodyguards, and their sole purpose was protecting one individual.

As I shifted my position, I caught a glimpse of the person they were guarding. The creature sitting behind them looked so alien, so unabashedly inhuman, I could hardly bring myself to look at him. At first glimpse, he looked like a very old man, dressed in rags. But as my eyes adjusted to the dim light, I realized he was shirtless, and what I'd mistaken for rags were swaths of sickly green algae and brown muck. His large mouth opened in a ghastly grin. His skin was bone white and his eyes were light gray, matching the color of his elongated teeth. Among the muck and algae, something white gleamed on his chest, bathed orange in the candlelight.

On either side of him sat two naked human women. The man's arms reached around the women, and he groped their breasts with his green, webbed hands.

Roan paused, leaning into me. "That's Grendel," he whispered. "But I don't know which of the women is Lucy."

I looked at the girls. Each wore a fixed smile on her face, though their smiles didn't reach their eyes. They seemed young—no more than twenty, perhaps even younger. I wondered if they were trapped here, or if they were escort girls, paid for their time. Either way, I didn't feel like leaving either of them here with this man.

"We'll take both with us," I said. "We can figure out which one is Lucy later."

"And how do you propose to take them from him?"

I didn't have a clue. "I suppose just killing him is out of the question."

Roan cocked his head. "It's typically my favorite approach. I can take the bodyguards." He nodded at a hall, opposite where we stood. "But I guarantee there are a dozen more outside."

"You think you can take out these four bodyguards?" I asked, raising my eyebrow.

He looked almost hurt. "Of course."

Damn it! We had to get the girls right now if we wanted a chance of getting to the Sheerness Docks in time, and even that was cutting it close.

"We'll talk to him," I said. "Perhaps we can cut a deal. There must be something he wants."

"It doesn't look like he's lacking for anything here."

We crossed to him, and as we approached, the rotting smell grew stronger. The guards parted, and Grendel's murky eyes fixed on us.

"Well," he croaked. "Roan of Taranis. And a lovely play-thing. You always could pick them, Taranis."

"Grendel." Roan's voice was stony.

"What's your name, plaything?" Grendel asked, looking at me, his mouth opening and a long purple tongue emerging to lick his thin lips.

Bile rose in my throat, and I stared at the ornament on Grendel's chest. It was a bone. A human pelvic bone. Well, that was... unexpected.

Grendel stroked the bone. "Admiring Lucy, I see?" He grinned at me, his sharp teeth glinting in the light. "She was something special. The most beautiful woman I ever owned. But, of course, human, and like all of your race, she aged too quickly. Still, I keep her best parts with me." One of his webbed paws caressed the bone lovingly. "Reminds me of old times."

"We just wanted to pay our respects," Roan said. "Thank you for your hospitality."

Grendel smiled again, staring at me. Roan grabbed my arm and pulled me away.

"Lucy is the fucking bone," I hissed at him when we were far enough.

"So I noticed. He won't give it away," Roan said. "Not without a fight."

"Maybe he'd be willing to trade—"

"If he would, the price would be too high."

I thought of Scarlett. "There isn't a price that's too high."

Something fierce flashed in his eyes. "Trust me, there is."

"We're running out of time." *Damn damn damn!*

A briny draft whispered over my skin, and I turned, catching sight of a small, wooden door, inset into a shadowy wall by the gilt-framed mirror. It stood not ten feet away. This door, inside the inner court, led somewhere important. To Grendel's private quarters, perhaps?

I pulled Roan closer to me, whispering into his ear. This close, heat from his body warmed mine. "I have a plan," I whispered. "You should get out, find Gabriel, and wait for me."

"No." His tone brooked no argument.

But I was already walking away from him. He reached for me, but I rushed out of his grasp.

The moment I moved away from his side, all the eyes in the room turned to stare at me, as the fae immediately sensed my pixie emotions. Their eyes widened, and I saw the mesmerized looks around me. Pixie emotions were like a

ALEX RIVERS & C.N. CRAWFORD

drug to fae—a mix of magic and human feelings. And it helped if the emotions were powerful. Which, considering my fear and revulsion, they were.

"A lilive." Grendel's tongue flicked out, licking his lips as I approached. "Imagine that."

I smiled at him. "That's right." I fluttered my eyelashes. "I've heard you're the richest fae in London. Is that true?"

"Yes." He quirked his head, entranced.

"I thought… we could spend some time together. Private-ly." I trailed my fingertips down my chest, between my breasts. "And maybe you could… reward me for my favors, later?"

"That's an interesting proposal." His grip tightened on the girls' breasts. "What did you have in mind?"

"Oh…" I looked around me at the sparkling rubies and diamonds. "I'm sure we can work something out."

He stood up slowly. He was completely naked, and I kept my eyes firmly off his crotch. I did *not* need any more fuel for my nightmares.

Roan growled behind me. "Cassandra. What are you doing?"

What I'm doing is saving my friend, and I will do whatever it takes.

I turned to look at him. Those antlers had reappeared, and his golden eyes burned into me, copper tattoos gleaming on his skin. "Cassandra!" He bellowed, his fists clenched. I had the feeling he was about to level this place, but I needed him to stay in control for just a few more minutes.

I widened my eyes in an expression that I hoped conveyed *trust me.* "I'll be *fine.*"

"I'll be gentle with her," croaked Grendel. "Perhaps." He nodded at the door by the mirror.

I plastered a smile on my face, and followed him to the door. He grabbed my arm, his webbed hands surprisingly strong. He dragged me toward the door, and his bodyguards followed. I could only hope they wouldn't be faster than me when I made my move.

"Oh, it's going to be a party?" I smiled at them. "That's good. I have enough emotions for all of you."

Grendel blinked, aware of his bodyguards for the first time since I approached. "Wait here!" he snarled. "I want her alone."

I tried to hide my satisfaction as they froze, hoping Grendel couldn't feel the sense of achievement I was emanating. Furtively, I glanced at the chain that held the bone around his neck. It was thin. I could easily break it. I just needed to time it right…

As we approached the door, I felt the mirror by its side merge with me, forming a bond. As fast as I could, I searched for a second reflection to jump through. My pulse racing, I grabbed the bone and tugged it hard.

But the chain didn't break, and my heart skipped a beat. Grendel let out a rough laugh, and flung me against the wall. My head snapped back, slamming into the stone, and pain cracked through my skull. I cried out, my vision darkening as I lost my grip on the reflection.

"Interested in Lucy, little fortal?" Grendel hissed at me, his webbed hands all over me. "Well, you're about to know her real well. We're going to have great fun, the three of us. And I won't be gentle."

Over his shoulder, I was dimly aware of Roan charging the bodyguards, roaring in anger.

Behind me, the door swung open, and Grendel shoved me inside, letting the door close behind him.

CHAPTER 12

He dragged me down a steep flight of stairs, much stronger than I'd imagined he'd be, his slimy hand gripping my wrist. Adrenaline burned through my nerve endings. If I didn't get the fuck out of this situation fast, some psychopath was going to burn Scarlett to death. Rage flooded my body. Someone was trying to play the puppet master, pulling my strings and sending me on a wild goose chase through the city. Someone knew I'd do anything for Scarlett, and wanted to watch me flail around. Did my tormentor know that I hated being underground, that I loathed the dank air?

This had gone terribly wrong, and my chest tightened. How was Roan faring against the bodyguards? He'd been completely unarmed.

Pain throbbed through my skull, and I struggled to concentrate. A cold, briny breeze chilled my skin. As Grendel took me lower down the dank stairwell, I could hardly see anything around me, and the rotten smell in the air grew heavier.

Finally, we reached the bottom of the stairs, and he pulled

me into a dark room. With a shock, I found my feet submerged in water. The sound of rushing water echoed off a low ceiling, but I couldn't see a thing. Icy water flowed over my legs, up to my knees, chilling me. Where the fuck were we? Fat drops of water dripped of a ceiling, dampening my dress. My best guess was that he'd dragged me into some sort of underground river.

I desperately tried to feel for a reflection in the water, but in the dark, I had nothing.

"Now…" Grendel shoved me against a damp wall, and my head smacked the brick. "Let's have some fun, little fortal."

The blow dizzied me, and I grimaced in revulsion as Grendel squeezed his slimy body against mine, pressing my wrists to the wall. I felt his slimy tongue lash my cheek, and heard his groan of pleasure, his excitement at my pixie horror apparent. He let out a small gurgle of pleasure, and he breathed on me, his breath full of rot.

When I had killed the Rix, I had used the reflection in his eye as a weapon against him, but in the dark, I had nothing.

"Your emotions are exquisite, lilive," he groaned. "Now let's feel your pixie body."

He pressed my wrists into the wall, which seemed to curve behind me. One of his knees nudged between my legs.

This had gone on long enough. I had a friend to rescue, and this rapey fucker was getting in my way. Hot anger blazed. Clutching the iron bullet I had palmed earlier, I head-butted him, and he dropped his grip on me. I slammed my knee into his crotch, his agonized howl echoing in the dark space. I thrust my right hand forward, feeling his open mouth, shoving it inside, driving the iron bullet into his throat.

He bit down on my hand, pain splintering my fingers. I kicked him in the gut and he stumbled away from me. I couldn't see him, could only hear the sound of his coughing and hacking as it echoed off the ceiling. His body splashed into the water, and I trudged toward him through the river, plunging in deeper, up to my waist. My feet brushed against a slimy body. It seemed the iron bullet had worked.

Holding my breath, I plunged under the icy water, feeling around his fetid carcass for his necklace. At last, my fingers brushed over the smooth bone, and I pulled it from his neck, struggling as it got caught around his head, my lungs burning. At last, I unhooked the thing and rose, gasping for breath. I shivered in the frigid water, moving back to the shallower edges of the tunnel.

As the rage and panic in my mind subsided, I heard shouts echoing in the stairwell. I tensed, ready to kick someone in the gut again.

"Cassandra?" Roan's voice.

I loosed a breath. "I'm right here." I caught my breath. "I got the bone."

"Are you all right?"

"I'm fine. Just soaking wet." I wasn't about to tell him I was terrified of tunnels. I didn't need to sound like a major wimp.

"What happened to Grendel?"

"He's in the river with an iron bullet lodged in his throat."

"Impressive."

As much as I wanted to bask in his admiration, we needed to get out of there. I trudged toward the sound of his voice. "I got Lucy; let's go." Please, let's get the fuck out of this tunnel before I suffocate.

"We definitely can't go back that way." He touched my shoulder, stalling me. "I killed four of the bodyguards, but there are more on their way."

My jaw clenched. "Down the tunnel, then."

Already, I was moving through the water, with Roan by

my side. The darkness here was so complete I felt disoriented, my eyes scanning for any hints of detail.

"Can you see anything here?" I asked, shivering.

"Faintly. There's not much to see. A round tunnel, dark stones. Moss on the walls. That's it. I can see you, faintly. You look cold. And your dress is sheer."

Of course that would be an important detail to him, though oddly enough, I felt better with Roan here. "I *am* cold." I hugged myself. "Let me know if you see a ladder or something. Maybe we can get out through a manhole."

"Are you going to allow this person continue to control you this way?"

"The abductor? I don't have much choice, do I?"

"If you allow yourself to become attached to people, you make yourself vulnerable. Others can easily control you, as you are demonstrating."

My feet splashed through the freezing water. "That's your theory, is it? What about Elrine? You're obviously attached to her."

"She's the only one."

I felt an inexplicable twinge of jealousy. "How can you be so old and have so few emotional attachments? What do you do with your time? Just live in the forest in total isolation?"

"I spend time at the court as well." His icy gaze slid to me. "And what I do with my time is none of your concern."

"Who is it you wanted me to speak to?"

He cut me a sharp look. "I needed to bring you to the Council. I don't know what will happen there, except that the Callach said it will help restore Trinovantum to its former glory."

The fucking Callach again. "What does that mean?"

He took a deep breath. "Have you seen the heraldic emblems in Leroy's bar?"

I nodded. Phoenixes, ravens, foxglove... "Yeah. What are they?"

"The six ancient houses of Trinovantum. Once, they ruled together. Six kings, who made decisions together. Six kingdoms, each with our own customs and gods. And now there's just one. The House of Weala Broc, ruled by the High King."

"The skulls under water, and the king who forbids dancing." I stumbled in the darkness, trying to hurry. How much time did we have left? "But I only saw five emblems. The sixth was there, but it was defaced."

"True." He declined to elaborate further. "In any case, once you come to the Council, your role here is probably over, and you should leave London. Return to your former life across the ocean doing... whatever it is that you do."

So, apparently, I was the key to restoring these six kingdoms, and no one had a goddamn clue why. If I had to guess, the Callach was full of crap—a weird old woman who uttered cryptic fragments before returning to gnawing on twigs, and everyone treated her ramblings like gospel.

We walked for a few minutes in silence, until the sounds of splashing and shouts echoed from behind us. We moved faster, running through the water. I knew Roan was slowing himself down for me, but I just couldn't pick up speed in the water. Ahead, I heard the sound of churning water.

"It's a dead end," said Roan.

Shit. "Are you sure?" I whispered.

"It's a wall of water. This is Grendel's doing. He's blocked our way. He can make river water do his bidding. He would have drowned us both already, except he probably doesn't want to lose Lucy."

"So I didn't kill him?"

"He isn't so easily killed. He's as ancient as the rivers themselves. But you definitely managed to piss him off."

The sound of shouting guards moved closer.

My heart thrummed. "What now?"

"Now, we hide." Roan grabbed my arm, pulling me into a tiny alcove in the side of the wall. Brick pressed against my back, and Roan squeezed in next to me.

What was the time now? I didn't have my phone to check anymore, but I was certain we'd been in this tunnel for over twenty minutes. I'd never get to the docks in time. Tears stung my eyes.

My teeth began to chatter, and Roan whispered, "Shhh," wrapping his powerful arms around me.

His body warmed mine, and I breathed in his smell—moss and sage, a hint of musk. I wrapped my arms around his neck, letting my body brush against his. He ran a hand down my back, his fingers warm on my skin, and his touch electrified me. I tucked my head into his chest, listening to the soothing sound of his heartbeat.

One of the bodyguards ran toward the alcove, slashing through the water, and I held my breath, certain he'd hear the frantic pounding of my heart. But he ran right past us, followed by another guard a moment later.

I heard one of the guards shout, "I think they got away!"

"I'm telling you," said the other. "They went down that side tunnel!"

"I didn't see anything there."

"There's nothing here either!"

"The frog will have our heads if we don't catch them."

"Don't call him that!" the other one hissed, horrified. "He'd kill me for just *hearing* you call him that."

"Fine. Let's check the filthy side tunnel."

I heard the sound of splashing water as they ran past us again. I waited, breathing softly. Roan's breath warmed the side of my face, his fingers lightly stroking me just above my hipbone.

Slowly, I pulled myself away from him, regretting the loss

of his warmth. I could no longer hear the fae guards, and the sound of churning water seemed to be abating.

"His magic is weak," Roan said softly. "The iron bullet poisons his body."

"Good."

We waited for another minute, until Roan judged the wall of water to be low enough to wade into safely.

And just on the other side, a tiny ray of sunlight streamed into the underground river through a manhole. I could see the rusted ladder that lead up to the opening. I climbed first, gripping the pelvic bone.

At the top, I pushed the manhole aside and hauled myself out onto a narrow alley. Water poured from my dress, and Roan had been right—it was completely transparent.

"Do you have any idea what time it is?" I asked.

He glanced at the sun. "Twelve forty."

My heart stopped. It took an hour and a half to get to Sheerness in a car. There was no possible way we could make it.

Fail to get her there on time,
And Scarlett burns alive.

CHAPTER 13

For a moment, I just stared at Roan, feeling empty and helpless. If the CIA had given me their support and a charted aircraft, *perhaps* I could have gotten there on time. But by land? An hour and a half drive—and the original estimate hadn't even accounted for traffic, which existed in real life. Getting the drive down to twenty minutes was impossible.

Frantic, I looked around me at the brick Victorian buildings, searching for some kind of brilliant idea. Behind us was a newsagent's, and the man behind the glass stared at us. He probably didn't see many women in sheer dresses climbing out of the sewers.

And then, a crazy idea bloomed in my mind.

I dashed into the shop, the bell ringing as I flung open the door into a tiny space, crammed with newspapers and boxes of chips. The old man behind the counter glared at me.

"Do you have a map of London and its surroundings?" I asked, breathless.

I heard Roan come in behind me. "What are you doing?"

"Most people use their phones these days." He rummaged

around behind the counter before handing me a map. "That'll be one pound," he said.

I ignored him, unfolding the map. It only showed London. Not good enough.

"I need a map that shows the area around London too. Like, the suburbs."

His eyes drifted down to my chest, taking in the sheer fabric and the fact that I was clearly cold. "Suburbs?"

"Kent." I was losing patience.

He sighed, then rummaged behind the counter, muttering to himself. I tapped my foot until he handed me another map, then unfolded it as well. Better. It had a large area around London, and showed the Isle of Sheppey as well.

"That'll be another pound." He held out his hand.

"Are you going to explain yourself?" asked Roan.

"Please find Gabriel," I said. "Tell him to get me from the Sheerness Docks."

"I need more of an explanation."

"And I need you to trust me."

He stared at me, his green eyes boring into me. "You need to know that the way you… travel can be dangerous."

I swallowed hard. "I don't have much choice."

Roan turned, walking from the shop without another word. I had no idea if he planned to do what I'd asked, but maybe I needed to trust him, too.

The old man thrust his hand closer to me. "Two pounds, miss."

"Do you have a mirror?" I asked.

He grumbled to himself, rifling around in a box of plastic tat until he found a plastic hand mirror. I glanced at the clock on the wall. I had about eighteen minutes to get there.

"Four pound fifty," he said.

I tucked Lucy and the map under one arm, and I stared into the mirror, letting my mind bond with the reflection.

When it did, I searched eastward, as far as I could go. I found another reflection, a mirror in a house. I felt the magnetic pull of the mirror, and I let it tug me into its surface, sucking me in like a black hole. The reflection's magic shimmered over my body, rippling over my skin.

I tumbled through the wall of liquid magic into an empty bedroom, where light shimmered through a dusty window. Dashing to the window, I opened it and looked outside. I could see the Thames lazily flowing a few blocks away. *Good.* Was I looking at it from its southern side, or northern? I glanced at the sun. Southern side. East was to my right. I rushed back to the mirror, felt for a bond with the reflection, and searched for another. East.

Jump.

A shopping window reflecting a London street. Passersby screaming as they saw me appear out of thin air. Checked the street name, found it on my map. I was moving in the right direction—east, east, east.

Jump.

Another bedroom. A bleached-blond woman screamed in bed.

"What's the address here?" I roared at her.

She blubbered incoherently, clutching her pink duvet.

"The address! Now!"

"Thirteen Tarling Road! Please don't kill me!"

I found it on the map, blocking out her shrieks. I glanced at her clock. Sixteen minutes.

"Which way to the Thames?" I asked, hoping she could easily point it out.

"Take the elevator to—"

"Just point in the general direction!"

She pointed. Gritting my teeth, I turned to the mirror, bonding with the reflection, then searching.

Jump.

The street again, another window, the Thames easily in sight. This time I took more care with my jump, searching for a reflection to the east.

Jump.

On the Thames walkway, people screamed as I leapt out of a dark window. I checked the sun again, pretty sure I could tell which way was east just by its location. I prayed I was right.

Jump.

Another street—a squat brick council estate, empty of passersby, a cool wind kissing my skin.

Jump.

Another shop window, and a man in a grubby T-shirt stared at me, blinking.

"Which way to Rochester?" I asked. Rochester stood between the Isle of Sheppey and me.

"I… Miss…" he stammered. "You can take the bus from the—"

"Just point the direction!"

"I reckon, maybe…" He gestured limply to the right.

Grinding my teeth, I fixed my eyes on the sky, trying to approximate *east.* I slipped back through the reflection.

Jump.

The next man couldn't form any words after I jumped out of his rearview mirror while he was getting into his car, but he did easily point the way, his finger trembling.

Jump.

The more I jumped, the more the reflections began feeling strange—sticky, as if I were moving through gelatin. With each jump, I started to feel slightly queasier, my head foggy. I clutched my stomach, letting myself fall through another reflection.

Jump. Jump. Jump.

Nausea welled in my gut as I tumbled through the reflection on the glass of a bus shelter. I'd lost the map during one of the jumps, but I still clung tight to the pelvic bone. Clutching it to my stomach, I fell to my knees on the sidewalk, hunching over. I heaved, puking up a thin stream of brown liquid. The tea I'd had earlier. I wiped the back of my shaking hand across my mouth.

It had to be nearly one now. I didn't have time to lie here in the street puking.

"Are you all right?" An old woman with silvery curls bent over, gently touching my shoulder.

I looked up at her, squinting in the sunlight. "Do you know which way is Rochester?"

"This is Rochester." She frowned behind her Coke-bottle eyeglasses. "Do you want me to call an ambulance?"

The Isle of Sheppey was northeast of Rochester.

"Can you point me in the general direction of the Isle of Sheppey?"

She straightened, a perplexed look on her face. "It's that way, but—"

I rose on unsteady feet, and fell back into the reflection. *Jump.*

Loud honking pierced my ears. Screeching tires. I'd jumped into the middle of the highway through a side mirror reflection, and a car missed me by inches, the air rushing past me. Another car swerved, nearly lost control, stopping at the side of the road, the driver opening his window, face red with rage, screaming at me. Dodging the cars, I ran to him, clinging to the bone. He stared in fright, rolling up the window. He began driving just as I got to his car. I grabbed the door handle, stared into his side mirror, feeling the bond with his reflection.

Jump.

It was like jumping through thick goo, my body forcing itself through the reflection, no longer quite welcome.

129

A small residential street, fields of scrub brush. A teenager stared at me, his eyes bloodshot and half-lidded, obviously stoned.

"Which way to Sheppey Island?" I barked, my nerves on fire.

"Mate… you look well mental. Did you just come out of that car mirror, or—"

"Which way?" I screamed, confirming his theory.

"Just up that road." He pointed.

Turned around to look at the car's window, bonded with the reflection, searched another one.

Jump.

The reflection pushed back, thick as molasses. I nearly couldn't get through. I could now glimpse the world between reflections, a world of *nothing*, and it gnawed at the inside of my mind. I could get trapped here, and I needed to push on. My body moved through as if swimming through drying cement. At last, I broke through, gasping for breath.

I tumbled to my knees, spewing more tea. Standing shakily, I turned around, getting my bearings. I'd jumped through a shiny metal fence and now stood by the side of a large road —fields on one side, and some sort of warehouses on the other. I needed to find out where the fuck I was, exactly.

A car was driving in my direction, and I stepped in front of it. The driver slammed on the breaks, screeching.

"How far to the docks?" I shouted.

A woman with frizzy brown hair stuck her head out the window. "Get out the road, you daft cow!"

Panic ripped through my body, and I waved Lucy in the air, marching toward her car. "I am holding a human pelvic bone, and I will kill you! Where's the fucking dock?"

"It's just a ten-minute walk that way." She pointed, her bottom lip quivering.

I stood by her window, staring down at her. "What time is it?"

"Twelve fifty-seven."

No time to get there on foot.

I bonded with her rearview mirror.

And I jumped.

CHAPTER 14

*T*he reflections clung to my body, trying to hold me there. My world tilted. I knew that staying in this world between reflections meant death. My death, Scarlett's death. I couldn't let that happen. I wasn't going to let Scarlett burn.

With what little willpower I had left I pushed through, my blood roaring in my ears, breath ragged in my throat, head throbbing…

I landed on my feet, and water shimmered in front of me. Dizzy, I tried to get my bearings. An abandoned brick building, broken windows… broken pieces of wood in the sand.

Was I in the right place? I tried turning my head to survey my surroundings, but a wave of vertigo hit me. I dropped to the ground, trying to throw up, nothing left in my stomach.

I raised my arm to my eyes, my vision blurry. It had to be nearly one o'clock.

Had I made it? The world blurred and darkened, but suddenly there was someone standing over me. I tried to ask which way the Sheerness Docks were, but couldn't speak.

The figure kneeled and plucked something from my hand. The bone. Lucy.

My mind whirled, and I struggled to stand up. I needed the bone. It could save Scarlett somehow.

The voice sounded far away. "Well, you made it. I'm surprised, I admit."

As my world dimmed, I heard the sound of footsteps moving away from me.

"Stop," I mumbled, and then everything went black.

* * *

"HORACE, DON'T!"

A wheeze, a gurgle, my mom's lungs bubbling as blood flooded them. I shut my eyes, suffocating in the cramped space. I was too big to stay under a small bed.

"Couldn't you save her?" It was my chief's voice, full of disappointment.

I opened my eyes, looked at him. He was shaking his head sadly.

"You're an FBI agent, Liddell, what were you doing under the bed?"

He was right. I should have saved my mother, but instead I'd hidden under the bed like a coward. As I crawled out from the bed, I let out a sob.

"Stop that! I want you to report back tomorrow, you hear me? Get on the first plane and report back about what you did."

My mom lay on the floor—in my room, for some reason. A trickle of blood ran down her chin. She opened her mouth to yell at me, but all she managed to get out was a wheeze, and a gurgle.

"I'm sorry!" I blurted.

Gabriel looked down at me, eyes full of regret. "I shouldn't have helped you, Cassandra."

My blood roared, and guilt pressed on my chest like a thousand rocks. "But…"

"Cassandra!"

Gabriel's deep voice pierced the nightmare and my eyes flickered open, the afternoon sun blinding. I squinted, and a figure knelt over me, blocking the harsh light. It took me a moment before my vision focused on his deep, hazel eyes. *Gabriel.*

Visions of my past flickered in my mind. Mentally, I scrambled to bury them again, to push them deep under the surface. I couldn't function with that gurgling noise ringing in my mind. At last, I cleared my skull of those dark memories, clamping them tightly underground. "What happened?" I asked faintly.

"You scared the hell out of me, that's what happened," Gabriel said, brushing the wet hair from my face. "When I got here you were hardly breathing, completely pale. I thought you were dying!"

"Are we in Sheerness Docks?" I asked

"Yeah. I drove here after Roan told me where to find you."

"Good." I groaned, pushing myself up until I was sitting. Dirt clung to my sodden dress. "I think I got here on time." I hazily recalled the figure, and her voice as my world had dimmed. It had been a woman, I realized, her voice full of malice. And it sounded familiar. I'd met her before…

"You delivered the bone?"

"I… think so. Roan told you about the pelvic bone thing?"

"Yeah."

"Is he here?"

"No. He said he had somewhere else he needed to be. What happened to you? Did someone attack you?"

"No." I thought of Grendel. "Well… yes, back at the club,

but he didn't do this. I used too much magic, and it started screwing with me."

Gabriel took my elbow, helping me stand. I was shaking, my whole body weak. I leaned into him, so grateful he'd come for me.

"I was hoping I'd get Scarlett back."

"Come. I'll take you to my car."

"Thank you for coming for me. Have I mentioned that you're fantastic?" I leaned against him as we walked to the road. He opened the passenger's door for me and helped me inside. I closed my eyes as he got in the driver's seat and turned on the engine.

The car hummed to life, and we pulled away.

"Do you have any idea what the abductor's next move will be?"

"I don't know," I said hollowly.

"Did you see him?"

"It was a woman." My mouth was dry, and I swallowed hard. "She said she was surprised I made it."

"That's it?"

"Yeah, I think so. I was busy fainting."

"Right. So what do we—"

"Gabriel, I can't think right now, I'm too…"

I searched for a word. When you don't eat for too long, you're hungry, or famished. A lack of water makes you thirsty. I had no magic. My body craved the vibrant sensation of magic that I'd never known I had until it was gone.

"I'm too weak," I said simply.

"Of course. Sorry. Close your eyes."

Before I drifted off to sleep, I looked at the rear-view mirror. I looked terrible. My hair hung tangled around my face, I had black circles under my eyes, my face was sickly pale. Dirt covered my wet skin and dress, forming muddy smudges. I tried to feel for the reflection, desperate to form a bond with it.

I could feel something there, but I couldn't bond with it. I tried for several minutes, biting my lip in frustration. Nothing. Had I destroyed my magic? The thought filled me with a strange dread.

As we drove, an emptiness gnawed at my chest, too terrible to bear. I shifted uncomfortably in my seat yearning for… something, I didn't know what. Until, suddenly, I could feel it. To our right, there was something I needed, I starved for. I could feel it washing over my skin in faint waves.

"Take that exit," I said, my voice hoarse.

"What?"

"Do it. Now!"

I was about to grab the steering wheel and twist it myself, consumed by desperation. But there was no need. Glancing at me with concern, Gabriel steered the car to the exit from the highway.

"Are you going to explain this?"

"It's there…" I pointed out the windshield at another road. "To our right! Get us there!"

"What is there?"

"I don't know! Please! I'm so… I *need* it."

He turned right again and I guided him, the sensation tugging me like an invisible cord. My eyes could hardly take in where we were going until Gabriel stopped.

"Okay," he said. "Why are we at the hospital? Do you need medical help?"

I stared wide-eyed at the blue sign in front of a squat brick building. *Sheppey Community Hospital.* There was something here I needed.

"I'll be right back." I opened the door, stumbling out, following the tug at my body.

I pushed through the hospital doors, oblivious to everything but the magnetic pull. *So close now.* I ran down the blue-walled hall into a large room, full of chairs. People milled about, their faces serious, worried. Tears stained the cheeks of some.

A toddler screamed, clutching his ears. A young woman clutched her bleeding hand, her clothes stained with blood.

The emergency waiting room.

Energy vibrated through the room, feeding my body. I took deep breaths, relief washing over me, just standing there, feeling the rush. A banquet of fear.

Everywhere around me, people were worrying for their loved ones, terrified of bad news, anxiously waiting for the doctors to tell them what was going on. A boy with an ear infection didn't understand what was happening to him.

The only one enjoying themselves in here was me—the fucking terror leech—as my magic built inside me.

I wanted to stop, to leave, and yet I stood there and fed.

Finally, my body was satisfied, drunk on fear. I could tell my magic was far from its former self—just a fragment of what it had been. Filling the well would take a long time. But it was there, and now I could feel the reflections around me, let my mind bond with them.

I walked outside, my body whole again, but my soul a little broken. In the parking lot, I pulled open the car door, ignoring Gabriel's concerned stare.

I knew who I was now, and I would never be the same.

CHAPTER 15

*I*n Gabriel's bathroom, the ransom note was still scrawled on the mirror, written in blood. It had dried to a deep brown. I had an overwhelming desire to wash it off, but maybe I'd be able to get it tested for DNA or fingerprints.

I turned my back to the reflection as I pulled off the muddy dress, and threw it into the trash. When I'd originally stolen it, I'd thought of returning it, perhaps. But I had waded in the murky river water in it, and probably vomited tea on it, and finally, I'd lain on the dirty docks for several hours in it. There was no coming back for that dress.

I turned on the shower—hot enough to turn my skin red —and stepped into the stream. Steam billowed around me, and I let the hot water run over my body. What was Scarlett doing now? And why had that woman's voice sounded so damn familiar?

I couldn't place it. She had a British accent, but there'd been nothing remarkable about it. It was a generic sort of accent—nothing regional. I scrubbed my body all over, working up a soapy lather, scented of lilac, then rinsed off the suds.

After a few minutes, I turned off the shower, and stepped into the steamy bathroom. I toweled off, then pulled on my underwear, a pair of jeans, and a cotton T-shirt.

I stood in front of the mirror and felt for the reflection, testing my magic like someone trying to stand on a sprained ankle. I did it gently, my body tense as if expecting the pain of rejection. But within a few moments, I felt the reflection click in my mind, bonding with me. From here, I could even bond with another reflection, looking through the toaster in Gabriel's kitchen, watching the kettle steam.

I didn't dare trying to jump through the reflection. Not yet. When I thought of how it felt to get trapped between reflections, a shiver ran up my spine. I dropped the link to the kitchen reflection.

Through the maroon smears, I stared at my own face, feeling as if I was looking at a stranger. This woman, with her pink, unkempt hair, was not Special Agent Cassandra Liddell. The woman before me was a lilive, a fortal. A terror leech. Someone who thrived off human suffering, her own feelings a drug for fae. Wanted by the CIA.

I had a thousand ideas of what should be done. I could try and find Roan, discuss our next step. I could try and contact the FBI, who could hopefully help me reach out to the CIA. Maybe get a forensic crew here, analyze the note.

I stared at myself, wondering if the abductor would contact me again. I had a feeling she would. There was something… personal in the way she'd reached out to me the last time, watching me through the bathroom mirror, her magic similar to mine. I must know her, right? I'd recognized the voice.

I bonded with the reflection again, searching for Scarlett. Nothing. The same result for Roan.

I frowned, stepping back to take in the whole note. Written like a nursery rhyme, just like the Rix's note. Gabriel had asked me about the chances that the Rix and the abductor both happened to communicate in nursery rhymes.

Was there a significance to the similarity, or just a quirk of how the fae communicated with humans? It was, of course, entirely possible that this had all been orchestrated by someone loyal to the Rix, enraged that I'd killed a petty king.

But then why the whole puppet-master charade, getting me to run around London with a pelvic bone? Why not just murder me?

I needed to do some research. I crossed into the bedroom, searching for my laptop before I remembered I'd left it in the kitchen. My hair dampened my T-shirt as I crossed into the kitchen. Being clean felt glorious.

As I stepped into the kitchen, I smiled to see Gabriel frying eggs in a pan, barefoot in jeans and a gray T-shirt.

Music filled the air, a jazz tune—a variation, I thought, on a song called "Naima."

I sat at the table, opening my laptop. "Hey, gorgeous."

He smiled, his cheek dimpling as he scooped scrambled eggs onto toast. "How are you feeling?"

I hesitated. "Fine."

"Are you hungry? I'm making you something to eat."

"No. But did I thank you already for picking me up in Kent?"

"Yes, and eat anyway." He slid a plate in front of me, sticking a fork in a mound of scrambled eggs.

I took a bite dutifully, and swallowed. On my laptop, I opened the browser, and began searching for articles about nursery rhymes, fae, and psychopaths.

From my experience so far, there was significant overlap in the latter two groups.

"What is this music?" I asked. "It's nice."

"The Lauren Gardner Quintet."

"Never heard of them."

"Yeah. We were never very successful."

I raised my eyes from the screen, smiling at Gabriel. "You're a part of this quintet, I take it?"

He slid a cup of tea over to me. "I *was*. Years ago."

"Let me guess… piano?"

He sat across from me, in front of his own plate of eggs. "Nope, that was Lauren. I was on drums."

I glanced at his athletic-looking arms, realizing that might be why his shoulders and arms seemed so strong. "Ah. Drums. You still play, though, on your own."

He frowned. "How did you know that?"

"Just…" I swallowed hard. "Your arms. It's either that or you spend a lot of time in the gym."

That dimple appeared again in his cheek.

"Anyway, the music is lovely," I said. "I'd love to hear more. Once…"

"Once your friend is safe."

I nodded, and took another bite of the eggs. I looked at the screen again, sighing as I scanned through a bunch of useless articles about the dark origins of nursery rhymes. I sighed, shaking my head.

"What are you doing?"

"Trying to understand the note in the bathroom. You said Lucy Locket was an old nursery rhyme. And the Rix's note had been based on the Queen of Hearts."

"You're trying to profile the abductor?"

"That's what I do. That reminds me." I rubbed a knot in my forehead. "I don't think I can stay here long. The CIA knows I'm fae, and they think I have something to do with Scarlett's disappearance. I was the last person she was seen with."

"I'm not sure I like where this is going."

"When I went to the CIA's London station, there was a bit of a kerfuffle, and they tried to shoot me."

"Wonderful."

"So, it probably won't be long until they connect the dots to you and come sniffing around here."

He leaned back in his chair, scrubbing a hand over his mouth. "Mmm-hmm."

"I should probably find somewhere else to stay."

He frowned. "I'll get you a hotel room."

Tears stung my eyes. Gabriel was unbelievably generous. "Why are you helping me?"

"Because I'm not an arsehole and I don't want your friend to die."

"Right." I dropped my fork on the plate, unable to eat anymore. "Thanks. I had another thought. You should get a forensic scientist in here, have them test the mirror for—"

"Already called Gracie this morning. She took what they needed. She couldn't get a print, unfortunately."

I felt a surge of panic. "If the CIA interviews her about what she saw—"

"She won't say anything to anyone, Cassandra. I trust her. And she's under no obligation to give information to a foreign intelligence agency."

I let out a long, measured breath.

He nodded at my laptop. "Did you find what you were looking for?"

"No. I need to know more. This abductor. This woman. Why did she target Scarlett? Was it an attack on Scarlett? Or was it aimed at me?"

"Perhaps both."

"Right. And what does she want? Her first task seemed so arbitrary. Why would she need an old bone? It makes no sense."

"*First* task? So you think there will be more?"

I sipped my tea. "Yes. I think so. Very soon."

"What makes you say that?"

"This woman enjoyed the thrill of the race. She likes it when things are fast, unpredictable, intense. We'll get another message in no time. And before that happens, I need to know more about her. I need to find a way to talk to her, to negotiate with her."

I turned to the laptop again, clicking on another link. So far, I'd found zero scholarly articles about psychopathy and nursery rhymes, or even poems. Nothing but a bunch of bullshit blogs. I read them anyway, feeling my eyes droop as I struggled to make sense of the information. My mind seemed to be drifting, and if I could just close my eyes for a few moments....

"Cassandra." Gabriel gripped my shoulder.

I started, raising my head. I had fallen asleep on the table.

"What?" I blinked.

"Look."

On the kitchen window that overlooked the street, words had begun materializing.

CHAPTER 16

$\mathcal{A}$s the words appeared on the window, my body froze. The sentences scrawled over the glass, the blood trickling down the pane.

> *Three blind mice. Three blind mice.*
> *See how they run. A bull in the sun.*

My heart thumped, and I tried to avoid thinking about where the blood had come from. I highly doubted it was the abductor's.

"A bull in the sun," Gabriel read aloud, his voice piercing the fog in my mind.

As another line of red smears began to appear on the glass, I shot out of the chair, knocking it over with my momentum. I rushed for the guest room, and rummaged through the discarded clothing on the bed and floor until I found the wand-shaped magical scanner.

"Cassandra!" Gabriel called. "What are you doing? There are more words appearing."

My pulse racing, I dashed into the kitchen, trying not to

get distracted by the lengthening smears of red. Hurriedly, I waved the scanner across the window, praying that I'd gotten there in time for it to capture a magical imprint.

"What's that thing?" asked Gabriel.

The scanner let out a high-pitched tone, and a small green light blinked.

I sighed in relief. "I got a magical imprint. If I can find some way to get the CIA to cooperate, maybe we can identify the source of the magic." Maybe even find Scarlett.

Stepping back, I stared at the gory message on the window as the last lines of the poem materialized, and I stood back to read it all out loud.

> Three blind mice. Three blind mice.
> See how they run. A bull in the sun.
> You all chase after the little spy,
> Did you ever think you would watch her die?
> At six forty-four, if you don't bleed the boar,
> Scarlett's sacrificed.

Sharp claws of panic raked through my chest. These were supposed to be our instructions, the way to save Scarlett, and it made no sense whatsoever. The only clear thing was the part about sacrificing Scarlett. "What the hell does that mean?"

The blood from the letters trickled down the window in a gory trail, pooling on the bottom sill.

"Hang on." Gabriel jotted down the words on a notebook, which was wise, since the entire message was becoming an incomprehensible mess. "The bull in the sun," he muttered.

My fists tightened. "Does this make sense to you?"

"Not particularly."

I closed my eyes, replaying the words in my mind. "The three blind mice are all chasing after the little spy. Me, you,

146

and Roan, maybe? The three of us were working together. Maybe the abductor is letting us know that she was watching us. She knows about you and Roan."

"And she's enjoying watching us run around blindly."

"Exactly."

"What is this boar we're supposed to bleed? And where? Last time, she gave us a very specific location."

Gabriel scrubbed a hand over his mouth. "Let me think. The last time she gave us a hint about where we needed to go. The Winchester Geese. That linked us directly to the palace. But there's nothing so straightforward here."

I pulled his notebook from his hand, staring at the message. "Why six forty-four? It's weirdly precise. A normal person would have said six forty-five."

"Quite clearly, she is not a normal person."

"But there's a method to her madness. 'Winchester Geese' was straightforward to you, only because you happened to know about it. To anyone else, it would have been a code. She wants us to figure out her code, to mull over her words." I was already forming a mental picture of her. "She's someone who was probably starved of attention, and now she wants as much of it as possible from us. She relies on her intellect, and it boosts her ego to know that other people will appreciate her cleverness. She's desperate for affirmation, for approval."

Gabriel leaned against the counter, crossing his arms. "Be that as it may, I still don't know what we're supposed to do."

I began pacing in the small kitchen, my thoughts whirling. "The Winchester Geese were alive... what, five hundred years ago?"

Gabriel's eyes were closed. "Something like that."

"So maybe she's a history nerd. Is there anything in London's history connected to bulls?"

His eyes snapped open. "A bull in the sun... yes." He

stared at me. "At the museum of London. There are relics from the Temple of Mithras. It's a Roman-era ruin in the center of the city, left by participants of a mystery cult. He was associated with Sol, the sun god."

"And the bull?"

"There were images all over the original temple—Mithras slaying bulls, then sharing a feast with the sun god. Some believe that actual bulls were sacrificed at the temple. Supposedly, the bull was sacrificed above ground, and the blood from the bull's throat poured over the supplicants below. Something to do with astrology." He pulled out his phone, scanning. His brow furrowed as he read. "Maybe the number four is significant. There are twelve astrological ages. Taurus, the bull sign, happens to be the fourth. The slaughtering of the bull might have represented the end of the Taurean age." His gaze met mine again. "I'd say the Temple of Mithras is definitely our place."

I could have hugged him. "Good. I knew you'd come up with something. So where do we find the boar?"

"I have no idea. But maybe we start at the temple."

I checked the time. It was half past four. "We've got just over two hours." I bit my lip. "Why do I feel like this won't be a straightforward, run-of-the-mill, everyday London boar sacrifice?"

"Maybe we shouldn't try to play her game," Gabriel said softly. "We're letting her control us. Maybe we should try to strike back instead of letting the puppet-master pull our strings."

He was right, and I knew it.

I'd only handled one kidnapping case as a field agent, and we'd managed to return the child to her parents within fourteen hours. During that time, we'd had to constantly hold the parents in check. They wanted to do *everything* to make sure that the abductors were happy, and wouldn't harm their daughter. At the time, I'd felt a mixture of sympathy and frustration with their behavior. We were the professionals. Couldn't they see that letting us do our job was the best way to get their daughter back?

Now, *I* was the one frantic over a loved one. And instead of acting like a pro, following time-tested methods of handling these cases, I was acting instinctively, doing whatever I could to keep the abductor happy.

I tried to rationalize my behavior. I still had no direct line of communication. The abductor was fae, which meant all prior profiling research was out the window. I was treading new territory—one with magic. Who knew what would happen if I didn't meet the demands of a fae? They didn't think like humans, and I had no research to reference.

On the other hand, I could rationalize anything my heart wanted me to do. My heart was telling me to comply with the abductor's demands, and I was doing everything I could to convince myself.

My fingers tightened into fists as I tried to get a grip. I *had* to talk with the abductor.

I leaned down, staring into Gabriel's chrome toaster. I gazed at the surface, searching for Scarlett, thinking of her vibrant hair, her sparkling green eyes. The way she waggled her eyebrows after a dirty joke.

Nothing.

Then I tried to search for the woman I had glimpsed in the docks, thinking of her mocking voice, the hazy outline of her figure.

Again, nothing.

She hadn't responded earlier, when I'd showed her the note, and didn't respond this time as well. Maybe she didn't have Scarlett at all?

I considered my options. The best way to gain control of the situation would be to ignore the abductor's instructions and wait until she contacted us again. If I'd been acting dispassionately, that would have been my choice. But I simply couldn't risk sacrificing Scarlett just to gain control.

The second option was to follow the abductor's demands to the letter, resulting in a new demand. That was out of the question, too.

I had to find a third option. A negotiation without communication. Find a way to comply, while clarifying that she wasn't calling all the shots.

"You're right. Under normal circumstances, you're right," I said. "But I can't get back in touch with her. If we wait for the abductor to contact us again, it might be after she's slit Scarlett's throat. We'll have to follow the instructions, buy some time, and figure out a way to outmaneuver her."

Gabriel frowned, mulling over what I said. "Fine. Let's go to the temple."

* * *

As Gabriel drove, his car crawling down Threadneedle street, I used his phone to look at some images near the temple. It looked like the center of one of the busiest parts of the city—by Walbrook and all the banks. At this point, I had no idea where the damn boar would come from.

"Maybe it's not a literal boar," Gabriel suggested.

My mouth went dry. We were clueless. "Do you have an idea as to how we can sacrifice a metaphorical boar? I don't suppose they'd sell a boar in a pet shop, would they?"

"Are you joking?"

My heart thundered. "No. I'm just desperate."

I pulled out my phone, glancing at the time. It was seven minutes past five. The car wasn't even moving, stuck in London's traffic. I considered dumping the car and trying to get there through reflections, but the mere thought made my stomach turn.

"What the bloody hell is going on with the traffic?" Gabriel muttered, honking.

"It's rush hour right now."

"Yeah, but we're practically at a standstill." He pulled out his phone and pressed it to his ear. "Hello, Constable Taylor? Threadneedle Street is at a complete standstill. It's been like this since Bishopsgate. Has there been an accident or—" Gabriel paused, his eyes widening. "Okay… who's in charge? Wright? Yeah, thanks."

He hung up and looked at me.

"A wild boar has been set free by Moorgate Station. Two injured. There is a blockade, and they're bringing in a specialist to take it down."

I grabbed Gabriel's arms. "We have to get there before he does. We *need* this, Gabriel."

"Right." Gabriel nodded. He swerved the steering wheel, honking his horn as he slowly drove his car onto the sidewalk, ignoring the shocked stares from the pedestrians. Both of us jumped from the car, Gabriel pulling out his badge and waving around.

"Police business!" he shouted.

As we sprinted through the intersection, I asked, "How far?"

Gabriel moved swiftly, weaving through the traffic. "About fifteen minutes. Or less, if we're fast." He clamped his phone to his ear again.

"Wright? This is DI Stewart. I'm temporarily replacing DCI Wood… That's right. Yes, I heard you were handling the wild animal situation…"

We careened into a narrow lane called Old Jewry and pounded down the narrow sidewalk. "Move!" I shouted at a group of pedestrians who were in our way. They parted in panic, and I ran past, jostling one of them, Gabriel close behind. A string of tuts and sighs followed our wake.

"Don't let him approach the animal!" Gabriel shouted. "No, it's... Wright, listen to me, this is no ordinary boar... Fuck!" He shoved the phone into his pocket. "The specialist is already there," he rasped. "The constable said he's already past the blockade, and the situation is nearly over."

"Is he about to kill it?" I asked, my breath ragged in my throat.

"Not sure," Gabriel said. "Maybe they want to tranquilize it. They think it escaped from the zoo."

I gritted my teeth, hoping that the English distaste for guns and violence would prevail. I needed that animal alive.

CHAPTER 17

*I*n front of Moorgate Station, four police cars formed a blockade, with at least a dozen police surrounding the cars. Honestly, it felt like an excessive show of force for one wild boar. To the London police's credit, handling wild hogs probably wasn't in their basic training. I could envision a scenario where a fifteenth-century French king would have boar-wrangling experience, but for your everyday London cop, it just couldn't be in the standard playbook.

Gabriel still managed to stride confidently forward, already flashing his badge as if he knew how to handle a wild boar.

"DI Stewart," he said authoritatively. "Where's Sergeant Wright?"

"Right here." A squat, stocky, square-headed man walked over, his face grave.

"What's the situation, Sergeant?" Gabriel asked.

Sergeant Wright scratched his stubble. "We evacuated the station, shut down the tube, and sent in the specialist in fifteen minutes ago. I haven't heard from him in seven

153

minutes, when he said that the darts he brought were malfunctioning. He said he was heading back out, so I'm not sure what happened."

Gabriel's brow furrowed. "Malfunctioning? Did he say why?"

"No. He should have been here already, and we're working under the assumption that he was hurt by the animal. We have an AFO team on their way. They'll put down the animal and get the specialist out."

AFO were the Authorized Firearms Officers, the equivalent of the American SWAT force—the only British police who carried firearms.

"The animal needs to be kept alive, Sergeant," Gabriel said. "It is crucial that—"

"All due respect, DI Stewart, but this isn't your unit, and you're not in command of the patrol police. I have a possibly hurt man there, and I need to get him out. That giant bloody pig is out of control, and I don't give a fuck if it's a precious zoo animal, or if it's on an endangered list, or even if it's the prime minister's pet. The thing's got tusks the size of your arm. It's going—"

"Sergeant." I stepped forward, hoping no one would recognize me. I hadn't spent much time with the patrol police, and in any case, the pink hair might throw them off. "I'm Fiona Tursten, the zoo's vet," I said, doing my best to fake a British accent. "Give me ten minutes. I'll take care of the animal for you."

He shook his head. "Miss Tursten, I can't risk—"

"The AFO might not get here on time to save your specialist," I said. "And without weapons, you can't risk sending any more men in. I'm here right now."

He glared at Gabriel. "DI Stewart, I hope she knows what she's doing."

Gabriel blinked. "Ms. Tursten is the best in her field. It's why I called her. She knows how to..." He cleared his throat. "How to calm a boar."

Wright turned to one of his officers, a tall man with a mustache. "Radio!" he shouted. "Our vet here needs it."

The officer lumbered over and handed me the radio.

Wright arched a cautionary eyebrow at me. "Once the AFO get here, I'm sending them in, Tursten, and you're coming out. Don't make me regret it."

"Of course."

Wright turned, shouting at the other officers. "Vet's coming through!"

With dozens of officers' eyes on me, I crossed through the police blockade, Gabriel following close behind me.

Silence welcomed us as we crossed into the station, the fluorescent lights flickering. A strange energy hummed through the station, and the hair rose on the back of my neck. I could still hear the chatter of radio and the occasional shout from the officers outside, but inside, nothing but my own footsteps and a faint dripping noise.

"Stalking a boar in a tube station," muttered Gabriel. "I feel like my life took a wrong turn somewhere."

"You and me both."

I scanned the abandoned space—the gates, the empty ticket booth.

Gabriel turned to me, pulling his wallet from his pocket. "Follow close behind me through the gates."

We crossed to the gates, and he swiped his wallet over the scanner. The gates beeped, sliding open and breaking the silence. I stuck close behind Gabriel as we moved through, my body brushing against his.

From the wide stairwell in front of us, I heard a faint shuffling in the darkness. Someone had cut the electricity on the platforms.

I pointed. "I heard something down there."

As we hurried down the stairs, faint yellow lights briefly flickered, and for just a moment, I caught a glimpse of something dark laying on the far corner of the platform.

Gabriel pulled out his phone, using it as a flashlight. "Look," Gabriel said softly, pointing. The white sphere of light from his flashlight illuminated a motionless figure. As we moved closer, I could see it was a bald man, neatly dressed in black trousers and a corduroy jacket. A few feet away lay a long black case, probably his tranquilizer gun. A thick puddle of blood glistened all around him. Was he dead?

Gabriel knelt, pressing two fingers to the man's throat. "Alive. Barely."

The light moved down his leg, and I caught a glimpse of the blood pumping from his wound, and I thought I glimpsed a bit of bone. Taking in his deathly pale face and his mangled left leg, I wondered if he'd survive. Without immediate help, he'd probably die of blood loss within minutes.

My fingers clenched. "We need to get a tourniquet around his leg."

"Right." Gabriel rose. "If you can get some cloth, I'll find something to apply the pressure. Do you have anything to use as a light?"

"Yeah." As Gabriel ran off, his footfalls echoing off the ceiling, I reached into my handbag, pulling out the mini flashlight attached to my keychain. I rested it on the floor to illuminate the man.

Then I knelt by his torso and pulled the cursed iron knife from my bag. Immediately, the blade whispered in the depths of my mind, *Bathe me in blood.* I ignored the knife's macabre glee and grabbed the man's jacket. Using the blade, I sliced through a large strip of corduroy.

With the twisted blade, it was clumsy work, yielding a ragged and tattered piece of cloth. Still, it would work for what I needed. I twisted it several times, forming a makeshift rope. As I worked, I tried to keep my ears attuned for the sound of animal grunts and footfalls. If I wasn't careful, at any moment, the boar could come hurtling out of the shadows and gore me to death.

Moving to the man's leg, I wrapped the cloth rope just below the knee. His blood soaked my fingers.

I tied the rope tightly, and goosebumps rose on my skin. From another part of the station, I could hear a snuffling noise, and something like the smashing of tile. I swallowed hard, energized by my own fear. From what I could tell, the boar was around a corner. I tried to keep an eye on that direction as I worked.

I tightened the rope, pulling as hard as I could. The man groaned, the pain penetrating his unconscious mind. Footsteps echoed through the station, and I caught a glimpse of Gabriel moving toward me, gripping something in his hand.

As he approached, I held out my hand, and he thrust something like a broken broomstick into my palm.

I slid the stick between the rope and the man's thigh, then snatched my knife from the ground. "I heard the boar. Just around the corner, I think." I looked up at him. "Can you twist it? I'm gonna cut more cloth."

While Gabriel knelt, twisting the stick, I worked the knife through another strip of the man's corduroy jacket.

Gabriel tightened the pressure, and the man let out a whimper. Then, Gabriel held the stick firmly, and I used the second strip of cloth to tie the stick in its position. I shoved the knife back into my bag.

Around the corner, the boar's grunting and heavy footfalls were getting louder. The damn thing was probably panicking, trapped in a dark subway station. How it had managed to get beyond the ticket gates was beyond me.

I rose, wiping my bloodied hands on my jeans. "Get this man out of here. I'll handle the boar."

Gabriel shook his head. "I can't leave you—"

"He'll die if he doesn't get help, Gabriel. And I need you to run back to the temple for your car. We're going to need it to get this boar back there. I can handle one fucking pig." At least, I *thought* I could handle the boar. Right now, I felt the thrilling rush of my own fear, and I wasn't entirely sure how accurate my perception was. "Once I get the boar, we'll need to get to the Temple of Mithras as fast as we can. And I don't think we can take him in a police car."

In the dim light, I could see a struggle flickering across his features. It wasn't in his nature to leave a partner in danger, but he knew I was right. If he didn't get the victim medical help immediately, he'd die.

At last, Gabriel nodded. He grabbed the man by one arm and hefted him on his shoulder, grunting in effort. He took a step, nearly slipping in the puddle of blood. Then, catching his balance, he walked away, leaving behind him a trail of bloody footprints.

I walked over to the black case and opened it, using my flashlight to illuminate the contents. Inside, I found a long gun, three darts, a plastic bottle of liquid, and a syringe. The bottle probably held tranquilizer fluid, and the syringe could be used to fill the darts. When I held the darts up to the light, I could see that the specialist had already prepared them— each half-filled with clear liquid.

In the dim light, it took me a minute to figure out how to load the darts into the rifle—just one at a time. Carefully, I slid a dart in the rifle, then slung the case over my back.

I flicked off the flashlight and shoved it into my bag. Slinking through the shadows, half-crouching, I crept to the place where I'd heard the grunting. I left the light behind. Slowly, with the fear blazing through my nerve-endings, my eyes were starting to adjust to the dark. If I shone the flashlight around, the boar might come charging right for me.

I rounded the corner, adrenaline blazing. There, against the tile wall, I caught a glimpse of an enormous form, emitting a low growl.

When the lights flickered again, my blood roared in my ears. Twenty feet away stood an immense boar, its flesh and fur the ivory color of bone. The thing was nearly as tall as me, with two curved tusks the size of my arms, spattered in blood. Its eyes were the size of baseballs, dark as the opening of a cave.

The lights flickered off again, and my heart slammed against my ribs. I tried to make out its form in the dark again, my eyes slowly adjusting. In the ancient, primitive part of my brain, a voice screamed at me: *Run.* I tried to marshal my calm, using my FBI training. With fear whispering over my skin, I lifted the rifle in a fluid motion and shot.

My aim was perfect, the dart hitting the boar in one of its shoulders—but the damn thing bounded off, as if hitting rock. *Shit.* How had that dart just bounced off it? Maybe I'd hit its shoulder bone.

With an enraged grunt that echoed through my bones, the boar charged for me. I dove out of its path, rolling on the floor. I was already inserting the second dart into the gun, my pulse racing. As I fiddled with the gun, I heard the boar turning, grunting. I strained to see him in the dark. To get it, I would need to shoot it somewhere soft, like his stomach.

The boar screeched, a sound that turned my gut. I tensed, preparing to roll away when it charged. But instead of charging me, I heard its feet clack against the stone floor, the low growl as it ran past me. For a moment, the lights flickered on, and I seized the chance, taking aim at the boar's haunches. My pulse racing, fired, just as the lights flickered off again. I heard the dart clatter to the floor again. *What the shit?*

I strained to see in the dark, my raw fear helping me

penetrate the shadows. Through the dim light, I could see the boar turn again, its dark eyes glistening with rage. My mouth went dry, and I loaded the third and last dart into the gun. I'd have to wait for a sure thing with this one.

I crouched, keeping my gaze on the creature's dim silhouette, but my body felt strange, my fingers clumsy. I had the strange sensation that a layer of thick lead was encasing my body, my movements slow and cumbersome. I struggled to keep my eye on the boar. Panicking, I tried to re-aim my gun but realized I couldn't move my arms. It felt as if a thick layer of metal were locking them in place.

"All right, Cassandra?" a voice said to my left.

I couldn't turn my head to look, but I knew the voice.

"Alvin?" I struggled to get the word out.

"Right here." A note of sadness tinged his voice.

"What are you doing here?"

"You didn't keep your promise," Alvin said. "I have to say, I'm a bit vexed."

My blood roared in my ears. Through the darkness, I could see the glint of the boar's terrifying eyes, ready to gore me to death.

"Can we talk about this later?" I slurred. "I need your help… something's wrong with me. Feels like metal all over me."

"Right. You can't move. I know."

Understanding dawned in my mind. "You did this."

"You were supposed to ask your mate to delete my name from the database. You had the chance. You didn't do it. My name's still on there, innit?"

A drop of sweat tricked from my forehead as I struggled to move. Apart from my lips, Alvin had completely frozen my body. I'd broken my promise to him, and it gave him power over me. Power to do *this*.

"Alvin. This boar will kill me if you don't free me."

"The king will kill *me* once they discover what I did!" Alvin said sharply.

Underneath the heavy lead weighing down my body, terror raked its claws up my spine. "We can think of something. If I die now, it won't do you any good."

"Nah. Sorry, but it will. Grendel has quite the prize on your head. With his money, I might be able to buy the silence of the fae technomancers."

"Alvin—"

The boar's feet clacked over the floor, his furious grunts echoing off the ceiling as he charged.

Alvin sniffled. "Goodbye, Cassandra. I actually liked you."

"Alvin! Give me more time! I'll get your name off that list! Just a bit more time!"

I could hear the boar moving closer, charging for me, its lethal tusks about to impale my chest.

"Please!" I shouted in desperation, willing my body to move from under the heavy lead weighing it down.

Suddenly, a pulse of warmth flooded my body, melting the feel of lead from my body. I was free. Just before the boar slammed into me, I rolled, swiveling the gun and taking a shot. Once again, I heard the dart bounce off its hide, clattering on the stone.

"Fuck!"

"Iron!" Alvin shouted. "You've got to use iron!"

I threw the gun on the ground, grasping desperately around me for the case. My fingers brushed against it, and I popped it open, feeling for more darts. Still, I didn't want to attract the boar's attention by turning on my light.

In the case, I felt nothing. No tranquilizers, and no iron. I felt around for the syringe, then plunged it into the plastic bottle with the tranquilizing liquid. My breath came in shallow gasps as I filled it up. I shoved my hand into my bag, feeling for the twisted iron knife. I yanked it out, squirting some liquid onto the blade. The sound of the boar's enraged shrieks echoed off the ceiling. For a moment, the lights flickered, and I saw it charging for me.

I held the syringe in my left hand, the knife in my right, trying to predict the trajectory of the beast's charge as the lights went dark again.

When I thought it was right next to me, I lunged sideways, turning to slam both my hands down at once. I slammed the knife into its flank, and the syringe a fraction of a section later.

The boar screamed, bucking its tusks with a furious motion, and agony splintered my leg. Blocking out the pain, I depressed the plunger on the syringe, emptying some of it into the boar's blood before its furious motion tore both the syringe and the knife from my hands, running off over the platform.

I fell back, moaning in pain, gripping my ankle. I could feel it wasn't too deep—not down to the bone like the other man's—but it hurt like a bitch.

"Fuck." I clenched my teeth, trying to take the pain. "This is a shit show."

Alvin crouched by my side, his fingers tracing around the wound at my ankle. The lights flickered, and I saw him, drawing a small bottle from within the flap of his tattered jacket, his shaggy blond hair hanging in his eyes. When the light blinked off again, I felt him pour a cool liquid over the wound. The entire area instantly went numb.

"Analgesic," he said. "That's all I can do."

"That boar..." I swallowed hard. "Is it... magical?"

Instead of answering, I heard him heave a heavy sigh.

"Alvin?"

"Do you know what I just helped you do?" he asked, his voice cracking. "Bloody hell, Cassandra, I should have stayed away from you. I'm absolutely fucked now!"

"Why?" I asked. "What—"

"Two days!" Alvin said, and already I could hear his voice moving away from me. "You have two days to keep your promise, or I'll deliver your head to Grendel myself!"

I heard his footsteps echo over the floor. My leg throbbed, still losing blood, but with the analgesic Alvin had given me, it was manageable. I reached into my bag, pulling out my flashlight. With the boar injured, I was less worried about it charging me.

I flashed the light around me, scanning the ground for the knife. I found it a few feet from me, covered with the boar's blood, and I heaved a sigh of relief. I gripped it hard, shining the flashlight around the darkened station, searching for the boar, my stomach churning.

It took me only a few seconds to find the thing. It charged for me again, but this time, its movements were erratic, and it stumbled. About fifteen feet from me, it fell to the floor with a final grunt, its eyes slowly closing.

From my bag, my portable radio screamed, and I suddenly realized someone had been shouting into it for a while. I pulled it out, my hand shaking.

"This is Cassan… Uh…Tursten."

"Tursten!" Wright shouted. "Why didn't you answer earlier? Get the hell out of there. We're sending in the AFO."

"No need." On trembling limbs, I limped over to the boar. "The animal is down. Just send in DI Stewart and several people to help us carry it."

CHAPTER 18

*A*fter four of us had hauled the boar up an escalator, using a stretcher that groaned under its weight, we loaded the creature into the back of Gabriel's car. Gabriel had explained to them that I needed to get the boar back to the zoo, and as long as we were taking the thing off Wright's hands, he didn't seem to care.

While Gabriel hurried off to speak with a paramedic, I plopped down in the passenger's seat, the window down. Alone with the unconscious boar, I clutched my ankle, my blood streaming over Gabriel's floor. All around, red and blue lights flickered over the stone walls. I tried to imagine how this boar sacrifice would work in the center of London's financial district, surrounded by bankers and rush hour traffic.

Gabriel hurried back to me, thrusting a roll of gauze into my hands. "Let's go."

As Gabriel slid into the driver's seat, I haphazardly bandaged my ankle, staunching the blood flow. Slowly, Gabriel rolled into traffic, heading back to the Temple of Mithras.

By the time we got to Gresham Street, by Guildhall and the fae bar, the traffic started to ease up. The smell of blood overpowered the car, both from my bandaged ankle and the bleeding boar, its ivory hide stained maroon. That, coupled with the earthy smell of unwashed boar, made me want to gag. I swallowed my revulsion. The idea of adding vomit to this ungodly stench horrified me.

Gabriel turned to me. "How are you doing?"

"Okay." I pulled out a syringe and unbuckled my seatbelt, turning back to the boar. "I'm just gonna make sure this thing doesn't wake up."

I held the syringe just over the sleeping boar's body. If it moved, I'd have to plunge the syringe into its back, filling it with more sedatives, hoping it wouldn't gore me to death. I didn't even want to think about what would happen if it overdosed. The idea of giving the boar mouth to mouth made me want to hurl.

After a few moments of staring down at the dirty animal, I noticed a small metallic chain encircling its neck.

"There's something on this boar," I said. "A necklace."

"Can you get a closer look?"

I tried to unclasp it, but the blood covering my fingers made the slippery.

"No. I'll try again later after I can wipe off my hands. I'm guessing our culprit put the chain there." I glanced at the window, recognizing the intersection near Bank Station. Somehow, everything kept leading back to this neighborhood. Gabriel turned onto a large street, pulling up his car in the bike lane. To our right stood a raised stone platform. On the platform, a low railing surrounded a rectangle of rocks, about one foot high. Modern buildings loomed behind the temple ruins, their glass surfaces gleaming in the city's lights.

I frowned at the stumpy rock foundation. "This is it?"

He unhooked his seatbelt and turned on his blinkers. "This is it."

I checked the time. Six twenty-five. We had twenty minutes. Plenty of time to kill an unconscious boar, I thought. I put the syringe in my bag.

I stepped out of the car, gripping the syringe. "There's no altar here. Just a plateau with some rocks."

"There *was* an altar." He pointed at a curve of rocks on the near side. "We just need to heft this thing to where it used to be."

A shiver of dread snaked up my spine. "What if we got all this wrong?"

Gabriel pinched the bridge of his nose. "I don't know, Cassandra. But it's the only solution we have, and we're running out of time."

I nodded, then stepped out of the car, my stomach clenching. Hurriedly, I pulled open the back door to where the boar lay.

Gabriel grabbed the animal's rear feet, while I pushed its head. Slowly, we shifted the enormous creature over the seat, its body leaving thick smears of blood over Gabriel's car.

"Don't let its head smack the ground!" Gabriel grunted.

"How many laws… are we breaking right now?" I slid my hands under its enormous head.

"Illegal parking," he grunted. "Animal cruelty."

I clutched the head just as the body dropped off the rear seat, and nearly gave myself a hernia.

Straining, we shifted the boar into the sidewalk, my body trembling with effort. A woman striding by glanced at us, then walked on with barely a shrug. You had to love big cities.

"One, two… three!" Gabriel said.

We lifted the monstrous boar, then stumbled toward the plateau of stones. I'd never carried anything so heavy before.

Blood pooled in my bandage, making the wound tingle. I hoped Alvin's analgesic wasn't about to wear off. I took deep breaths, my lungs filling with the scent of boar as we hefted the creature up a short set of stairs.

Passersby in business suits simply walked past on their cell phones, barely glancing at the two people hefting an unconscious boar into the ruins of an ancient Roman temple. *London.*

I gritted my teeth as we got to the low fence between us and the raised rock of the temple's foundations. We could have easily climbed over it—if we hadn't been carrying a wild boar.

"Ready?" I asked through gritted teeth. "I'll slip over the fence as we lift it." Easier said than done.

Gabriel nodded, and we hoisted the boar higher into the air. With the boar held aloft, I stepped over the low fence into the shallow space between the fence and the temple's foundations, my body groaning with the effort.

I strained, using my legs to lift as Gabriel followed me over the fence. Once we'd passed that barrier, we just had to get it onto the temple's foundations—only about a foot off the ground. Groaning, Gabriel stepped up onto the temple's surface, and I followed after him. Slowly, we lowered the boar onto the smooth, rocky surface of the temple's floor, in the gentle curve of stones where an altar had once stood.

Once the boar's enormous ivory body touched the temple's surface, the world around us shimmered.

No longer did modern glass buildings loom over us; no longer could I see the modern thoroughfare. Instead, we stood in a curved stone hall, the walls painted white. Ornate tile mosaics spread across the floor, depicting astrological signs. Moonlight streamed through an oculus above us onto a pedestal altar, its surface carved and brightly painted with an image of a sacrifice: a man in a Phrygian cap, cutting a bull's throat. Silver chalices lined low benches around the hall.

"Fucking hell," Gabriel muttered, gaping. "What the hell just happened?"

"I don't know," I said, still catching my breath. "Magic. I guess we have the right place." I pointed at the altar. It was narrow, and about four feet high. Not the kind of thing we could rest a boar on. "I guess we just sacrifice him near the altar."

"Time?" Gabriel asked.

I checked, my pulse racing. "Six forty." *Shit shit shit.* "Four minutes."

He wiped his hands on his jeans. "Let's finish this."

I shoved my hands into my bag, pulling out the knife, and its gleeful whispers echoed around the inside of my skull. *Bathe me in the blood of fae.*

I clenched my jaw in resolve, gripping the knife tighter. I knelt in the narrow space between the benches, where the boar lay nestled, and I put my hand on its head, watching the slow rise and fall of his chest. "I'm sorry," I whispered to the boar, as I drew the blade closer to it.

"Stop!"

A deep voice boomed off the temple walls, and my hand froze. I whirled around, still crouching.

"Roan?" I said in disbelief, holding the knife near the boar's flesh.

Dressed in black, Roan stood at the other end of the temple before a set of oaken doors. He wore his sword slung over his back. By his side was a beautiful woman whose red hair cascaded over a gold gown. It took me a moment to identify her as Roan's friend, Elrine.

"How did you get here?" My thoughts were whirling.

"We followed the news about a wild boar roaming free in London." His green eyes seemed to root me in place. "When we got there, you were already gone. But there was enough blood for Elrine to track you."

Right. Elrine had magical tracking powers. She had once helped Roan track the Rix using the internal organs of his victims.

I could see Gabriel's body tensing, his fingers clenching. "We're running out of time."

"Get that iron knife away from King Ebor," Roan said.

I glanced at the boar. "What are you talking about? The boar?"

"He isn't just a boar." Elrine's voice dripped with distaste. "He's a fae. King of the Elder Fae in the Hawkwood Forest, in fact. Unfortunately, you have no idea what you're doing."

The boar grunted, his feet beginning to twitch. I pressed the knife harder against his fur. "I have to do it. The message from the abductor—"

"Cassandra." Steel edged Roan's voice, and he drew his sword. "You're a pawn in a war you don't understand. If you kill him, you will break the fragile peace in Trinovantum."

He wouldn't stab me, would he? Either way, I had to risk it. "Listen, I have a plan..."

The boar grunted again, his body bucking. I had to do it now, or I'd be fresh out of time and luck. My heart slammed against my ribs.

"Get that cursed knife away from him!" Roan clutched his sword, pointing it at me. "Listen to me. He's not a boar. He is a fae. Like us. On top of killing a king, you'd be killing an innocent fae."

"Put the bloody sword down," said Gabriel. "It's six forty-three. We've got one minute before Scarlett dies."

Roan ignored him, refusing to lower his sword. His eyes burned holes into me.

I bit my lip. The boar grunted in panic, his feet kicking.

"Six forty-four," said Gabriel.

I moved the knife quickly, plunging it into the boar's rear leg. He squealed, bucking violently, blood pouring from the wound onto the stone floor. Roan moved swiftly toward me, but I'd already dropped the knife.

"That's it." I rose. "Six forty-four. I bled the boar. That was the only thing the abductor demanded. That was all I intended to do."

Roan stared at me, his eyes icy with a cold rage. "You just stabbed the king of the Elder Fae." His gaze slid over the boar's body. "More than once."

"What would you have done differently?" I whispered. "If it was Elrine?"

Instead of answering, he moved past me, kneeling by the boar's side. He stroked he boar's fur, whispering in the strangely lilting fae language.

Then he noticed the metal chain around its throat. He touched it and hissed, pulling his fingers back. "Iron. That's why he didn't change."

"I'll take it off," I said hurriedly.

"How kind of you," Elrine sneered. "Now you're helping, after stabbing him with iron."

I fumbled at the clasp until I managed to unclasp it. The iron chain slipped to the stone floor, and a rush of magic burst from its body.

I stepped back, gaping as the boar began to transform before my eyes with a sound like the stretching of tendons and the snapping of bones. The boar's body elongated, its ivory fur retracting into its skin, tusks shortening. His hind legs lengthened, and his body began to straighten. Popping sounds echoed off the stone walls, sounding as if they came from within its body, where the bones twisted and reshaped to accommodate the new body. It sounded... *painful*.

Finally, a man was standing before us, staring down at me. Two tusks emerged from his mouth—the only remnants of his boar form. Straight blond hair hung to his chin, and apart from the tusks, his face was almost handsome. A crown of yew sprigs sat atop his head. His back was slightly hunched, under his black and gold doublet. On his collar, he wore a golden brooch—three suns. An array of rings gleamed from his fingers. He twisted his pinkie ring, staring at me, his dark gaze powerful and penetrating. A tendril of fear coiled though my gut, and I cast a nervous glance at Gabriel, whose jaw hung open.

Roan bowed. "King Ebor."

My gaze lowered to the king's leg, stained crimson.

King Ebor inclined his head. "Taranis. Do you know this fortal who cut me with iron?"

"Yes. But it's more important that we know who put the chain around you. Did you see who it was?"

He shook his head. "Someone snuck up on me in the Hawkwood Forest while I slept." He glared at me again, his eyes darkening with shadows, and he pointed at me. "Who *is* that?"

At the sound of his wrathful voice, dread tightened my stomach. "I'm sorry I hurt you." I tried to steady my voice. I'd nearly cut this man's throat. "The person who abducted you is threatening to kill my friend if I don't do what she wants."

"King Ebor," said Roan with reverence. "She's just a pawn, a fool. She's not your real enemy."

Maybe he was trying to help, but his words stung.

Roan sheathed his sword. "You're injured, Your Highness. I'll help you return to the Hawkwood Forest."

The king curled his lip with disgust, stepping away from me, and the three fae walked to the oak doors at the far end of the temple.

Before pushing through the doors, Roan cast a final glare at me, his expression positively glacial. Flanked by Elrine and the king, Roan pushed through the oak doors. Elrine didn't even bother looking back at me. Just a pawn and a fool.

"Guy's a fucking bellend," muttered Gabriel before turning to me. "Are you okay?"

I smiled weakly. "No."

"You took a risk, not killing that boar."

I shook my head. "We had to show the abductor that she needs to talk to us. Now she knows that as long as she doesn't talk to us directly, she isn't in complete control. And that's what she really wants. Complete control."

He ran his hand through his hair. "Come on, let's get out of here."

I heaved a breath, turning to leave through the doors—but something shimmered in the corner of my eye. I turned, watching one of the silver cups glimmer with a moving image. Frozen in place, I looked at it, my heart beating wildly. As before, I couldn't feel the reflection, couldn't bond with it. It belonged to someone else.

"Gabriel," I breathed, picking up the chalice. On its surface, an image appeared of Scarlett, sitting in the same room as before, just below the mirror, her hands tied, mouth gagged. Except this time, her left foot was bare. Something glimmered underneath. It took me a moment to realize what it was—a round mirror.

I tried to take in all the details I could, but once again, the abductor had placed the mirror I was looking through too close for me to take in any details. Just a stone floor, a dimly lit room.

Then, a figure stepped into the reflection, next to Scarlett. I couldn't see her face—a dark fog floated around her, obscuring her features, barely showing her silhouette. Through the murky fog around her body, one of her hands materialized, holding a pair of garden shears.

The woman turned away from me, and I could see Scarlett's eyes widen in fear at the sight of the shears. I'd never seen Scarlett scared before—and she looked *terrified* of this woman.

"Gabriel," I breathed again, my heart stopping. "Something terrible is about to happen."

Gabriel leaned over my shoulder, watching the images on the silver surface. He touched my back, as if trying to soothe me.

I clenched the chalice tightly, sweat dampening my palms. Frantically, I tried to feel for the reflection, to jump through, to help my friend. I could have tried to jump through a wall for all the good it did.

I stared as the woman knelt by Scarlett, and grabbed her foot with one hand.

"No," I said, choking.

"It's going to be okay, Cassandra," said Gabriel, but by the tone of his voice, I could tell he knew it wasn't.

The woman slid the curved blades of the shears slid around Scarlett's toe. A drop of blood dropped on the mirror under Scarlett's foot.

"No!" I screamed at the reflection.

The woman snapped the shears shut, and Scarlett's toe dropped on the mirror's surface, blood streaming from the wound. Scarlett threw back her head, screaming silently, her eyes wide with pain.

My world tilted, and I faltered. Gabriel slid a hand around my waist to steady me. I was trembling, aghast, feeling Gabriel's hands around me as he tried to pull the chalice from my hand. I pushed him off roughly.

White hot fury blazed through my body. "I will find you, and I will put you in the ground. I will put you in the *ground*!"

Her face clouded in dark mist, the figure turned to look at me, even though reflections didn't carry sound. Then she looked down at Scarlett's foot, still bleeding profusely on the mirror. The figure touched the bloody mirror, dipping her finger in the blood.

And it was gone. The mirror was clean, its surface gleaming. Another spurt of blood from Scarlett's toe stump splashed on the mirror's surface, only to disappear completely. What the hell?

Then I realized what she had done. Mirror magic let one connect between two reflections, enabling objects to be sent from one to the other.

Somewhere in London, blood was pouring through a reflective surface. A puddle, a window, a car mirror, soaked in Scarlett's blood. And the abductor didn't have to clean a single drop of blood on the floor. An efficient, clean job.

Gabriel grabbed me as my knees went weak. The chalice's surface went dark, my own horrified face reflected back at me. My mind lunged at it, searching for a bond with the reflection. Frantically, I searched for Scarlett, for the abductor, for that dimly lit room... but I found nothing.

"I think the abductor just clarified what happens if we stand up to her." Tears streamed down my cheeks. "I tried, Gabriel. I tried to do what needs to be done. And look what happened."

"Come on." Still supporting me, he nodded at the door. "We have to get out of here."

I walked a few steps, and then felt something wet dripping on my leg. Staring down, I looked uncomprehending at the red stain soaking through my pants, sticking to my thigh.

"What is it?" Gabriel asked.

I touched my pants, then raised my fingers, frowning at the blood that stained them red.

Gabriel frowned. "Are you hurt?"

"Just my ankle," I said in confusion. I traced the trail of blood with my fingers upwards until they brushed the bottom of my bag.

It felt wet.

Fingers shaking, I opened the bag, staring inside.

Blood pooled in my bag, streaming from one of my hand mirrors, staining everything red. And between a blood-soaked gum pack and my keys, I could just glimpse a small, pale toe.

CHAPTER 19

Some images can't be forgotten, no matter how much time has passed, no matter how hard you try. The memory of my bag, and Scarlett's small toe in it, would be etched in my mind until the day I died. It would haunt me in my quiet moments and my nightmares.

I couldn't remember getting back to the car, or watching the temple walls disappear around us. I dimly remembered Gabriel taking my bag from me and putting it in the car's trunk, which was probably for the best. I'd wanted it as far from me as possible.

As we drove back to Gabriel's home, the only thing that pierced my fog of horror was the strangely discordant sight of people dancing in the streets. While dread was eating a hole in my chest, every few blocks, someone was dancing ecstatically on the street corners. Probably a stupid flash-mob, I guessed, their jubilation completely at odds with the endless screaming in my head. If Scarlett's toe in my handbag had this effect on me, how terrified must she be right now? Her suffering at the hand of this lunatic was more than I wanted to think about.

When we reached Gabriel's home, I went straight to the guest room and pulled off my bloody clothes, shoving them into the trash. I tried to clear my mind as I hurried to the bathroom and turned on the shower, letting the bathroom fill with steam. Smears of blood from the abductor's first message still stained the mirror, and I tried not to look at them. If I was going to get Scarlett back, I needed to stay in control of my emotions.

I stepped into the scalding shower, feeling the hot water wash over my skin. Blood and water mingled over the porcelain, and I scrubbed my skin violently. After a few minutes, I stepped out of the shower and toweled off, keeping my gaze off the bloodied mirror.

At least I had proof that Scarlett was alive. And that the abductor really had her.

Naked, I crossed into the guest room and pulled out a clean pair of underwear from the pile of clothes on my bed, then slipped a black sundress over my head. My hands shaking, I hoisted my suitcase onto the bed and opened it, hastily throwing everything I had into it. As I packed, hot tears slid down my cheeks, and I clenched my jaw, trying to think clearly.

My best friend had been mutilated because of me. I wouldn't have Gabriel targeted by the CIA or the fae because of me, too. He'd already done enough for me, and it was time to leave. I was an FBI agent, and I could figure out how to get Scarlett back on my own.

It took depressingly little time for me to pack my belongings. Once I had everything stuffed into my tiny suitcase, I grabbed it off my bed and headed out to the living room.

Gabriel sat on the sofa, leaning over his coffee table. While I'd been in the shower, he'd been cleaning the contents of my bag, laying them out to dry on a towel.

"I cleaned everything I could," he said apologetically.

"And, uh... I put Scarlett's..." He cleared his throat. "In some ice."

I nodded numbly, wondering if we'd get her back in time for that to do any good.

"I'm leaving," I said quietly. "I can't stay here. The CIA is looking for me, and they'll find out we're connected."

"What if the abductor contacts you here?"

I shook my head. "She knows to find me. There are mirrors everywhere. Thanks for everything you've done."

I walked over to the table and picked up the pouch, my purse, and my keys, and shoved them into the pocket of my suitcase.

I hesitated, looking at the knife. "Did you touch it?" I asked.

Gabriel shook his head. "I used gloves. And even with them I could feel its... voice. Why do you keep it?"

"I don't know." I picked up the knife. Instantly, it began whispering in my skull. *Whore. Filthy pixie whore.*

Ignoring its voice, I slid it into my suitcase pocket. Then I took the rest of my possessions, leaving the phone and the mirrors on the towel. "You can throw out everything else. The phone should probably go. I don't need the CIA tracing me."

"What's your plan?" Gabriel asked.

"I don't have a plan."

"Cassandra—"

"Thanks for all your help, Gabriel."

He rose, his eyes glinting with sadness. "I'll take you to a hotel."

I shook my head. "It's better if you don't."

"You're in no shape to be alone right now. I'm taking you."

I looked at him tiredly. He was wrong. He thought I was falling apart. Maybe that was true, just a little. I'd heard people claim the human body was made of ninety percent water, which couldn't be true. But right now, I was ninety percent sorrow.

But underneath it all, there was something else simmering.

Molten rage.

I could feel it kindling, knowing that it would take a few hours to become full blown, an inferno of anger. I could wait. I needed that rage. "Fine. Take me to a hotel. Somewhere at least a few miles away."

He nodded, pulling the suitcase from my hand—the perfect gentleman. I followed him down the stairs, endlessly grateful for his presence in my life.

Downstairs, he pulled open the back door of his car and slid my suitcase into the back seat. I plopped down in the passenger seat, my body racked by fatigue.

As my mind drifted, simmering with anger, Gabriel started the car, taking off through the dark East London streets. I stared out the window, feeling the anger slowly boiling through my veins. I could already feel it in my jaw, clenched tightly, my teeth grinding. My dentist used to say that I would eventually grind my teeth to dust. Right now, it felt likely.

As we pulled onto Bethnal Green Road, I stared out the window at a crowd of dancing people. This time, I studied them more closely, my pulse speeding up. What I'd thought had been an ecstatic expression before wasn't—not at all. Their mouths were wide open. But they weren't smiling— they were grimacing, their movements strangely jerky, faces glistening with a sheen of sweat.

Their heads lolled, a haunted look in their eyes. One of the dancers we passed by was an old lady. She flailed and twitched in her spot, her face a mask of pain. Tears ran down her cheeks.

"What the hell?" said Gabriel.

"Are you seeing this?" I asked.

"I'm seeing this." He slowed down his car, and we rolled slowly past the sidewalk. "I thought they were dancing before. This seems like a... like a spell or something, doesn't it?"

"Yeah." I took a shaky breath. "And it probably affects humans, so I wouldn't slow down too much."

We drove on in silence. Despite my warnings, Gabriel pulled over twice, to ask two different dancers if they needed help. He didn't get a response either time. When he pulled up close to the dancers, I could feel their fear pulsing wildly, igniting my body with power. I drank it in without hesitation. I felt a flicker of guilt at feeding off their terror, but I'd need all the power I could get to get my best friend back.

* * *

THE PRETTY BRUNETTE receptionist at the Tower Bridge Hilton found me a single room. At this point, I had no idea how much money I owed Gabriel, but as soon as I got access to my bank account again, I was going to pay him back with interest. While I was checking in, Gabriel's cell phone rang, and he stepped outside to take it. I was sure someone was reporting exactly what we'd seen on our drive here.

The receptionist handed me my keycard, and I rolled my suitcase to the elevator.

As it carried me up to the third floor, I closed my eyes, my body humming with that wild energy that came from the fear I'd absorbed. The elevator doors opened, and I walked a few doors down the white-walled hallway. At room 303, I inserted my keycard, getting a high-pitched squeak as a reward.

When I pushed the door open and flicked on the lights, I

found the message from the abductor already waiting for me on the room's body-sized mirror.

I stared at it in horror, my heart slamming against my ribs, then quickly shut the door behind me. I read the text, understanding the basics almost immediately. I still didn't have a phone, so instead I snatched a pen and paper off the bedside table, then hurriedly copied the message. Moving as quickly as I could, I rushed to the bathroom, grabbing a small towel. I rinsed it in the sink, then hurried into the room to clean the message off the mirror before Gabriel found his way to my room.

When I'd cleaned half of it from the mirror, a knock interrupted me.

"Cassandra?" Gabriel's voice.

"Just a second!" I called, panic rising in my chest. "I'm in the bathroom!"

As fast as I could, I finished wiping the mirror, then shoved the blood-stained towel in the cupboard under the bathroom sink. I rushed back to the door and opened it, barring the way with my body.

Gabriel stood in the doorway, concern etched across his features. "Everything okay? You still look quite shaken."

"Getting there," I said.

"Okay. I got a call from the station. There's a meeting about the latest development. The dancers. I think it might be another attack. Our forensics teams are debating if it's a toxin from some kind of chemical weapon, or if it's some sort of shared psychosis."

"And you think it's another fae terrorist attack, like the explosions?"

"It wouldn't be the first time. Strasbourg in the fifteen hundreds. The dancing plague killed hundreds. At the time, they blamed fairies."

I nodded, recognition dawning. We'd studied it in an

abnormal psychology course. "Modern science attributed it to a shared psychosis—*folie à plusieurs*, 'the madness of many'—or to the hallucinogenic fungi. The same bullshit ergot theory that people think explains the Salem Witch Trials."

"And the debate still rages, but you and I know better. I don't suppose you have any idea what's the purpose of all this?"

I shook my head. "To instill terror. Someone must be feeding off it, I guess." *Someone other than me, that is.*

He nodded slowly, considering this. "Okay. I have to go. You'll keep me informed when the abductor calls you again, yeah?"

"Sure," I lied. "If you need me, just call the front desk and ask for my room. I'll get a new mobile phone as soon as I can."

He nodded, his hazel eyes studying me. Then, to my surprise, he wrapped me in a warm hug. I leaned against him, breathing in his clean smell, listening to his heartbeat.

"This wasn't your fault," he whispered.

"I know," I said.

With one last glance, he turned and left, and I watched him walk down the hall to the elevator. A tear rolled down my cheek, and I wiped it away, stepping back into the room.

I surveyed the space—the clean, white walls, the enormous white duvet. My gaze trailed over to the paper where I'd written down the message. That molten rage burned through my veins, fueling my mind, my desire for revenge.

And with that simmering rage, a plan began to spark in my mind.

Even so, I'd need more time, which meant I had to complete the next task.

And there was no way in hell Gabriel would be on board for this one.

CHAPTER 20

$\mathcal{D}$arkness surrounded me as I gazed up at the Tower of London, the rough stone walls that had stood here for nearly a thousand years. A fortress with four towers stood in the center—the White Tower, the oldest part of the structure. Around the White Tower were two concentric rings of stone walls. It was three in the morning, and hardly anyone lurked here at this time of night.

The Tower walls loomed high above the Thames, cast in a bright, white light. I paced the pedestrianized walk by the river, choosing my point of entrance carefully. I was dressed entirely in black, a large, nearly empty backpack slung on my back. Right now, I stood just above the Traitor's Gate—the tunnel that ran from the river, under the street beneath me into the Tower walls, where terrified queens had once cowered in boats, on the way to their executions.

As I surveyed the stone walls, my body pulsed with raw energy. Waves of fear floated on the wind as the dancing plague terrorized London. On the way here, I'd lingered in the shadows by some of the dancers, feeding myself off their terror. I didn't feel great about it, but now, strength coursed through my blood.

The message had been clearer than the rest, or maybe I was getting used to the abductor's style. This time, I didn't need Gabriel to work it out with me.

> *Sing a song of six birds,*
> *They're yearning to be free.*
> *Ravens in the tower.*
> *Scarlett is with me.*
>
> *Walk them past the stone gates*
> *Until the birds are gone.*
> *The White Hill's beckoning:*
> *You have until the dawn.*

After spending countless hours listening to Scarlett ramble about the history of London, I'd heard plenty about the ravens. Supposedly, they guarded the city, and if they ever escaped the Tower, terrible things would happen. However, considering the city was currently being torn apart by the fae, I didn't have a great deal of faith in the ravens' ability to ward off disasters.

Still, before leaving the hotel, I'd logged onto one of the lobby's communal computers, and googled the Tower Ravens. According to legends, a British king named Bendi-geidfran had ordered his followers to cut off his own head. They then buried it under the White Hill, where the Tower now stood, as a talisman to ward off enemies. He was also known as Bran, which meant "raven." Other legends described ravens flocking toward the smell of corpses left to rot at the Tower after executions, the enemies of the crown. Too bad none of this was going to help me figure out how to break into the Tower and get a small flock of ravens beyond the walls without any guards noticing.

I had until dawn to get them out, and this time, I'd be working on my own.

Gabriel had been complicit in our little zookeeper ruse with the London police, but asking him to look the other way while I broke into the Tower of London to commit a burglary was another thing. In fact, it was probably some type of treason, and there was no way he would have let me go through with this if he'd known what I was up to.

The Tower of London's security was tight and impressive because of the Crown Jewels. Lucky for me, most of the security was meant for the jewels, and not for the ravens. What sort of lunatic would want to steal a bunch of ravens?

As far as I could tell, no clever alarm systems protected the Tower grounds, where the rookery stood. I just had to avoid the fifty or so armed guards who patrolled the premises, carrying automatic weapons. Oh, and I had to scale the Tower's walls, which had been built to repel entire medieval armies.

My first problem was that a bright, white light illumined the entire outer wall. In my pack, I had a rope and grappling hook that I'd picked up from a hiking store earlier. But it would take a few minutes to scale the wall, and during that time, I would be very, very visible to anyone walking past, and to boats in the Thames. Granted, there weren't many people out at this hour, but I couldn't risk it.

No one would see me down at the moat, though. In the shadows, I slipped along the southern side, where I found a shallow, dry moat. Furtively, I looked around me, making sure no one was watching. I saw only shadows. Carefully, I climbed the iron bars that stood at the edge of the moat for public safety, and dropped down ten feet or so, landing on the soft grass.

From there, I walked toward the Tower wall until I found what I was looking for. The southeastern corner of the tower had a spot that was cast in shadow—a good place to climb without being seen.

My heart thumping, I pulled out the grappling hook and rope from my backpack. I checked to make sure the rope was uncoiled, and fixed my eyes on a spot at the top of the wall. I tossed the grappling hook, my senses sharp and focused.

It hit the top of the wall with a painfully loud clang. I waited for a few seconds, my heart in my throat, to see if anyone would show up to investigate. Taking a long breath, I grabbed the rope again, and rappelled up the wall.

I felt completely helpless on the wall. Despite the shadows and my dark clothes, I was sure someone would spot me. As I pulled myself upwards, one arm over the other, I waited for the inevitable shout of "Stop, thief!" or "Freeze!" But none came. Finally, I reached the top of the wall and hoisted myself over the edge, standing on the battlement—a wide stone path, with walls on either side. Crouching, I moved along the battlement, peering over the edges until I found a part of the wall where I could most easily climb down without a rope.

I hoisted myself over the edge, using the gaps in the wall, my fingers white with effort. Without the energy that pulsed through my bones, I doubt I could have managed this. But blazing with the city's terror, I felt like I could do anything. At the bottom of the wall, I crouched to a point shrouded in shadow, and glimpsed the first guard patrolling through. He was tall, well-muscled, and his movements were alert and sharp. I held my breath as he walked past me, his footsteps slow and measured on the stone floor. Once he walked around the bend, I left my hiding spot, skulking though the shadows.

The rookery was in the inner yard of the Tower, and I had

to get over the second wall to get there. It took a while to find the right spot, and I'd needed to duck into the shadows as a guard patrolled past me. By the time I began climbing the second wall, my body was so jacked on adrenaline, I thought I might have a heart attack.

I climbed the second wall with no rope, too nervous about the loud clang of the grappling hook. I managed to find a pipe that helped me part of the way, and from there, it was a steep climb to the top using shallow fingerholds and footholds.

After crossing over the second battlement, it was only a few more minutes before I was in the inner yard. It took me a few moments to spot the rookery—the black metal cages abutting a stone wall, with large alcoves for the ravens.

I moved across the grasses, flooded with amazement and disbelief. I had successfully broken into the inner yard of the Tower of London.

"Stop!" A gruff voice pierced the silence, and I could hear the click of a gun's safety switch.

$\mathcal{I}$ froze in place, my heart sinking. The rookery was only a few yards away, but it might as well have been miles.

"Turn around. Slowly."

I turned around, keeping my face as blank as possible as I faced the gray-bearded yeoman. My eyes went to his gun—an SA80. If he pulled the trigger, there would be no more Cassandra to save Scarlett. The man holding the gun was dressed in the dark blue and embroidered red of a Yeoman Warder's uniform—a Beefeater, but without the hat. Maybe he didn't bother with the hat at night. Or maybe he didn't want to get blood all over it when he shot me. His keen, dark eyes glistened in the dark, piercing me.

I held up my hands, feigning a British accent. "Don't shoot. I'm from MI6. I am going to reach very carefully for my identification."

He raised the gun just a fraction, enough to clarify that he wasn't about to mess around. With snail-speed movements, my hand went to my collar and, ever so gently, dipped into my neckline.

I saw his eyes widen as they met Alvin's crystal, tied around my throat. Alvin had said this pendant would make a human follow my commands—presumably a sort of hypnosis. Would it be enough for this man to lower his gun?

"Okay," I said. "Now, when I say—"

"Oh my," he gasped, his eyes widening.

It seemed to be working, so I held the pendant aloft. "Right. What I want you to do—"

"I am not worthy."

"I… what?"

He lowered his eyes. "Please don't strike me down."

"Well, you're the one holding the gun."

"My apologies, Goddess!" He quickly lowered the gun. "I meant no disrespect!"

I stared at him, at a loss for words.

"I'm a terrible man." He stared at the ground. "I never truly believed in the power of the gods. I was a fool!"

I swallowed hard. I hadn't quite expected the pendant to work this way. "You think I'm a god?"

"Think? No, Goddess." He clutched his hand to his chest. "I *believe*! I know it with all my heart! Shall I call all the other men in the tower to bask in your glory?"

I held out a hand. "No! Definitely not. Your basking is plenty for me. And now I have some god-business to attend to, over there by the rookery."

"Of course." He bowed low.

I crossed the grass, my mind whirling. I couldn't believe Alvin had wanted me to use this on Scarlett. As I moved closer to the cages, I heard footfalls behind me, and I turned to see the yeoman following me.

I frowned. "You are disturbing my divine rookery work."

"Of course." He bowed his head. "Can I be of any service?"

"Do you have keys to the rookery?"

"Of course."

"And to the gate?"

"Yes, my Lady of Divine Terror."

I wrinkled my nose at the nickname. "Wait here, okay?"

"Of course, O Wrathful One."

"Please be quiet. Are there any patrol guards who might show up here?"

"I am the only one stationed here until six, Mistress of Dread, Mother of Death."

He was obviously talking crap, and yet his words sent a strange lick of fear up my spine. The buried memories, deep under the surface of my mind, began to rumble—the fevered hammering of the dark things underground. I clamped down on them as tight as I could, shoving those dark thoughts under the surface of my mind.

"If you don't stop it with the nicknames, I will smite the shit out of you. Be quiet for a second. I need to do something."

If Scarlett were here, she'd be laughing her ass off. She'd probably have asked the yeoman to invent a hymn in my honor. As soon as I got her back, I was going to tell her all about this.

I rummaged in my backpack, finding the raisins I prepared earlier. I tossed them through the rookery's metal bars, moving from one cage to another to toss them into each cage. I tapped the metal bars to wake up the ravens, and they squawked, jumping around, pecking at the raisins.

"Praised be the divine Goddess who feeds the hungry birds..." the man muttered to himself, rocking back and forth.

"They're not hungry," I muttered.

"Then why are you—forgive me, I didn't mean to question your divine will."

"It's fine, don't worry about it." I could be a kind god, who shared her wisdom with her believers... believer. "Did you ever read the book *Danny, the Champion of the World*?"

"No, divine Goddess."

"It's a fantastic book. By Roald Dahl."

He nodded eagerly. "It will be my holy scripture."

I considered it. I could think of worse scriptures. "Sure. Well, in the book, they put sleeping pills in raisins to knock out all the pheasants in the forest."

"Why? If I may ask, O Glorious—"

"Because... I actually don't really remember. But it's a great book. And I'm really happy that I read it."

One of the ravens wasn't sharing the feast. I looked at it, annoyed, and tapped the bars by its head.

It looked at me. "Squawk! Nevermore!"

I jumped back. "It can talk!"

"Yes, Goddess. Ravens with proper training can learn to speak extremely well. I've been teaching them."

It whistled, fixing its eye on me. "Goddess! Squawk! Nevermore, Goddess!"

"Good morning," I said. "Eat your raisins."

"Squawk! Darkness there and nothing more. Squawk!"

"So you've been teaching them Poe."

"Poe, and some other things..." he trailed off.

"Squawk! He pulled up the hem of my dress!"

I took a deep breath. "Romance, by any chance?"

The yeoman nodded.

"Wonderful," I said. "What's his name?"

"Odin."

"Of course it is. Odin, eat your raisins."

"Squawk! His hot mouth claimed mine. Nevermore!"

"*Ravished by the Captain*," the man explained. "A terrible book."

"Shhh... look." I pointed to one of the ravens, who stood on a perch in the rookery, its body slumping. It suddenly dropped down to the floor, unconscious. I let out a long sigh. Hopefully, it was asleep, and not dead from overdose. I'd filled each of the raisins with a drop of the tranquilizer, but I wasn't sure how much it would take to knock out a raven.

"Squawk! Nevermore, Goddess!"

That seemed like a forbidding portent, but I pushed my reservations to the back of my skull. Slowly, the ravens dropped to the ground, until only Odin remained standing.

"Okay, Yeoman, please open the doors of the rookery, and hand me the sleeping ravens."

"Of course, Mother of Terror. I am happy to serve..."

As he unlocked the cages doors, he muttered quietly to himself. I slung the backpack off my back, unzipping it. Gently, the yeoman began handing me the ravens, one by one. At last, the yeoman handed me Odin.

"I need you too," I said.

"Squawk! Take off your dress!"

"Not now, Odin. Come on." I made a grab for it and it hopped away, squawking angrily.

"Allow me, O Glorious One." The man grabbed Odin and held him nestled under his arm.

"Okay." My stomach clenched. "Listen. It's my divine command that you don't tell anyone about this night, and that you continue your life as if nothing happened."

"I want to worship you. I can pray morning and night—"

"No need for that, really." I felt as if I needed to impart some sort of wisdom to him. "Just be decent to people, and try not to be a jerk."

"Should I fast one month every year?"

"No, seriously, that's a terrible idea. Just be nice to people, okay?"

"Can I at least have one day every year to honor your glorious presence?"

"Sure." I gave up. "And on that day, eat and drink and have fun."

"Thank you, Goddess of Horror."

"Please show me to the gate. And remember… not a word to anyone, okay?"

CHAPTER 22

"*N*evermore, Goddess. Squawk!"

My eyes opened and I blinked, trying to understand where I was, who I was, and who was talking to me. As I rubbed my eyes, the events of last night slammed into my mind. I glanced at the time—eleven in the morning. I never slept that late. Panicking, I scrambled from the bed and checked the ravens. Apart from Odin, they all still slept in the corner of the room.

They seemed okay. Their chests rose and fell slowly, and I could feel a pulse at their necks.

I sighed in relief. Once Scarlett was home safe, I'd return the ravens to the Tower. I wondered if the yeoman would still want to worship me, or if that was a temporary situation.

Odin eyed me from his perch on the window sill. It felt as if his stare was accusing me of something.

"Good morning, Odin," I said blearily.

He hopped from leg to leg. "Squawk! I think it was his eye! Yes, it was this. Squawk!"

"Take it easy, Poe," I muttered, pulling on a black T-shirt and a swishy cotton skirt. I found the remote control and turned on the television, flipping the channel until I found the news. A blond reporter stood just outside Liverpool Street Station.

"Eighty-seven cases have been reported of Londoners affected by this … muscular problem. This mania. We don't really know what to call it. We don't know the cause yet. As I said before, we don't know if it's caused by chemical warfare, but the police are suspecting terrorism, and people are being asked to stay in their homes. Thirteen people are reported in critical condition. We've also had reports of numerous floods on the Thames' shores. Three have drowned, and seven have gone missing, but as I said, authorities—"

I switched off the TV, my chest tightening. We were powerless against the fae, and didn't even know who was attacking us, or why. I was being strung along by an insane puppet master, and meanwhile, the fae were torturing humans across the city with the dancing plague. I needed to speak to Roan— assuming he was still willing to talk to me after I'd stabbed the forest king. Maybe he'd have a clue who was attacking the city.

"Quoth the raven, betraying wetness. Squawk!"

I sighed, but I found the raven's rantings oddly soothing. As long as the bird was chattering, I wouldn't have to think about the mania claiming the city. Wouldn't have to think about mirrors soaked in blood, or that spluttering, gurgling sound…

Odin fluttered his wings, and I caught a glimpse of color around his leg—a tiny green ring. In fact, each of the ravens had a different colored ring on their legs for identification.

"Tell you what." I rummaged in my suitcase, searching for my toiletries bag. "Your behavior is utterly inappropriate."

"Squawk! He thrust into me!"

"Right. That's what I'm talking about." I found a pair of small scissors. "I'm not sure you belong at the Tower. You're not stuck-up like the other ravens. I'm thinking of hiring you as an accomplice."

He hopped away from me as I walked over to him. "I have dreamed of joy departed!"

"You and me both, buddy." I grabbed him and carefully cut the ring off his foot. "Congratulations. You're free."

"Squawk! Good morning, Goddess!"

I brushed my teeth quickly, eyeing the mirror nervously, but no bloody letters appeared on the glass. I combed my hair, pulled on my shoes, and carefully tucked the sleeping ravens back in the backpack. Then I left some raisins on the windowsill for Odin. He glared at me suspiciously.

"They're fine," I said. "You can trust me. We're friends, right?"

"Nevermore!"

I shut the room's door behind me. I had some urgent things I needed to do before I got another message.

* * *

CLUTCHING MY NEW CELL PHONE, I scanned the street around the police station. The late afternoon sun slanted over the street, glinting off glass buildings.

The warnings issued by government officials about chemical warfare had nearly cleared out the center of the city, and the crowds had thinned a bit, which would make it a little harder to go unnoticed. If the CIA had been asking the police about me, I didn't want any of them spotting me. But by now, I was sure, the CIA had marked Gabriel as a person of interest, and if I had to guess, his phone was tapped. If it was, I'd find it out soon enough.

I dialed his number, and he answered after two rings. "DI Stewart."

"Hey, it's me. We need to talk. It's urgent."

"I can't." He sounded troubled. "Things are insane here. Two people have died now from exhaustion and heart attacks, and the hospitals are overloaded. Not to mention that the EDL is stirring things up, blaming chemical weapons brought in by immigrants."

"The EDL?"

"English Defense League. A far-right organization. From Whitechapel to Luton, they can always be relied upon to be utter fucking pricks. And apparently, someone stole the ravens from the Tower, which they're all up in arms about. I don't know why anyone would give a toss about birds when people are dying, but they're using it as a symbol. An attack on our nation or some shit. They're claiming that refugees are feasting on the queen's ravens while poisoning the city with Iraqi weapons."

My throat tightened. The abductor had me playing right into the chaos. "I'm near the station. Meet me outside. It'll be quick." I hung up.

How long until the CIA got here? Ten minutes? Fifteen? They had no authority here, and I doubted they'd use the local police. I was still an FBI agent. They wouldn't want me taken in by British law enforcement—I hoped. I crossed the street to the police station, keeping my head down and staying at a respectable distance from the cop at the entrance. I rummaged in my bag, palming the small mirror I'd bought on the way here—my emergency getaway if the CIA showed up. Since the day I'd emptied my magic, I hadn't tried to jump through any reflections, and the thought of doing it now made me feel clammy all over. That feeling of the empty void between reflections still gnawed at me. Still, I might have to disappear fast.

After two minutes, Gabriel pushed through the doors, frowning at me. "What is it?" He asked, his voice low. "I have to go back inside. The mayor and the chief of police are here. They're demanding answers that I don't have, and—"

I leaned in closer to him, whispering. "I took the ravens."

He stared at me, fingers tightening into fists. Nearby, a car horn pierced the air.

I touched his arm. "I had to."

"You broke into the Tower of London?"

"The abductor contacted me. It was my next task. If I didn't do it, Scarlett would have been hurt again, or killed. I couldn't tell you because I knew you'd try to stop me, and I didn't want you to be complicit."

"Well, now I am, Cassandra, because you've just confessed to me!" he hissed. "You're a bloody liability at this point. You're under the control of a maniac, and I don't know what she's going to ask you to do next. What if she tells you to kill someone, Cassandra? Not to mention that innocent people are already taking the blame for what you've done."

Guilt coiled through me. "I'll return them," I said hurriedly. "Once Scarlett is safe."

He grabbed my arm. "I'm taking you in."

I yanked my arm from his grasp. "Gabriel. If you take me in, the abductor—"

"The abductor will get you to do even worse. I can't trust your judgment anymore, Cassandra. You'll do whatever she tells you to do, and you'll drag me down with you."

"I deeply appreciate your help, and I treasure you as a friend. Your support means the world to me—"

"You covered up the message, didn't you? When I got to your hotel room yesterday. You were lying to me." He shook his head. "I can't trust you, Cassandra. I'm sorry, but you're on your own."

I blinked away the tears. "I did what I had to do. And I have a plan. To find Scarlett, and get her back, I swear, but—"

I caught something from the corner of my eye. A businesswoman, briskly walking down the street, glancing at us for a moment too long. Sloppy work.

"Listen," I lowered my voice. "The CIA is tapping your phone."

"How do you know that?"

"Because they just showed up here, like I expected. I just wanted you to know. About the ravens. They're safe."

"I don't care about the sodding birds. I care that you broke into the Tower, that you lied to me, and that as long as this woman is controlling you, you're a danger to the city."

I glanced over his shoulder, catching a glimpse of a man walking towards us about thirty feet away. He was talking on the phone, looking sideways. Movements too precise to be accidental. The agents were about to grab me on the street. The bastards had nerves of steel.

Just as I was about to move, the mayor pushed through the station doors, the breeze toying with her tidy gray hair. The CIA operative stopped walking, talking animatedly on his phone. He didn't want to grab me in front of the mayor. Good.

She crossed to Gabriel. "DI Stewart. I'm leaving, but as I said before, I want results within twenty-four hours."

He turned to look at her. "Of course, Madam Mayor."

She glared at him, her gray eyes piercing. "The explosions, the floods, the ravens, the plague… they're all connected. It isn't vague, Stewart. I've seen zero progress so far."

She had an odd way of speaking—probably the years of learning to sell her ideas to the public.

Gabriel held out a hand. "I assure you—"

"I'm going to get my car." She turned, her kitten heels clacking over the pavement. Gabriel turned toward me while the CIA operative was hastening his steps, only a few yards away.

I touched Gabriel's arm. "I'll be in touch."

CHAPTER 23

The CIA agents were gaining ground when I reached Dirty Dick's Pub, which quite frankly needed a better name. I pushed through the door and rushed to the bathroom of the old wooden-walled pub. I found my way to the loo, and shoved open the door to the women's room, letting it swing wide open. But I didn't go through that door. Instead, I quietly slid into the men's.

An overweight man stood at the urinal, his face lost in concentration. When he glimpsed me, his eyes widened, and he turned sideways to shield himself. I ignored him, and slid into the last stall. I locked the door behind me and pulled off the tank cover.

Good. The airtight nylon bag I'd left in the tank a half hour ago still floated in the water, and I pulled it out, dropping it on the toilet lid. I unzipped the bag, and pulled out a red tank top and a black wig.

I pulled off my T-shirt, swapping it for the red tank top. Then, using a hair band from around my wrist, I quickly wrapped my hair into a bun and pulled on the wig. Finally, I put on the sunglasses. Cassandra Liddell, master of disguise.

The skirt I left the same, but it wasn't particularly memorable—just a short, black skirt. I thrust my shirt into the bag and put it back in the tank, closing the lid.

I pushed through the bathroom door and slipped past the bar. One of the CIA agents was arguing with the bartender, but I couldn't see the two others. If I'd been managing the pursuit, one would be looking for me in the bathroom, while the other would have gone into the kitchen. I skulked though the front door and left, loosing a sigh of relief.

Thirty yards down the street, I dropped my phone into a Metro Newspaper stand. Unfortunately, there were no trash cans in this part of the city—a relic of the IRA bombings years ago.

I moved swiftly past a woman in a suit, her body just starting to jerk and twitch with the first signs of the mania, and my throat tightened. This would just keep getting worse —more victims, more terror.

A thought nagged at the back of my mind, and I slowed down my pace, mulling it over. Something the mayor had said caught my attention.

The explosions, the floods, the ravens, the plague.

The floods?

The newsreader on TV had been talking about the Thames flooding, too. I crossed back to the Metro stand, pulling out a copy of the free newspaper from under my phone. I skimmed the articles—the biggest story was about the dancing mania. But after that, an article about a possible terror attack on the Thames barrier, causing the flooding.

I skimmed the article, and dread crawled through my gut. The article was describing towers of water, inexplicable waves, and strange surges of river water.

Grendel.

I had no way to be sure, but my gut told me it was him. After all, I'd just stolen Lucy from him. Today, there were floods all over the Thames. He was punishing the citizens of London, letting his anger take hold. And it was all my fault.

I crumpled up the newspaper and hurried off, my stomach flipping. No. This didn't make any sense. Grendel knew I was a pixie, and I'd been aided by a fae—Roan. We weren't human. So why would he attack humans as retribution?

The explosions, the floods, the ravens, the plague.

I began walking again, shoving the crumpled-up newspaper into my bag. As I moved deeper into the oldest parts of the city, I could feel the fear washing over me in waves. It thrummed through me, filling me with power. Someone was doing this—all one plan, to spread panic. Just like the Rix had done, but on a larger scale.

And they were using me.

Grendel wasn't flooding London out of rage. He was doing it because someone had told him to—someone who held something very dear to him. The bone.

Whoever the abductor was, she was acting out a plan. Grendel's flooding created panic—just like the dancing mania. The disappearance of the ravens was fomenting discord in the city—an attack on an ancient symbol, that the EDL could blame on immigrants. More chaos, more terror—and more power, for terror leeches like me.

And the boar yesterday—King Ebor. Roan had said he was the key to keeping the peace with the Elder Fae. But this abductor didn't want peace.

The tasks had been personal, vindictive, hateful. But they also served a purpose. Whoever had abducted Scarlett was also responsible for the explosions and the dancing plague.

I was so caught up in those thoughts that I almost didn't notice the fourth message as it appeared. A murmur of surprised gasps and cries finally penetrated my mind and I blinked, looking around me. A young woman pointed at a shopping window, just to my left. Words were appearing on it, one after the other in the same erratic handwriting I'd seen before.

It was the moment I had been waiting for, but when it finally happened, it caught me unprepared. I nearly missed it.

Fumbling in my bag, I ran to the window. I got the scanner out just as the final word appeared on glass, waving the thing frantically.

It let out a small beep, and I inhaled.

Got you, bitch.

I now had two scanned samples. If I was right, that would be enough to find Scarlett's location. Only then I focused on the message.

> *To Guildhall, to Guildhall, to kill who you find,*
> *Three fifteen, three fifteen, Scarlett is mine.*

I checked the time. I had twenty minutes.

I began to run.

* * *

IF I HADN'T BEEN CONSTANTLY FEEDING on the fear overlaying the streets, I could never have reached Guildhall in time. But the Londoners' raw fear blazed through my body, and I sprinted past a dozen people caught in the grip of the dancing mania, their bodies jerking helplessly, muscles contracting.

Their fear was palpable. And for a terror leech like me, it was a total feast.

I ran fast, hardly feeling the pain in my lungs, the fast beating of my heart, knowing that I just needed to complete this one last task.

Once I got through this, I could use the scanner to track down Scarlett. I would end this once and for all.

Pumping my arms, my breath ragged in my lungs, I tried to imagine what kind of creature she'd put me up against. A monster from the Hawkwood Forest? A dragon, perhaps? The iron knife hissed in anticipation, stroked alive by my growing battle fury. Whatever lay before me, I had to handle it. I had a loaded gun full of iron bullets, and I wouldn't hold back.

I peered through the window into Guildhall's entrance, looking for a guard. Just to my right was a bag scanner—like the kind they have in airports—but no one stood guarding the entrance today. It seemed the abductor had taken care of everything.

I pulled open the door, striding through the empty entrance hall. My pulse racing, I crossed over the flagstones and pulled open the arched wooden doors into a towering medieval hall. A shiver of awe ran up my spine: the vaulted ceiling that arched high above me like ribs, the blood-red carpet, the sunlight pouring in through tall stained-glass windows. The dais, where kings and queens had once sat in judgment over the broken bodies of heretics and traitors. Apart from that, the hall was empty. No roaring monster, no elder fae. Just my own fear, curling through the room like a ghostly presence, my heart thumping like a war drum.

As I turned in a circle, searching for my opponent, the world flickered.

The towering ivory walls and stained glass shimmered away, giving way to oak trees and tall grasses that tickled my ankles, rustling in the breeze. Sunlight streamed through oak boughs, flecking the ground with amber light that danced over the grassy earth. A jackdaw chirped, and woodlarks trilled.

In a clearing to my right, a serene lake reflected the dark

blue sky, its clear surface interrupted only by crimson water lilies that dappled the surface like drops of blood.

I whirled around. As I surveyed the scene, a voice in the back of my mind whispered, *Trinovantum.*

I breathed in the humid air, thick with the scents of moss and oaks... Not unlike the way Roan smelled. I could almost picture his golden skin, his muscled body, those perfect lips. His piercing green eyes, like chinks of emerald. He was too beautiful to live, and I wanted to destroy him, to bite into his flesh. Nature killed beauty, and so would I.

I blinked, trying to clear my mind. What the hell was I thinking? My thoughts, focused and sharp only a minute ago, were suddenly jumbled and confused, my body strangely hot. I pulled the wig off my head, tossing it to the ground, and tugged the elastic band from my hair, giving it a chance to breathe. My hair fell over my shoulders.

A new sensation coiled through my ribs, making my limbs tremble—battle fury. I wanted to feel the hot rush of blood dripping down my arms. I wanted to lick it off my fingers.

I pulled out my knife, and its anger seeped into me, infectious, poisonous. I needed to plunge this twisted blade into the hearts of my enemies.

From a copse of hemlocks to my left, the trees rustled, and I crouched, holding the knife aloft, ready to kill.

My heart skipped a beat as a towering, golden figure stepped from them—Roan, moving toward me, gripping his sword.

Slowly, I straightened, my grip on the hilt tightening, hands shaking.

"Roan," I managed, feeling strangely compelled to slice his perfect face with my knife, although I had no idea why. "What are you doing here?" I gritted my teeth, trying to marshal my control.

Shadows slid through his eyes, but there was something else in them as well. Concern.

"Elrine has been taken."

"Imprisoned? Did the High King capture her again?" We'd already broken her free once. I wasn't sure we could manage it a second time.

"No." His entire body was tense, his thickly corded muscles coiled tight, like a snake about to strike its prey. "I think it's the fae who took your friend. She took Elrine. She left me a note, on the mirror. A note in blood."

Bony fingers of dread tightened their grip on my heart. "What did the note say?"

"It said I should come here, and kill whoever I met if I wanted Elrine to live."

No. I swallowed hard, the realization slamming me in the gut. I pointed my knife at him. "That's what my note said as well."

His eyes widened, and I could see he understood. The abductor wanted us to choose between our friends and each other.

His jaw tightened. "I told you that you were in over your head. You should have done what I said. You should have come to the council, and then left London for good. You can't survive among the fae. You don't belong here, and you can't protect yourself."

"Really? Because right now I feel like I could slaughter an entire army." Blood lust was still blazing through my body, and I had to fight the urge to hurl my knife at Roan's chest. Sweat slicked my palms. "I'm not thinking clearly. Something is wrong with me."

A muscle twitched in Roan's jaw. Without taking his green eyes off me, he pointed to the lake, where red water lilies floated on the surface. "You see those flowers? We're by the Lake of Blood."

My heart slammed against my ribs. "And what does that mean? It doesn't look like blood."

His fingers were tightening on his sword. "It's not the lake itself. It's the lilies. They provoke fae to lose ourselves to our baser instincts."

My legs were shaking, my body desperate to attack. But there was no way in hell I'd ever win in a fight against Roan. I had seen him fight. Even with my gun, he could probably disarm me in a fraction of a second. And besides—even if I could kill Roan, I didn't *want* to.

The abductor had been watching me, knowing that Roan had helped me get the bone from Grendel. And she'd put us in an impossible situation—having to choose between slaughtering each other, and keeping our closest friends alive. I snarled. I wasn't going to let her control me this way. We had to find a way out of it that didn't involve killing each other—assuming the Lake of Blood didn't overpower us. But Roan smelled amazing, and I wanted to devour him…

No. I tried to pick through the angry fog of my thoughts to something clear and logical. I knew something about my tormentor. Something crucial…

I took a deep breath. "She's using mirror magic. To watch us." I didn't see any mirrors around us, but the lake was perfectly still beneath the lilies. It would make the perfect reflection. Battle fury ripped through my nerve endings, and my teeth began to chatter. "We can fake fighting."

"And fake dying?" Roan asked.

"Well, maybe we lead the fight into the woods and…" A vision of carnage danced in my mind—my iron knife, plunging into Roan's chest, my hand around his throat, his green eyes locked on mine as he took his last breath. I shook my head, clearing the thought. What was I talking about? "We could fake…"

"I can't fake fighting," Roan said. "Whoever has Elrine would know it wasn't real."

"What do you mean?"

"When I fight, I change. Like I said. You have no idea what we're really like."

I shuddered. *Unveiling.* I'd seen a flicker of his true form in the fae club—and it had been terrifying. "Can't you just... change?"

"I can't control it. And if I unveiled fully, I'd probably kill you." His muscles were tense, knuckles white on his hilt, as if he were hanging on to his sanity. With what appeared to be a great deal of effort, he sheathed his sword.

Fiery rage blazed through my veins. The abductor had known that just telling us to fight wouldn't be enough. She had to tilt the scales, pushing us to the edge of the precipice until she had a proper slaughter on her hands.

"I... think I know how to find Elrine and Scarlett," I said slowly. "At least... I knew. I had a plan."

"Good," Roan said. "But there's only one way out of this." Unlike me, his voice wasn't slow. It was sharp, angry. Underneath his controlled demeanor, he was a bubbling volcano of rage, and it was now threatening to erupt.

"And what's that?" What did the abductor want? To get rid of me? Or Roan? I felt my rage as well, simmering inside me. That bitch... I wanted to rip her fucking heart out and bathe in her blood. I wanted to beat her fucking head in with her own bones.

Roan growled, his eyes glowing amber. He could sense my rage. And out here, by the Lake of Blood, it fed his own rage, with nothing to stop him. "We need to find this woman, and rip her organs from her body." Steel laced his voice.

"Right." Battle fury blazed through my system, and teeth chattered. "But I have no idea where she is." I clenched my teeth to stop their frantic chattering. "We can't let her win. Elrine needs you, Roan, and we have to focus."

A chill rippled through the air, and Roan's eyes flared with gold. My free hand crept into my bag, fingers brushing against my gun. Somehow, I knew that if I turned my back to him, he'd unveil immediately.

"We need to get out of here." I took a step back from him.

Ivory antlers appeared on the top of his head, and my stomach swooped as he prowled closer. His arms, thickly corded with muscle, tensed. "You can't run from a hunter, Cassandra. Don't turn your back to me. As soon as you run, you look like prey. And don't ever pull an iron weapon on me, because you will die. I am Death, and I will destroy you."

"Roan!" I shouted. "Snap out of it!"

He closed his eyes, taking a deep breath. After a moment, he opened his eyes, and they were green once more.

I let out a breath of relief, trying to think clearly through the carnage in my own mind. "We don't want either of our friends to die." Anger blazed, igniting my body. "We need to find the monster who is doing this, and rip her rotten spine—"

I stopped mid-sentence, staring at the lake. Under the clear, blue sky, it shimmered, and an image began to form on its surface. The abductor was showing us something, and the immensity of it took my breath away. I could never have manipulated such an enormous reflection, and her power sent a shiver of fear up my spine.

"Roan. We have to go. I don't want to... Roan?"

He was staring at the lake, his eyes wide. The air had thinned. I followed his gaze, staring at the image on the lake. It was a pair of coppery butterfly wings, severed at the base. They lay in the dirt, ripped and bloodied. Jagged, gory bones protruded from them—like severed finger bones. No... they weren't butterfly wings. They were wings ripped from a fae's back. Why was she showing us this? The image shimmered again, showing a knife, soaked in blood. It had a dark, rusted tone; I thought it might be iron.

"Roan," I said, my voice shaking.

He turned to stare at me, and fear ripped through my skull. He glared at me with eyes the color of fiery lava, his savage tattoos glowing metallic copper. White-gold hair draped over his shoulders, and his antlers shone in the sunlight. His fingertips ended in white claws, and his ears had lengthened into points. He snarled, his canines lengthening. Shadows seemed to thicken around him, making my stomach clench. He had completely unveiled—a pure predator, with me as his target. At the sight of his raw, animalistic fury, terror slammed into me, so powerful I no longer knew my name.

CHAPTER 24

*R*un, my mind screamed. Vaguely, I remembered telling me not to turn my back to him, that it would provoke his hunter's instincts. But I wasn't in control anymore. The ancient part of my brain had taken the helm, and it was spurring me on through the forest, propelling me away from him. My blood roared in my ears, the world seeming to tilt as I ran from him, my feet rushing over the undergrowth. As I sprinted, my body shook with an over-whelming mixture of fury and terror. My own panic increased my speed, and the wind whipped over my skin, tearing at my hair. I ran, fast as a hurricane gale. But Roan was fast too, and I could hear his footfalls moving behind me, snapping twigs, pounding the earth.

I needed to get away from the Lake of Blood, but I had no idea where I was going. I was being hunted. Panicking, I moved blindly through the oaks, desperate to save my own life.

A voice in the hollows of my mind whispered, *Time to fight. Kill.* I shoved my hand in my bag, snatching the gun, and I whirled to face my attacker. In a blur of white and copper, he lunged for me. Before I could get my finger on the trigger, he tore the gun from my hand, hurling it away from me, deep into the woods.

It arced through the air, far out of my grasp. I looked frantically around me, realizing where we were for the first time. The Lake. Somehow, it had pulled me back to its shores, the blood lilies luring me back like a savage siren song.

Roan's sword was still sheathed, but that did little to comfort me. He could kill me with his bare hands.

Afternoon light glinted off his pale horns, his lethal claws. His fiery eyes burned into me, ancient and demonic, demanding submission. I struggled to hold his gaze, compelled by an instinctual force to lower my eyes. And yet, somehow, I knew that if I did, he'd go in for the kill.

A chilly breeze rushed over the Lake of Blood, and strands of platinum whipped around his face in ghostly wisps. He took a step closer, growling, his eyes locked on me. My stomach swooped, and I took a step back from, completely helpless without the gun.

"Iron," he snarled. "You brought iron."

The air thinned. He *hated* iron. It had enraged him, and something about that vision—the iron sword covered in blood, the severed wings—those images had made him snap. They'd broken something inside him.

I stumbled back, away from him, my back slamming into a tree. Now, pure terror had burned away my battle fury, and I only wanted to survive.

Roan lunged for me, and the next thing I knew, his hand was around my throat. He wasn't squeezing—yet—but his enormous hand encircled my neck, pinning me in place, taking complete control. His other hand clamped around my hips, his claws nearly piercing my flesh through my skirt.

For just a moment, I tried to move away from him, but his fingers tightened on my hip, claws pressing against my soft flesh. His low growl slid through my bones—a rebuke. He was in control here. Behind those fiery eyes, I could see nothing human, nothing gentle.

He pressed his body closer to mine, his enormous hand encircling my throat, and my blood roared.

I still had the knife in my bag. Slowly, my hand crept toward the blade, and I heard the gleeful whispering of the warped iron. If I could just get it out without him realizing, I might be able to fend him off. I slipped my hand into my bag, feeling the cool hilt under my fingertips, calling to me. *Kill*, it whispered through the fog of my mind. *Kill the fae monster.*

Yes. My own thoughts responded. *It's time for him to die.*

I gripped the hilt, but as I did, Roan's hand darted from my neck, clamping around my wrist. In the next second, I felt his canines threatening to puncture my skin— a threat. Then, for just a moment, a sharp pain seared my neck. At the same time, he slammed my wrist against the trunk and a jolt of pain shot through my arm.

He pulled his mouth from my throat. "More iron," he snarled, pinning me to the tree. "I told you. Someone would get killed." Venom laced his voice, and something else, too—a deep sense of betrayal. "You should never have come here."

Maybe Roan had been right. I was in way over my head, and I didn't understand the fae at all.

Unveiled, Roan was terrifying. And yet, something in his expression was changing. His eyes still blazed with fire, but his lips parted slightly, sensually. His strange beauty mesmerized me—the blazing copper tattoos that snaked over his muscled body, and shimmering locks of pale hair, like an ancient god. Slowly, his fiery gaze raked up and down my body, as if he were memorizing every curve.

Heat from his body warmed mine, and I could no longer

remember why we were here in this forest. I inhaled, breathing in his delicious, musky scent. Suddenly, I had the strongest desire to kiss his skin, to taste the salt with my tongue. Now, another primal desire was caressing my ribs with licks of fire, and I could remember nothing except for the intensely carnal appeal of the man staring down at me. Why were we here? Roan's body called to me, a primal song I couldn't ignore.

"Roan," I said softly.

His grip softened on me, just a little. He moved in closer, and with the feel of his body pressed against mine, liquid heat pooled in my belly. He inhaled, and another low growl emerged from his throat, this one softer, nearly inaudible. Around me, the air seemed to thicken, growing heavier and fuller, and Roan's hard body glowed with a pale amber light, so staggeringly beautiful, and strangely erotic. Suddenly, my body felt constricted in my clothing, my breasts swelling against the fabric. A wave of desire washed over me. My body was too hot in these clothes, burning up.

I had the strongest desire to see what Roan would do if I stripped off completely right now, wanted to tear my clothes of and stand naked before him. Except, one of my hands was still pinned.

Instead, I craned my neck to look up at him; I licked my lips, a silent invitation. I wanted his powerful hands all over me, needed to feel him possessing me. He stared at me, his eyes a deep gold, flecked with ruddy brown.

With my free hand, I reached for him, my fingers brushing over his waist. Instantly, I felt him respond. His grip still possessive on my body, he moved his hand from my waist down to my thigh, searing me with his touch. His fiery eyes locked on my face, searching. Slowly, his fingers slid up my skirt, sliding over my bare skin. Higher, higher... Then, in one swift movement, he ripped through my panties with his claws, as if he'd intuited my desperation to strip off my clothes. As the forest air caressed my skin, I felt completely naked before him—a sensation that sent a hot thrill swooping through my belly. His gaze scalded me.

My breath heaved, and he moved his hand to the top of my shirt. *Yes, Roan.* My eyes implored him to strip me bare. I hardly felt him rake a claw down the front of my body, his movements precise and controlled. He slashed through my shirt and my bra, cutting through the fabric. Slowly, he trailed his carnal gaze over my peaked breasts, as if examining his prize.

He moved his hand to my thigh, his claws retracting. Electricity rushed over my skin where his fingertips curled around the inside of my thighs, and I groaned. I wanted his hand *higher*.

He leaned down, kissing my neck—exploring, tasting, caressing the place where his teeth had been. My breath hitched in my throat. As he kissed my neck, he slid one knee between mine, forcing my legs further apart, and my pulse raced. I slipped my free hand under his shirt, feeling his powerful back, his muscles flexing as my fingers stroked his skin. I rocked my hips into him again, and he grazed his teeth against my neck, warning me to stay just where I was, that he was in control.

Slowly, his grip loosened on my wrist, and his hand brushed down my arm, his tongue flicking against my throat. Heat claimed my mind, and I wrapped my arms around his neck. My back arched, my nipples grazing against his chest, and I let out a low moan. At the sound, he growled, and moved his hand further up my skirt, cupping my bare ass. My breath sped up, and molten heat pooled in my core.

I thrust my fingers into his pale hair, and pulled his mouth to mine. He kissed me hard, his lips crushing mine, fingers possessive. I opened my lips, letting my tongue brush against his. Moaning, I pressed my body against his, and his hand slid further up. At the feel of his hand between my thighs, I lost all sense of control. Writhing against him, I threw back my head, gasping—

But when I did, I saw something moving in the corner of my vision—white light dancing over the Lake of Blood.

Reality slammed me in the skull, and I froze.

"Roan," I breathed, trying to think clearly through the haze of desire.

His body tensed, went still, as if he were waking from a dream.

"Roan," I said. "The lake. It's shimmering."

He still seemed dazed, his gaze lingering over my bare skin, his horns fading away, eyes returning to emerald green. He pressed his forehead against mine. Gently, he ran his fingers over the tattered edge of my tank top, frowning. "Cassandra." There was an unspoken question in his voice, a trace of despair.

He seemed to be recovering.

"Are you with me, Roan?"

"I could have killed you." He stared at my neck, where he'd bitten me, his brow furrowing. "It was the lilies, and that vision in the lake…"

"I'm fine." I glanced at my tattered silk panties on the ground. "Though I can't say the same for my clothes."

With a final glance at my body, he stepped away from me. He pulled off his sword and scabbard, then pulled his black T-shirt over his head, showing off the savage tattoos that snaked over the muscled planes of his body. As I pulled off the remnants of my tank top and bra, he handed his T-shirt to me. "I'm sorry."

I slipped his shirt over my head, smelling his delicious, oaky scent. "I'm fine," I said again, though a deep fatigue began to burn through my body, making my legs shake.

I took a step closer to the lake. Slowly, the blood lilies were closing their petals, but beneath them, an image was crystalizing on the lake's serene surface. When I saw the vision stretched over the lake's surface, my knees buckled. Roan slipped an arm around me to steady me.

CHAPTER 25

In a dark room, Scarlett and Elrine lay on wooden tables, bound by thick straps, their shirts torn at the back. They nearly looked like sisters—both with red hair. The only difference was that Elrine was significantly taller than Scarlett, and her hair a deeper shade of red, nearly the color of cherries.

The abductor stepped behind them, shrouded in the dark mist that snaked around her body, only her hands visible. She held a long iron bar, ending in a flat, orange surface. My heart stopped.

No. The tip of the iron burned red-hot—a branding iron, its surface shaped like a skull under water.

"No!" Roan roared, reaching for the water. He turned to me. "You have to jump through the reflection and stop it!"

Panic tore my mind apart. "I can't—"

His eye burned into me. "You have to stop it!"

"I can't! I can't bond with the reflection. She's blocking me!"

His fists clenched, his face taught with rage and fear. This woman was going to brand Scarlett—she was tormenting my friend, forcing me to watch. Letting me know it was my fault. I heard the sound of helpless sobbing, and it took me a moment to realize it was me.

The branding iron descended, pressed against Elrine's bare back. She thrashed against the straps, trying to get away, but she couldn't move an inch. The iron remained set against her back for what felt like ages, a wisp of black smoke rising from her skin. My body shook, my mind numb. My breath had left my lungs.

Finally, her head dropped as she lost consciousness, going limp. The abductor lifted the branding iron from her back.

I looked at Scarlett, her head turned, staring at Elrine. She'd seen the entire thing, and I could see the terror in her green eyes. But there was fierceness there as well. I tightened my fists, trying to marshal control over my mind. I had to remember that she'd been trained to withstand torture—that she'd think of this as part of the job.

The torturer stepped into the darkness, and I thought I could see a flicker of flame for a moment before she returned, her iron blazing red again. She pressed into Scarlett's back. A dark tendril of smoke curled from Scarlett's back.

Instantly, Scarlett tensed, her eyes wide. I could read the struggles on her face, her desperation to resist. For two seconds, she managed to sustain this rigid pose, but then she snapped, bucking, her innate reflexes taking hold of her body. I whimpered in pain as the monster seared my friend's skin—my punishment for failing to kill Roan. Raw horror slammed into my gut.

Then, the image simply rippled away.

Sorrow gnawed at my chest. The abductor didn't know Scarlett. She didn't know that Scarlett drank nearly two liters of water every day, or that she needed black coffee every morning to wake her up. She didn't know that Scarlett had once punched a man who'd grabbed my ass in Brooklyn, or that she could make toddlers laugh by pretending to think they were stuffed animals. She didn't know that Scarlett read poems every night before she fell asleep, or that she imitated robots talking dirty to make me laugh whenever I was having a shitty day.

The abductor didn't know or care—she was simply using her, like a thing. I was dealing with a pure psychopath. Or maybe that's just how the fae operated. Using humans. Feeding from them. Terror-leeches. Maybe Scarlett had been right about us.

Somehow, I'd found my way to the ground, sitting in the dirt. I was crying into my hands, my body racked with fatigue. This was my fault. For whatever reason, the abductor hated *me*. I was the target, and that meant it was my fault Scarlett had been taken in the first place, and that I'd failed to rescue her. As my body trembled, all those things I'd buried under the surface of my mind came clawing out again, rampaging through my skull—my parents' blood-spattered room, my mother's half-dead body, gurgling on the floor. *Mistress of Dread.* Why couldn't I manage to *help* anyone?

I tucked my head into my knees, the tears flowing. *Mother of Death.* I hadn't cried like this in years, not since my mother had died.

"Cassandra," Roan said sharply.

I ignored him. I couldn't lift my face, not when the pain and anger ripped my mind apart.

"Cassandra!" I could feel Roan's warmth radiating off his body, his firm hand on my back.

I couldn't get that image from my mind—the tendril of smoke rising from Scarlett's skin, her body straining as she fought to keep control.

Strong arms grabbed me, pulling me close, and Roan's

scent enveloped me. "Focus, Cassandra. You told me you had a plan. I need to know what it is."

Tears blurred my vision, and those memories clawed their way out of the dank and rotten ground: my mother's body on the floor. The tendril of smoke from the hot iron. The brand itself, a skull under water. Thoughts risen from the ground raged through my mind. That symbol felt like it belonged to me. I'd heard the screams of terror when I'd walked over the subterranean Walbrook, beckoning me to them like a long-lost lover. Why had the yeoman called me the Mistress of Dread? What had he *known*? Did he know that I'd hid under the bed, feeding off my mother's fear as my father stabbed her?

"Cassandra." A powerful hand on my back. "The plan."

"I can't think clearly, Roan. I can't think."

"You need to focus, Cassandra. We need to get them back."

Even now, I could hear my mother's last sharp rasping breath, hammering in my skull like an accusation. "I let my mother die. I fed off her fear. I let her die, and I hid under the bed."

"What are you talking about?"

I couldn't stop my body from shaking. "I could have saved her! And I didn't. I just hid under the bed. I felt her fear rippling through the house. I didn't know what was happening but I... I was scared, and I hid under the bed like a coward, and felt her fear. Like a terror leech. I can't save anyone, Roan."

The air thinned, and I felt his finger tense on my back. "What are you talking about? This is nonsense. You're wasting my time."

Desolate. I stared into his eyes, clutching my knees. "I once believed that evil was something you learned, not something innate in people." I'd needed to believe that.

Otherwise, what did that mean for me, given what my father was? But I couldn't convince myself of this fiction any longer. "I thought monsters were created, not born. It was all nurture, not nature." My fingers tightened on my knees, my nails piercing my skin. "That was before I knew about the fae, and creatures that feed off terror. That was before I knew what I was—a Mistress of Dread. A terror leech, evil and cowardly. I thrive when others suffer. I help no one—"

"Enough." He said, his voice quiet and controlled, a hint of a threat under the surface. He was losing patience. "You are not evil. The only thing you are is exhausted and feeling sorry for yourself. You're stewing in your own misery." He nodded pointedly at the lilies, now closing as the sky darkened. "This is the Lake of Blood, where fae lose their minds. And you've seen something designed to break you, and it's working. Besides that, the battle fury is wearing off."

"Why is it wearing off?"

"The lilies are closing, and their spell is leaving the air. The aftereffects will leave you drained. And of course, you don't seem like you've slept enough to handle any of this. You're always tired, or hungry, or freezing. I honestly don't know how you've managed to stay alive this long."

I stared at him sullenly. The air had cooled ten degrees, and my teeth chattered, my body shaking. Already, the sun was dipping below the tree line, casting long shadows over the forest, and the air chilled around us. In Trinovantum, the daylight and the temperature didn't seem to follow the normal rules.

In any case, I certainly felt drained. "I'm half human, half terror leech. And it's nice of you to say I'm not evil, but *you're* the one who called me that in the first place. Remember?"

Something fierce flashed in his eyes. "You're not evil. You came back for me, into the depths of a Trinovantum prison. And you're brave. I saw you slit the Rix's throat. I called you a terror leech before I knew you. It's different now. Get a hold of yourself."

I wiped the back of my hand across my cheeks. "Okay."

"Okay?"

"Yeah." Exhaustion washed over me. I wasn't entirely sure what we were arguing about, or what I'd just agreed to, but I was too tired to care at this point. I could feel my eyes drifting closed. The air was cooling, and a cold breeze whipped off the lake, streaming up my skirt, raising goosebumps. I suddenly realized I wasn't wearing underwear, and I pulled my legs in tighter. Shivering, I rested my head on my knees, and the tears kept streaming down my cheeks.

As my tears dripped onto my knees, I felt Roan's powerful arms envelop me, pulling me into his lap, against his bare chest. Heat radiated from his body, warming me.

I opened my eyes to look at him. "What are you doing?"

"Sleep here. When you wake up, you can tell me about your plan. You're no use to me until you've slept."

I blinked away the tears, staring at the lethal-looking tattoos covering the golden planes of his chest—the vicious-looking ogham slashes, the whorls that ended in sharp points. One of the designs by his heart caught my attention, and I gently traced my fingertips over the shape. It almost looked like three leaves, their edges spiked.

"What's this?" I asked, fighting to keep my eyes open.

"Wild strawberry leaves." I saw something cross his features—a flicker of pain, nearly imperceptible.

I wanted to ask him about the vision in the lake, but it seemed too risky. Too much raw pain lurked beneath the surface for him.

Gently, he ran his fingers over my throat, whispering something in his fae language. Slowly, I felt some of the sharp sting subside from the bite on my neck.

"Out here in the woods, you must spend a lot of time in silence," I said. "Don't you get lonely?"

"Mmm. Why do I get the feeling that you hate silence?"

He wasn't wrong there. My eyes grew heavy, and I leaned against his chest, his heartbeat thudding rhythmically against my ear. His hand slid higher up my back, resting behind my head.

I didn't trust him yet. He'd nearly killed me not that long ago, and he kept more secrets than I could imagine. And yet, his skin felt amazing against mine, his scent so intoxicating. My body relaxed in his arms. "You said you're only attached to Elrine. What happened to the rest of your family?"

He tightened his powerful arms around me, warming the shell of my ear with his breath. "Go to sleep, Cassandra. You're safe."

Slowly, my eyes drifted shut, and I fell into a deep sleep on the bare, tattooed chest of Roan Taranis, dreaming of wild strawberries growing by the edge of a woodland path.

CHAPTER 26

J'd slept for hours in Roan's arms, probably drooling on his bare chest. He hadn't complained. When I'd woken again, feeling refreshed, six hours had passed. We spent a half hour traveling through the woods to get to the oak portal. After a quick trip to my hotel for underwear, a shirt of my own, and my backpack, I took off for West London. I stopped in several stores on the way to buy some supplies for the tense upcoming night.

When I reached the embassy, it was nearly midnight. I could only hope that the CIA's London station was mostly empty by now. I imagined there were some CIA operatives working late into the night, but it was a risk I had to take. I'd already spent far longer sleeping than I'd meant to. Now, every minute I wasted was another minute the abductor could demand another task from me. I *had* to do this now.

Standing across the street from the embassy, hidden in shadows, I pulled out a small hand mirror from my backpack. I gazed into it, praying the abductor wouldn't contact me now. Once I bonded with the reflection, feeling it click with my mind, I reached out and felt for the reflections in the CIA Fae Unit offices.

Nothing. I could feel a bunch of reflections in the building, but when I imagined the office where Scarlett had taken me, I sensed no other reflective surface.

The CIA had seen what I could do, and they had taken precautions, covering up the reflective surfaces. It didn't matter. I could work around it. Oddly enough, I found it reassuring that at least part of the American government was capable of protecting themselves from someone like me.

However, there was a large mirror in the elevator that went down into the CIA offices.

I stared into the compact mirror, searching for the elevator. It appeared in my tiny mirror, and I immediately bonded with its reflection. For just a moment, I hesitated. What if I got stuck between the reflections, in that painful, gnawing void? What if my magic wasn't strong enough to get me through?

Still—Scarlett was in trouble, and I didn't have time to panic. I dipped my finger into the cool reflection, feeling its cold, liquid surface. I let the reflection pull me in, like a black hole, and its surface skimmed over my skin.

My heart pounding, I stumbled into the elevator. Frantically, I looked around the cramped space. Was there a CCTV screen somewhere, showing me inside? Probably. How long did I have until the embassy's security noticed me, called for backup, sent some guards after me?

Not long at all.

I gritted my teeth and turned to the keypad. Concentrating, I focused on the moment two days ago, when Scarlett and I were in the elevator together. She'd keyed in the code, and I'd looked, of course—reflexively, as I'd been trained to do. I keyed in the same code. Slowly, the elevator descended, and I backed into a corner, my pulse racing.

If I fucked it up, Scarlett and Elrine would die.

The door opened into the CIA branch and I hurried inside. It wasn't entirely empty. I could hear a keyboard tapping from one of the open doors, and in another room, someone cleared his throat. But there was no one in the entrance. I hurried down the hall that led to the Fae Unit offices, keeping my footsteps as soft as possible.

It took me only a few seconds to reach the large steel door, which unfortunately had a thumb scanner. My thumbs wouldn't do any good, and I wasn't about to get anyone else's. I crouched down—just as I hoped, there was a tiny crack between the bottom of the door and the floor. I pulled a sheet of aluminum foil from my bag and slid it under the door—one half on my side, the other half in the room.

Taking a deep breath, I focused on my blurry reflection in the aluminum. Once I felt the mental click—the bond with that reflection—I searched for the other half of the foil, just on the other side of the door. I let the reflection pull me in, until I was falling into it, feeling the cool metal wash over my skin, slide over my body like icy water.

When I found myself emerging from the foil on the other side of the door, I loosed a long sigh of relief. I quickly pulled the aluminum sheet from under the door, leaving no trace behind me.

As I crept down the hall, I approached an open door, and I could hear someone tapping away on the keyboard, just on the other side of the doorway. Chances were, they were facing the hallway.

I crept forward, intent on glancing inside. If I had to, I'd pull my gun on the person in the office, tie him up. But it was a huge risk; one that I wasn't prepared to take just yet. I was just two steps from the door when I heard the unmistakable sound of a chair shifting across the floor. Whoever it was, he was standing up, and heading out of the room.

Frantically glancing around, I spotted another door labelled *Unit Chief*. I hurried to it, opening the door and sliding inside. As quietly as I could, I closed it behind me. In the darkness, I could make out the shapes of office furniture. A desk, a file cabinet, a large potted plant. I pressed my ear to the door, listening to the sound of footfalls echoing in the hall, and they were getting closer. Whoever it was, he was probably on his way to the elevator, but I wasn't about to take any chances. I crossed to the desk and hid behind it, crouching low.

Of course, he'd been heading right for this room. As my heart raced, the door creaked open, and the light flicked on. I tensed, terrified, one hand in my backpack, clutching my gun.

The man's boots clacked slowly over the floor, and he hummed to himself as he moved in the room. What was he doing here? Had he come inside to search his chief's files? Maybe look through his desk?

I heard a strange sound, and it took me a moment to place it. It was the sound of a zipper being unzipped.

And then, the sound of liquid splashing into something soft. Unable to help myself, I lifted my head a bit and peeked.

It was my friend Fulton, standing with his back to me.

He was peeing into his chief's potted plant.

I sank back into my hiding spot, a deranged giggle threatening to emerge. I forced myself to think of what would happen if they caught me. I would be charged with treason, or perhaps they'd just shoot me right there. Scarlett would die, and... and...

The peeing trickled down into short, happy spurts, and I bit my lip to stop myself from laughing.

Finally, Fulton's act of rebellion was done. He zipped up and left the office, shutting the light behind him. I wondered how often he did this.

Once he left, I shot up, walking softly to the door. Carefully, I opened it, peeking outside. Fulton was returning to his office. As soon as he moved through the doorframe, I rushed past the doorway, heart thumping, sure that he'd notice the shadow cast into the floor of his office.

He didn't. His thoughts were probably still lingering on his chief's plant.

It took me only a few more seconds to reach the armory door. Here, an eye scanner blocked my entry. I pulled out the aluminum sheet, ready to slide it under the door...

There was no crack.

Desperately, I looked for anywhere I could slide the sheet through. Nothing. The damn thing was airtight.

I needed an eye. Fulton's eye.

I swallowed hard. I had no other choice. I'd force him down to the door, push his face to the scanner and...

And then I had another idea.

Walking back, I pulled one of the mirrors from my bag. I threw it across the hallway, and it landed on the floor just beyond Fulton's door, clunking as it did.

I heard the sound of his chair shifting as he stood back, and I skulked back to the armory door. I pulled another mirror, staring into it until I felt that bond. Then, I frantically searched for the mirror I'd just thrown. For a moment, I could only see the hallway's ceiling, the mirror facing up. Then it shifted, and one of Fulton's brown eyes stared back, trying to figure out where this object had come from.

I quickly held the mirror up to the eye scanner, and the door clicked open.

My relief was short-lived. At this point, I was nearly out of time. Fulton would make some calls, maybe search every room in the hall and scan the CCTV, hunting for the mirror culprit.

I hurried to the console, pulling the magic scanner from

my backpack. A USB cable dangled from the computer, and I connected it to the scanner, then looked at the monitor.

A folder with two files appeared onscreen. I double-clicked the first. It took a moment to load, and the scan details showed up in a plain white window with black text. Without reading through the analysis, I scrolled to the top and clicked *print*.

I opened the second file, scrolling up to click *print* again. Lucky for me, the printer worked nearly silently.

A muffled voice in the hallway sent my pulse racing. From here, it sounded like Fulton on the phone, his tone urgent. Then, the sound of a door slamming.

Taking a deep breath, I searched in the application's menus until I found the option *Database Crosscheck*.

Bingo. A progress bar began crawling on the screen slowly, and I restrained myself from punching the computer in its face. While I waited, I dashed to the gun rack. I picked up two Uzis, shoving them into my backpack. As I did, the computer beeped and a dialogue box popped up. *Match Found.*

I clicked *OK*, and a report popped up on screen. I clicked *print* again.

As I was snatching the printouts, I realized I had one more task to complete here.

I moved back to the database, clicking on the search bar at the top of the application. Frowning, I typed in *Alvin*.

The dialogue box popped up immediately: *Seven Matches Found.*

A list of all seven appeared on screen. Just outside, Fulton's voice was getting closer to the door. I selected all seven, and clicked *Delete Records*.

Are you sure you want to delete those records?

I clicked *Yes*.

The progress bar began running, but I was already diving into my backpack for a compact mirror, forming a mental bond with it. Just as the door clicked open, I felt myself fall into the cool, sweet embrace of the mirror's reflection.

CHAPTER 27

*O*utside the embassy, I moved through the shadows, crossing past a woman who stared at the moon, her body jerking, jaw slackened. Shivering at the sight of her, I chucked the rest of my mirrors onto the pavement. I needed to go offline. The abductor could watch me and get to me at any time through reflections, and I wasn't about to give her the chance. Not now.

Hyde Park was only a minute's walk away, and I crossed the distance quickly, slipping through the shadows. I felt as if every window, every rain puddle was a pair of eyes staring at me. As I got to the park's edge, I slipped into its reassuring darkness. I stayed away from the paved paths, crossing the dark stretches of grass. Once I'd moved far enough from the street, I searched around me for reflections. I didn't find any. I was at least temporarily hidden.

I pulled the printed papers and my keychain flashlight from my bag. Clicking the flashlight on, I illuminated the reports.

The first two detailed the scans of magic imprints I'd scanned from the gruesome notes in Gabriel's house.

Quickly, I skimmed the long list of metrics and percentiles, most of which meant nothing to me.

When I turned to the third page, I found what I was looking for, and my pulse raced.

Name: Siofra (Family affiliation: unknown)

I'd seen this name before.

I'd always believed that my father had murdered my mother before killing himself, but Roan had claimed someone named Siofra was responsible for their deaths. The realization that she was real slammed into me, knocking the breath from me. At the time, he hadn't seemed to know a thing about her, so I'd dismissed it. After all, the police had thought it was my father. My hands shook as I held the paper. Was it true? Had she murdered my parents?

Was it a long vendetta with my family? One of my parents was fae. Maybe Siofra had gone after him for some sort of vengeance, and had been following me since then, planning to kill me as well.

Name: Siofra (Family affiliation unknown)
   Aether Imprint: Classification A, ID: 254093987
   Known Connections: None
   Known Powers: Reflection manipulation at a sophisticated level. Subject can move through reflections and change them at will.

She could do a lot more. The CIA's knowledge wasn't complete.

Activities:
   Suspicion of involvement in the assassination of Case Officer Nelson
   Suspicion of involvement in the assassination of Agent Vern, fae informant

Suspicion of involvement in the Edinburgh Massacre

Suspicion of involvement in the murder of Mr. And Mrs. Marron in Canterbury

Suspicion of involvement in the murder of Mr. And Mrs. Liddell in Arlington, Massachusetts.

I stared at the last line. The CIA had known that Siofra had killed my parents. Still, no one had told me anything, letting me believe that my father had killed my mother. They could have easily told me otherwise.

Grief washed over me, and I had to shut my eyes for a moment, to rein my roiling emotions under control. Siofra killed my parents—both of them. Not my father.

For the first time in years, I could think of my father without hatred. All those memories I'd shoved under the surface of my mind—they all came flooding back to me now. I could picture him mowing the lawn in the sun, stopping for a can of Diet Coke, the collar of his T-shirt soaked with sweat. Tinkering with his car in the garage, his arms covered in grease, tools shoved in the back pocket of his jeans. Cooking dinner in the kitchen, so distracted by the news on the radio that the catfish burned. "Oh, geez," his gentle voice hummed in the back of my mind. "Princess, can you turn off the rice?"

I'd thought he was a murderer. All these years, I'd thought he'd murdered my mom. A dark wave of guilt washed over me, threatening to drown me, and I fought to stay above water. I couldn't lose it now. I still had to get Scarlett back. Yet, all this time—why hadn't I *known?* He had just seemed so utterly, completely human.

And maybe he was. Maybe my mom had been the fae, though she hadn't seemed any less human than he did.

An image rose in my mind—my father sitting at the edge

of my bed, after he'd read me a story about witches. *Princess, monsters aren't real.*

The guilt nearly pulled me under. I'd hated my father for all these years... Hot tears spilled down my cheeks, and my fingernails pierced my palms. I couldn't give in to the guilt, not now. What did it matter if I'd been blaming him all these years? He'd been *dead.* He had no idea what I'd been thinking. And the person who'd put him in the ground was still out there, torturing my best friend.

I wiped a tear away with the back of my hand, trying to force my raging emotions under the surface again, my raw grief slowly mutating into rage. With fury blazing through my veins, I could at least think more clearly. I needed to get a grip right now, even if my entire world was coming apart at the seams.

My heart thundering, I read the rest of the report.

It simply listed the times and places agents had scanned magic imprints that matched Siofra's. The last two were the ones I'd scanned. The system had automatically added my scans to the database.

I took a shuddering breath, and shoved the report back into the bag. I'd deal with it later. Right now, I wanted to find out exactly where this bitch was hiding—the woman who'd murdered my parents, who'd made me think my father was a murderer all this time.

I pulled a map of London from my bag. The scale was 1:9,700, which made it fairly detailed. I carefully spread it on the grass, then checked the coordinates of both scans. Getting a pen from my bag, I painstakingly searched for the exact locations of both scans—one near the City of London police station, the other in Gabriel's home. I did my best to be as accurate as possible. The smallest mistake here could mean Scarlett's death.

Then I searched the scan metrics until I found what I

needed. *Angle of Aether Trace*. Q had said he could see the direction the aether had come from. The only thing that could describe a direction in this report was this angle. I was going out on a limb, assuming that the angle was from a vector that pointed north. I pulled out the goniometer and ruler I'd bought earlier that night. Using the goniometer, I determined the precise direction of the vector going out from the scan in Gabriel's home. I used the ruler to draw the line, then did the same with the second scan. As I worked, tears spilled from my cheeks onto the map. I assumed that both times, the abductor had been standing close to Scarlett when she'd used magic. She wrote the notes in blood, probably Scarlett's. To use the technical term, she was a sadistic, deranged bitch. That meant that the vectors would intersect in the place where Scarlett and Elrine were being held.

I was saving Scarlett with math.

I stared at the map, desperately hoping I'd got this right. The lines intersected on Mile End Road.

* * *

As I STOOD in the darkness of Hyde Park, I dried my tears on the back of my hand. Four figures were moving toward me along the path, Roan's tall form impossible to miss. Lurking in the shadows on the grasses, I hissed at them, and one of them let out a feral growl.

It was hard to see them in the darkness, but one thing was certain. These were quite possibly the four most intimidating people I had ever met—two other males and a very creepy-looking female, their enormous bodies faintly bathed in the dim park lights.

"Cassandra." Even in the dark, I could see his green eyes scanning my neck, looking for the tiny bruise where he'd bitten me. "Did you find the location?"

"Yeah, I did. What took you all so long?"

"Waking up Odette turned out to be… a difficult task."

"I sleep deeply," the woman whispered. She wore a green cloak pinned with a mourning dove pendant, and under her hood, I could see a glimpse of pearly white skin, and dark whorls of tattoos covering her cheeks. Her eyes were large, black pools. Strands of her hair escaped her cowl, flashing orange and yellow like wildfire in the darkness. I shivered.

Quickly, Roan introduced the other two. Morcant had deep brown skin and close-cropped hair. He wore jeans and a green sweatshirt. Apart from his size and the fact that he wore sunglasses in the dark, he seemed completely normal. Drustan was… well, I had no idea. For some reason I couldn't really focus on him. I could hear movement coming from his direction, like the faint sound of heavy wings beating the air. He had a vague sense of menace about him, but something stopped me from perceiving any real details, like a mental block in my brain.

"Okay," I said. "I have a name. The fae who abducted Elrine and Scarlett is called Siofra."

Roan let out a low growl at the name, but the rest didn't seem to find this name significant.

"What do you know about her?" I prodded.

"Only her name," Roan said. "That she killed your parents. I don't know anything else about her."

"Right," I said slowly. "I also have an address, but I don't know how we should get there—"

"I have a car nearby." Morcant's voice was silky, calming.

"Yeah, awesome. But Siofra has reflection magic. She can see us through reflections. She'll kill her captives before we get there—"

She won't see us, Drustan said. Except it was more like his voice rose up within my own skull, like a thought. *I will take care of that.*

Shivering, I swallowed. "Good. Uh. There's bound to be some security. I have no idea what to expect, but I know that she has several powerful fae with her."

They all stared at me, power radiating off their bodies, and suddenly I felt like I was telling a tank squadron to watch out for the guy with the slingshot.

Morcant tilted his head. "They have harmed Elrine. Branded her like a piece of cattle, or a slave. They should be running away, if they know what's best for them." His voice was pure, controlled fury.

I took a deep breath. "Where's the car?"

Wait, Drustan said. *For just a moment.*

As I waited, magic seemed to tingle and ripple over my skin.

Slowly, Hyde Park's lamps seemed to dim, the moonlight darkening. In the night sky, a cloud of shadows slipped over the stars. Darkness swallowed us, and my heart thrummed in my chest. Drustan's magic was leaving us in an endless, infinite void, all alone, where no one would hear us scream... Dread bloomed in my chest.

Roan touched my arm, his warm fingers reassuring on my skin. "Do not look straight at the shadows if you want to retain your sanity."

Heat radiated off Roan's body, and I moved closer to him, feeling the reassuring brush of his arm against mine. At least I could still see the other fae, as if we were in our own bubble of shadows, and the rest of the world fell away into a chasm of darkness around us. I focused on staring at the others.

It is done, Drustan's voice rose in my mind.

Even Roan and Morcant seemed slightly unsettled. Only Odette seemed at ease, as if these ghostly shadows were her natural environment. Morcant took off his sunglasses, revealing yellow, feline eyes, like a tiger's.

"My car used to be over there." He pointed to the street,

which was a void of blackness from here. "Before your bloody shadows swallowed it."

The car is still there, said Drustan.

As we walked, the shadows moved with us. It felt as if the darkness had a motion of its own, swirling and tumbling around us. It unnerved me, and I stayed close to Roan's warm body.

As we moved closer to the street, a silver Porsche stood by the curb. From my time ogling Porsches online, I knew it was a 911 Carerra 4S, that it had a top speed over two hundred miles per hour, and that it cost more than a hundred thousand dollars. And, most significantly for this particular moment, I knew it only seated four people.

"There it is," Morcant said, relief tinging his voice. "My baby."

Odette pulled open the passenger seat and slid inside.

Roan's gaze slid to me as he pulled open the door. "You'll have to sit on my lap." He took a seat in the car, while Drustan got in the other side.

"Right." In the tiny car, there was hardly room for me to fit on his lap, but I slid in on top of him, nestling in. His body felt hard and warm beneath mine, and as if by reflex, his powerful arms slid around me.

Crammed in the back of a sports car on the lap of a primal predator, I had to question the life choices I've been making lately.

Mordant glanced back at me, his yellow eyes gleaming. "Where are we headed?"

I bit my lip. "Forgive me for asking, but how do you plan to drive through the shadows? We can't see where we're going. And I don't have a seatbelt."

Roan pulled his arms tighter around me. "You won't need a seatbelt."

"And I have GPS," said Mordant.

I sucked in a breath. "Right. We're heading for the corner of Mile End Road and Cephas Avenue."

He started the car and we pulled away, the shadows drenching the streets as we drove through them. An image of my father flickered in the hollows of my mind, hunched over a newspaper at the kitchen table, the sunlight glinting off his reading glasses. I could feel the ghost of tears pricking my eyes, and I clamped down on my guilt, thinking of Scarlett. My father's killer was still out there, still torturing Scarlett. Bile rose in my throat.

"I can feel your panic." Roan studied me closely. "And something else. What's the matter with you?"

He always seemed to be annoyed at my normal, human frailties. "Siofra killed my parents," I said quietly. "You were right."

Almost imperceptibly, his arms tightened around me, and his emerald gaze met mine. "We will slaughter her, Cassandra."

"Right." Fear whispered over my skin, and I didn't manage to sound very confident.

"Cassandra," Odette purred, her voice hardly audible above the engine's hum. "Don't be so scared. If you're going to die, I'll probably be able to give you a few minutes' notice."

I swallowed hard. "How reassuring."

CHAPTER 28

*E*xhaustion hit me like a train, and for a few minutes, I nodded off in the car. Roan's gentle hand on my arm woke me. "Cassandra. We're here."

I glanced out the window, but of course I couldn't see anything—only a shadowy void.

"We're going to need to be able to see where we're going now," I said. "Instead of cloaking everything in shadows, can you just cloak the reflective surfaces?"

From Drustan's direction, I heard the sound of wings beating the air. At last, he said, *I do not know where they are.*

I took a deep breath. "Just every reflective surface. All the windows, any water puddle, every mirror…"

I don't know what reflective is. I know only shadows.

"Fine." I gritted my teeth. "We'll have to let her see us now, and we'll move fast."

A whoosh of wings, the feel of feathers brushing against my cheek. *Very well. I will lift the darkness.*

Slowly, colors seeped back into my vision, as houses appeared around me. I nearly wept in relief when I saw the streetlights washing wide sidewalks in yellow light. The world was still there outside the Porsche after all.

Buildings lined either side of the road, some of them squat and brick, others four stories tall, with colorful storefronts in the lower levels. Just to our right stood a three-story brick mansion, enclosed by a wrought-iron fence, overgrown with vines. Intriguing, but I had no way of knowing if that was the right place.

"All right," Morcant said. "Which building?"

I swallowed hard, trying to think clearly. It could be any of these places. How could I possibly know?

Then, an idea bloomed in my mind. Glancing at the side mirror, I let my mind bond with its surface, then searched for the other reflections around it. Every building had dozens of reflections. Mirrors, windows, silver cutlery—they were everywhere.

All apart from one, which was completely invisible to my senses. Siofra controlled all its reflections. That was the house.

"There." I pointed to the mansion, just on the other side of the overgrown fence. The mansion had twenty large windows. I had sensed none of them when I had searched for reflections.

"That's Malplaquet House," Morcant murmured. "I know of it."

"They're there," I said. "I think maybe we should enter shrouded in darkness. Get Elrine and Scarlett and—"

"No," Roan said. "No more secrecy."

"But—"

Roan opened the car door. "Odette. Can you please let them know we're here?"

Odette nodded, her mouth quirking in a cryptic smile. As she stepped out of the car, my stomach clenched.

"Anyone care to fill me in?" I asked.

No one responded as she slipped out of the car, onto the sidewalk.

In the next moment, I was scooting out after Drustan. Odette pushed through the gate, and it creaked on its hinge. What was going on?

Silently, Odette stepped into the courtyard, spreading out her arms. I followed her over the mossy stones. Plants snaked the fence and brick walls around us, rustling eerily, as if nature was trying to reclaim its territory.

As Odette raised her arms, the wind began to pick up, rushing through the vines and tree branches. At first, the wind blew quietly, then it whistled and shrieked around us, its strength nearly knocking me down. Odette's green cloak flapped in the wind, and her wildfire hair rose like flames licking the air around her head.

Then she screamed.

Odette's shriek vibrated through my ribs, my spine, my teeth, and my limbs. I covered my ears in horror, but it was useless—the sound penetrated my fingers. Around us, windows were shattering to pieces, her voice ripping through the glass. The scream went on for what felt like ages, until at last it died down again. I heaved a sigh as the wind died down.

On the other side of the fence, the mansion's door opened, and four large men emerged, holding guns, their expressions slightly vacant and bewildered. One of them noticed us and raised his weapon.

Before he could pull the trigger, Morcant raised his hand, and a bright orange bolt shot from his palm, hitting the guard in his chest. Instantly, the man burst into flame. Already, Morcant was unleashing more of the orange bolts, hitting the other guards.

One of the guards tried to take cover. As he did, Roan appeared by his side, his sword in hand, antlers gleaming in the moonlight. He brought the sword down, and the guard's head tumbled to the floor in a cascade of blood.

All four guards, dead within seconds. I guess Roan and his friends really hadn't needed my warnings.

Odette turned to me, her cloak billowing in the wind. "We're here," she purred. She held out her hand, and I stared as a gleaming, white scythe appeared in it.

Gripping his sword, Roan moved up the steps. He turned to me, his eyes blazing gold. "Stay here. You're in over your head."

Like hell I would.

Roan was ready to break down the door when a volley of explosions made me instinctively flatten myself into the corner of the stairs.

"Gun! Iron bullets!" I shouted. Panic surged in my chest.

I had no way of knowing, but if I had to guess, Siofra had armed her guards with weapons that could hurt fae. Cowering in the mossy corner, I raised my eyes, glimpsing the sparks from the house windows as someone shot from them. I counted at least three windows with guns. When I glanced around, I could see that Roan and Morcant had taken cover. Odette hadn't bothered to hid herself, but as bullets hammered her body, she somehow remained unharmed.

Then shadows crept around us, wisps of shadow curling from Drustan's body, reaching for the house in dark tendrils. Shouts of horror penetrated the brick walls, and through the windows, I could see Drustan's shadows seeping through the rooms, blinding the guards, robbing them of their sanity. Odette let out another ghastly shriek, and I shivered. The combination of those shadows and Odette's screams would drive anyone mad.

Roan stood and kicked the door open, plunging into the shadows. Once again, he turned to me, his eyes locking on me. "Stay in the car." He slipped into the house, and Morcant moved in after him.

There was no way I was leaving Scarlett in there. Cursing, I followed them up the steps, pulling the Uzis from my bag and slinging their straps on my shoulders. My heart climbed into my throat as I slipped into the darkness.

Drustan seemed to be pulling his shadows from the house as I moved through the open door. Somewhere deep inside, I heard Roan's roar, and another man's shriek. Morcant's bolts of orange light flashed in the darkness. As they lit up the decrepit hall, which was lined with paintings, I caught a glimpse of a figure charging at me—a man with large bat wings, holding an immense sword, his eyes flashing with white light.

I raised my Uzi. I could feel the recoil as I pressed the trigger, emptying half the iron bullets into the creature's chest. He screamed and fell back against the wall, his body still, eyes wide open. In here, the walls were crammed with mounted animal heads and strange paintings of woodland scenes.

I moved further into a dining room. Blood soaked the green walls and the threadbare rug, and a half-dozen corpses littered the floor. A head lay in stone fireplace, its blood staining the hearth. Roan swung his sword at a black-bearded fae who blocked the attacks with a club. A cold shiver of dread slithered up my spine as I stared at the carnage around me—the headless body slumped against the base of a marble statue; another on the other side of the room, his blood sprayed in an arc on a tall window. Roan had killed all these fae, and it had probably taken him less than thirty seconds.

Morcant was nowhere in sight, but his orange light still flashed through the doorway, and the scent of burning flesh curled through the air. We'd been here less than a minute, and it was a bloodbath in here. But where was Siofra? And more importantly, where was my best friend?

Odette slipped past me, her body seeming to float on a phantom wind, her wildfire hair slithering around her head like a pack of snakes. As I gripped my gun, an eight-foot hulk barged into the room, roaring. Odette swung her scythe, and it left a shimmering path of silvery light in its wake as it cut the hulk in two, like a hot knife through butter.

There was no time to lose. Any second, one of the guards might figure out they had leverage—the prisoners who could easily be used as hostages. I slipped through one of the open doorways, on my way to find Scarlett.

I had reached a flight of stairs when a red-eyed woman appeared from around the corner, nearly taking off my head with a curved sword. I ducked at the last second, the blade whistling above my skull, and hurriedly aimed my Uzi, pressing the trigger. The shots went wild, the recoil jarring my aim. The woman dove as the bullets cracked paintings all over the wall, piercing the plastered walls. The *rat-tat-tat* of automatic gunfire stopped abruptly as my magazine emptied.

The fae hissed, gripping her sword. I dropped the Uzi, grabbing the second one. I raised it, taking three shots at her body. This time, all three bullets hit their mark. She stumbled back, her red eyes bulging, sword falling from her hands.

And then Roan was by my side.

"You should have waited outside," he growled.

I didn't have time to argue. "Whatever." Ignoring him, I ran up the creaky wooden stairs, taking two with each step.

As I ran, two guards appeared at the top, raising hand-guns, and I unleashed a spray of bullets from the Uzi. They dove, and Roan rushed past me up the steps, his sword raised. I let go of the trigger so I wouldn't hit him. When he reached the top of the stairs, his sword carved a sharp arc through the air through the air, spraying crimson droplets of blood. He turned to look at me, his face spattered with blood, his eyes golden, a pair of antlers on his head. He hadn't unveiled fully, and yet the sight of him still made my stomach clench. One of the guard's heads tumbled down the stairs, leaving a trail of blood behind it.

In a dark-walled hall, Roan and I kept together. He kicked each door open, searching. From below, screams of terror floated on the air, as Morcant, Odette, and Drustan laid waste to everyone in their path. I shivered as I caught a glimpse of a dusty glass case further down the hall, filled with human skulls displayed like works of art.

Roan kicked a fourth door open, revealing a dark, familiar room—the place where I'd seen Scarlett in one of the reflections.

As my eyes adjusted to the dark, I saw Scarlett and Elrine lying on the floor, hands bound behind their hands, clothes in tatters.

I sighed with relief. "Scarlett!" I hurried to her side, tugging at the rope in frustration. I winced at the sight of her seared back—that image of the skull under water.

Elrine's eyes were closed, but Scarlett craned her neck to meet my gaze. Fear flashed across her features, then relief. "Cass," she croaked. "Nice of you to drop by. We were having a slumber party, but Elrine's not much fun anymore."

That witty remark was all she could come up with before bursting into tears. Frantically, I tugged at the rope. I had no blade except for the Rix's knife, and I didn't want the toxic blade touching Scarlett's skin.

Roan was lifting Elrine's body with one arm.

"Roan!" I shouted. "Sword!"

He tossed me his blade, and it fell to the floor by my side with a clang. It was so heavy I could barely lift it. It had to be sixty pounds, but despite its weight, I managed to cut Scarlett's binds with it. She sat up, rubbing her wrists. I'd never seen her looking so pale, her milky skin a sharp contrast with the bruises marring her face.

"Can you walk?" I asked.

"I think so."

I helped her stand up and let her lean against me. Her body felt like it was burning up, and sweat dampened her skin. I could hear her gasping for breath. It tore at my heart to see her battered face, her bloodied leg, the rough stump where her toe was missing. But what really made my stomach clench was the sight of the angry, red lines streaking her bare foot from her severed toe. Infected.

"We need to get you to the hospital," I said.

"No shit," she muttered, leaning into me. "I think my blood is infected. Sepsis. And I've got cracked ribs." Anger burned through my veins. With her blood infected, Scarlett could die of a heart attack.

"Okay," I said, struggling to carry Roan's sword in one arm, holding up Scarlett in the other. "Let's go."

Slowly, we moved out of the room. Silence had fallen over the house, though when we reached the stairs, a shriek of pain ripped through the calm.

Scarlett's body tensed against me. "Someone's hurt."

"Not ours," I said grimly.

We descended the stairs, Scarlett flinching with pain with each step. When we reached the bottom, her wide eyes flicked to the carnage in the dining room, the blood spatters over the walls.

"Jesus," she breathed. "What the fuck happened here?"

"Rescue operation got a bit out of hand," I muttered as we walked toward the front door. Blood soaked the wooden floors, making them slippery. Once this night was over, I'd probably be throwing away my shoes.

Outside, I found Roan, Drustan, and Odette standing in the overgrown garden. Roan held Elrine in his arms, gently cradling her. A pang of jealousy shot through me, but I pushed it under the surface. She was awake, shivering, her eyes staring at nothing.

"Who are your friends, Cass?" asked Scarlett, her voice sharp.

"Friends who just got you out of there. What about Morcant?" I asked Roan. "Did he…"

"Morcant is taking care of one last detail," said Roan.

"Detail?" I asked.

Odette pulled her cowl over her vibrant hair. "Humans are adept at ignoring us. But there are about two dozen dead fae in that house."

"So what exactly—" I began to say.

There was a sudden *whoosh*, and orange and yellow flames licked at the bottom windows. I stared, aghast, as fire consumed the house.

"But there could be wounded in there!"

Not any more, Drustan said in my mind.

"Damn it!" I shouted. "The fire could catch to other houses! People live here."

After a few seconds, Morcant appeared in the doorway, his suit blazing with flames. As he casually walked down the stairs, he ran his hands over his body, dousing the flames as calmly as if he were wiping off dust.

In the distance, sirens wailed.

"The human firefighters will get here before long," Roan said, the only one who even seemed to give a thought to the people living nearby.

Morcant nodded at his car. "And we need to go."

* * *

THIS TIME, Scarlett sat in the front seat by Morcant, while Elrine sat in Roan's lap in the back. Odette and Drustan had disappeared into the darkness—quite literally. Drustan had called up a cloud of shadows, and they'd just walked away, fading from sight.

I glanced at Elrine, curled in Roan's lap, and I had to bite down on my jealousy. What the hell was wrong with me? I wasn't Roan's girlfriend. And anyway, I still had a psychotic bitch to kill, and we had to get Scarlett to the hospital fast.

Scarlett turned to look at me, and I winced at the sight of her battered face—the black eye, the swollen lip. Her breaths were coming in short, sharp bursts, a faint whistle when she inhaled. She moistened her lips, and swallowed hard, trying to work up the strength to speak. "What did I miss while I was a captive? What's the news?"

I wasn't sure how much to tell her right now, when she was on death's door, but if we were heading to a hospital, she was bound to find out about London's chaos. "I think the terrorist who blew up London might have been the woman who took you. She's also been flooding the city. And does Strasbourg in 1518 ring a bell?"

Her eyes widened, and she grimaced. "Fuck. A dancing plague," she wheezed. "How many casualties?"

I shook my head. "I don't even know at this point. The numbers keep mounting, and I haven't been able to keep up with the news."

Morcant was driving slowly, well under the speed limit, and I fought the urge to yell at him to hurry. Since we weren't cloaked by shadows, Morcant would not want to draw unnecessary police attention.

Best to drive slowly. And as we did, rolling down Whitechapel Road, I stared out the window, chilled at the sight of deserted streets. From the look of the place, a few weeks ago, this road would have been filled with people moving between the bars and restaurants.

It only took a few minutes down to the Royal London

Hospital—a towering building of bright blue glass and modern angles that loomed over the rest of the squat, Victorian neighborhood. Slowly, Morcant pulled up at the ER entrance.

I helped Scarlett climb from the car, then cast one last glance at Roan and Elrine as I closed the door. I wasn't quite sure how Elrine would heal, but it probably involved Roan whispering in the fae language and stroking her skin. I shoved the thought out of mind as I slid my arm around Scarlett's back. Outside the ER doors, two middle-aged women in hospital gowns languidly danced and twitched, rattling the IVs in their arms. I had no idea how they'd ended up out here, but it wasn't a good sign if the patients were spilling out onto the streets.

"So that's what the dancing plague looks like," Scarlett mumbled.

"I think we're about to see a lot more of it."

As soon as we entered, chaos greeted us. At the front entrance, a mob of dancers blocked our path—some already in some kind of half-assed treatment, with IVs for hydration. Others simply lingered at the edges of the white-and-purple-walled waiting room. Some stumbled into chairs, groaning as their bodies convulsed.

"Holy shit." Scarlett faltered, and I gripped her harder, practically carrying her. "I'm not sure I can make it to the desk to check in."

I pointed to a white bench just behind her. "Do you want to sit for a minute? I'll run to the desk to check you in."

Groaning slightly, she eased herself down to the bench. "I'll sit for a second. I'll come with you in a minute. If they see what I look like, I might get to a doctor faster."

I glanced into the swarming crowd. The entire space was crammed with people whose bodies twitched and jerked uncontrollably, skin waxy, jaws open, eyes terrified. An elderly man swayed and shuffled, moaning, his lips pale. Only a single person in the waiting room *didn't* seem to have the dancing plague—a young woman gripped her hand to her chest, her shirt soaked in blood.

I wasn't quite sure where a severed toe and a skin-branding would fit in the triage cue, but we'd be here for a long time.

I swallowed hard. "Scarlett... I won't be able to stay with you. Not until you talk to your guys at the CIA."

Her forehead crinkled. "What are you talking about?"

"They think I had something to do with your abduction."

Her lips were pale. "An FBI agent? Who's the idiot who came up with that idea?"

"Fulton."

She wet her lips, straining to keep her eyes open. "What a moron."

"Scarlett." I swallowed hard. "He had a good reason to suspect me."

She blinked, her cheeks pink with fever. "What reason? What are you talking about? I don't understand." Her words were beginning to slur.

My heart slammed against my ribs. I shouldn't be this terrified to tell my best friend the truth. I needed her to trust me, but I had to trust her too. I needed to have faith that she wouldn't immediately turn me in. Truthfully, I just couldn't imagine that happening.

"I'm fae."

I watched as her grip tightened on the edge of the bench, her knuckles whitening. She stared at me, confusion etched across her features. I wasn't sure if that was the sepsis or the fact that her best friend had just confessed to being a monster.

I swallowed hard. "I didn't know until I got to London. I'm half-fae, half-human. A pixie. And I'm not evil. I swear I would never do anything to harm anyone…" My words trickled away as confusion clouded my own mind. I couldn't mention the whole *terror leech* thing. Save that conversation for some time when Scarlett wasn't near death.

For several seconds, Scarlett just stared at me, blinking. She'd spent the past few days being tortured by a fae. If anything, her hatred for my species had just intensified.

"You idiot." She winced, clutching her chest. "I know you're not evil. Except when you haven't had your first cup of coffee. Then you can be a nasty bitch."

I let out a laugh mixed with a sob, and crouched down to hug her. She hissed in pain as my hands touched her back, and I quickly stepped back.

"Sorry!" I wiped a tear from my cheek.

"It's okay. I'll get over it."

"We need to get you to a doctor. Now." I leaned down, helping her stand, and she held me around my waist.

"Did I say thank you yet for rescuing me?" she asked.

"You don't need to thank me. You'd do the same for me."

She shuffled by my side, her body burning up. "Who were the fae you came with? There was that hot guy from the pub. The hot one… his girlfriend…" She was rambling now.

Jealousy flared, and I pushed the feeling to the back of my skull. "I'm not sure if Elrine is his girlfriend." I took a deep breath. I hadn't wanted to rush Scarlett into giving details about her torturer, but I had to find out what I could before I left her here. "Scarlett, I know you're not feeling well, but this is important. Can you describe the woman who abducted you?"

"I caught a glimpse." Near the desk, Scarlett leaned in closer to me, clinging to my chest. "About our age. Brunette, shiny smooth hair, a straight nose. Thick eyebrows. Five-six. Familiar. I don't know why, where I would have seen…" She closed her eyes for a minute, resting her head on my shoulder. "It'll come back."

"Thanks. We'll figure it out later."

"Oh." Her eyes opened. "I heard a name. Siofra. And…" she hesitated.

"What?" I pressed.

Scarlett blinked, sweat beading on her forehead. "She said…" She closed her eyes, concentrating. *"Toll no bell for me, dear Father, dear Mother, Waste no sighs."*

If I hadn't known about Siofra's penchant for rhymes, I would have assumed this was fevered rambling. "That sounds like her."

A woman sat behind a desk frowning at us over the rims of her glasses. "Can you tell me your name?"

Leaning on the desk, Scarlett turned to me. "I'll take it from here. You'll work it out. Call me in a day. Don't let Fulton catch you before that."

"I won't." I pulled my fake police badge, faking a British accent. "She needs to be seen straight away. She's been tortured and her blood is poisoned, and she'll die without immediate treatment."

The woman nodded at me. "Of course."

But before leaving, I marched up to one of the guards, an enormous man who hardly fit in his suit. I flipped the badge again as I approached. Damn thing was handy as hell. "Police. Can I use your phone? Just a quick call; it's urgent."

He muttered something under his breath, but he pulled his phone from his pocket. I snatched it from the guard, then dialed Gabriel's number from memory.

"Hello?" he answered immediately, his voice rough, as if I'd woken him.

"It's me."

"What now, Cassandra? Please don't tell me you've stolen the animals from the London Zoo or blown up Big Ben."

"Good news, actually. Scarlett is safe. She's at the hospital in Whitechapel. And the ravens are in a storage facility called Big Yellow Self Storage Kennington with a whole bunch of bread and water. The container is listed under the name Edgar Allan Poe. They should be fine."

"Hang on. I don't give a fuck about the birds. You got Scarlett?"

"Yes."

"How? Who took her?"

"Finding her involved math, and…" Okay. I couldn't tell him about breaking into the CIA. "Mostly math."

"Math? That makes no bloody sense, Cassandra. Who abducted her? What can you tell me?"

I eyed the guard nervously. "Look, I can't really talk now. I'm at the hospital. I'll tell you everything I can in the morning. For now, I can just tell you the woman's name was Siofra, and she was keeping Scarlett in a mansion in Whitechapel. It's… the building is gone now."

"So the evidence is destroyed. Wonderful. You really know how to work a crime scene."

"Please tell me you'll send someone for the birds? I don't know how long they'll last in there."

"Give me specifics about the building being gone."

The guard was staring me down. "The fire department is there already. I think it's under control."

"Bloody hell. Listen, Cassandra. You'd better find some way to sort all this out with the CIA. They've sent someone 'round looking for you, and I don't fancy having to lie to them again. I've been having nightmares about orange jumpsuits and waterboarding. And if you're running around blowing up buildings in Whitechapel, I'm done lying for you, especially when you haven't done me the courtesy of keeping me informed about anything."

"I'm sorry." It was true, I was hiding things from him. And

yet, I wasn't going to tell him about the CIA break in. "But the more I tell you, the more you'll have to lie about. It's better if you don't know some of this. For your own benefit."

He let out a long sigh. "I'm glad Scarlett is safe. Just please tell me you're done with all the crazy shit."

"Siofra's still out there, Gabriel."

"Of course. And you're the person to stop her, right? I want more details tomorrow. You should be letting the police handle this."

"I have to go." I hung up, and handed the phone back to the guard.

CHAPTER 29

*I*n my hotel room, milky morning light pierced the blinds. I checked the clock next to my bed—just after nine a.m.

I rose from the bed, then rolled over to pick up the hotel phone. I dialed Gabriel, and he answered after the third ring.

"Stewart."

"Did anyone find the ravens?"

"Yeah. They're back where they belong."

"Good." I sighed with relief.

"And yet the city is still falling apart. There are more cases of the dancing plague. Additional floods. Thirteen dead last night. Can you tell me anything about those attacks? Is there any connection to Scarlett's abduction?"

"I think so. I think Siofra is doing it."

"And the fire last night in Whitechapel. Was that Siofra's house?"

"That was her house, but we didn't find her there."

"Looks like there are at least a dozen bodies inside."

"They were fae. Did the fire spread to the other houses?"

"Yes, but only minimal damage done beyond that house. Fire department managed to contain it," he said. "How exactly did it burn?"

"I didn't burn it, Gabriel."

"I didn't say you did, and yet you have a knack for leaving chaos in your wake. The EDL is still going on about the bloody ravens and travelers or refugees or whoever they're targeting this week."

In a battle against the fae, chaos sort of came with the territory. "I know. I'm sorry. But we're not going to solve this by using old-fashioned police work, Gabriel. This is a fae war."

"And that's how you see yourself now?"

"Yeah, I guess it is." Exhaustion punched a hole in my chest. "Here's what I can tell you. Siofra is five-six, brown bob, straight nose, about twenty-six. She uses incredibly powerful reflection magic. She's sadistic and likes to be in control. She probably thrives on fear. A terror leech, maybe connected to the Rix. Maybe not. She's known to the CIA. She's been targeting me specifically for reasons I don't understand. She's into rhymes and has a sick sense of humor."

"Anything else?"

"Yeah. She murdered my parents. I'll let you know if I find out anything else." I hung up the phone before he had the chance to ask me more about that particular fact. I didn't want to go into it right now, didn't want to picture my father and mother sitting in our old, cluttered living room, the comforting buzz of the TV on in the background...

Right now, I needed to stay focused on what was going on in London, and Siofra's attack on the city. Thirteen more had died of the dancing plague. Whatever her plan was, she didn't seem about to stop just because I'd freed her captives.

Why was she doing this? And why had she killed my parents in the first place? My initial thought had been that the abductor hated me because I'd killed the Rix, but Siofra had murdered my parents long before the Rix came into play.

None of it made sense.

I pulled my laptop from my bag and flipped it open. In the search bar, I typed in the line Scarlett had quoted last night: *Toll no bell for me, dear Father, dear Mother, Waste no sighs.*

The first result to pop up was a poem called "The Changeling," and a shiver licked up my spine. I read it twice —a sad poem about isolation, not fitting in. When I'd finished reading it, I searched for "changeling" and clicked the link to the Wikipedia page.

It seemed that, according to British folklore, when a human child was stolen and replaced with a fae lookalike, the fae baby was called a *changeling*. Changelings were supposedly unpleasant, difficult children. In the Victorian era, several children had been murdered for the crime of being changelings.

The Irish word Síobhra—and its English counterpart, Siofra—meant changeling child.

My heart skipped a beat. Siofra was a changeling: a fae who'd been raised as a human.

But this realization didn't answer *any* of my questions— namely, why she was after me.

I looked again at the Wikipedia article. Something nagged at the back of my mind, but I couldn't put my finger on it. I scanned it again, stopping when I got to a part about eggshells.

Supposedly, changelings could be uncovered if you boiled broth in an eggshell. If you stood near them when you did it, they'd burst out laughing. I'd heard something like this before. Alvin had once asked me if I ever stewed a broth in an eggshell. At the time, I'd thought he was just being weird. He hadn't been. He'd been giving me a hint about Siofra.

I opened my email account, finding ninety-eight unread emails, fourteen of them from my Unit Chief, most of them with a caps-locked subject about checking in. But the topmost email was from Scarlett. My heart beating, I clicked it.

Cass, attached is the sketch of the psycho. BTW the food here makes me yearn for death.
   Scarlett.

When I clicked open the file and it popped up on the screen, I felt like I had been kicked in the stomach.

It looked like a sketch of my mom.

Not exactly like her—the eyes were further apart, the lips a little fuller. But, aside from that, she looked just like my mom—same straight nose, same full, arched eyebrows. Hell, she looked a lot more like my mom than I did. Of course Scarlett thought she looked familiar—I'd shown her photos of my mom over the years.

Siofra was my mother's daughter. Either Siofra and I were somehow sisters or...

I swallowed hard, as a dreadful thought hammered in the back of my mind.

When Alvin had told me about boiling the broth in the eggshells, he'd said *you* should try it. He'd suggested that I would find it hilarious. And why would that be the case, unless I was also a changeling?

What if I was the other changeling, the one who replaced Siofra? Maybe it was possible for a fae to be swapped for a pixie. I didn't know.

My stomach tightened into knots. Maybe Siofra resented me for a life stolen—and maybe she and I were more alike than I dared to acknowledge. Two changelings; two terror leeches who fed off horror. Two sides of the same coin.

And if it were true, then who, exactly, were my birth parents?

hud. Something was pounding at the walls of my mind, my own heartbeat, perhaps. *Thud.* The thing I didn't want to name, didn't want to face, the whirling, shadowy possibilities of my own identity.

Thud. My dad's voice calmly intoned in the back of my mind, *Princess, monsters aren't real.*

Oh, monsters are real, Daddy.

I just wasn't sure if I'm one of them. *Thud.* I needed to know more about my past. A cold sweat broke out on my skin, and I clamped my eyes shut. Why did my past really matter? Why did it matter who my parents were? I believed in the power of environment to shape a person. Evil wasn't innate, right? I'd always said it was learned. *Thud. Thud.* So what the fuck difference did it make where I came from, or who my birth parents were--unless I no longer believed my own theories? *Thud. Thud.*

Maybe I didn't.

Whatever the case, the fact was, I needed to find Siofra. Something about me enraged her, and she was taking it out on innocent people in London. It wasn't my fault, exactly.

But somehow, I couldn't escape the gnawing feeling that it was *because* of me. Somehow, she was killing Londoners to get at me. She wanted my attention, wanted to torment me, wanted me to feel the blood on my hands. *Thud. Thud.* Perhaps she hated the fact that I'd lived among the humans, and wanted to torture me by slaughtering my own kind.

My heart was pounding in my skull. I had to get out of here. I needed the noise, the chaos of the London streets. Absurdly, I wished Odin were still here with me, to drown out my thoughts with his inane chatter.

To help me forget the blood on my hands. *Mistress of Dread, Mother of Death.*

I clamped my hands over my ears, trying to block out the sound of my own heart. *Thud. Thud. Thud.*

No—it wasn't my heart. That was the sound of a fist hitting the door.

Taking a long, shaky breath, I rose from the bed and crossed to the door, my thoughts still churning.

My body trembled as I stood on my tiptoes to peer through the peephole, shocked to see Roan staring back at me. How did he know to find me here? I pulled open the door.

"Cassandra. I nearly broke down the door. I could feel your emotions surging through." He peered at me closely, his body tensing. "What's wrong?"

"Nothing." I clenched my hands together to stop them from shaking.

"You look pale."

"I'm fine. I'm just trying to figure everything out."

"I need to talk to you."

I opened the door wider and he walked inside, dipping his head to avoid hitting it on the door frame.

I gestured at the rumpled bed. "Have a seat. Did you find out anything about this Siofra? She's still killing people."

He sat at the edge of the bed, and it groaned under his weight. "Only that she is a young fae. Not even a century old. Apparently, she grew up in the Rix's palace."

"The Rix?" A tendril of dread coiled through me, and I was having a hard time breathing.

Roan nodded. "I believe she was his servant, or slave. We're trying to find out more."

"Are pixies and fae ever exchanged for each other, as changelings?"

He shook his head. "No. A fae wouldn't be exchanged for another fae. Why are you asking about this?"

For a moment, my heartbeat slowed, but the seed of this dreadful idea had taken root in my skull, and I couldn't get rid of it. What if Siofra were human? Neither of my parents seemed particularly fae-like. They simply seemed human— they were too frail to be fae, too skittish, too flawed. Gray hair and creases around their eyes, my dad snorting when he laughed.

I paced in the small room. "Is it possible for a human to use magic the way a fae does?"

"What does it have to do with anything?" He frowned. "Cassandra, what's wrong? I can feel your emotions whirling out of control."

"Is it possible?" I demanded, nearly screaming now.

"Yes. It's just very complicated."

My gut dropped. If Siofra and I had been exchanged at birth, she could be the daughter of the two human parents who'd raised me. And that meant—I was the daughter of the man who'd raised her. The Rix. The monster I'd killed, the one with the poisonous soul.

I clutched my stomach, fighting a wave of nausea, trying to convince myself I could be wrong. I didn't have much to go on yet—just a comment about eggshells, and the fact that the parents who'd raised me seemed human. It could *easily* be wrong. My racing pulse began to slow slightly.

Roan's gaze pierced me. "You really don't look well."

I swallowed hard. "I'm just trying to figure everything out. Based on some things she said to Scarlett, I think Siofra could be a changeling. And I think I could be linked to her somehow. I'm just not entirely sure how."

"But she's fae, raised in the fae realm."

"Right." I loosed a sigh. "So you're certain she's fae. It's unlikely that she could use this powerful magic if she was human, right?"

He cocked his head. "Unlikely, but not impossible. A human must harness power from a particular tree in the fae realm. A human can channel the power of the spirit who lives in that tree. It takes years of practice for it to work. If the link to the tree is severed, the power is gone. They'd have to start over, building that relationship up again. The Rix would know how to do that. If she were human, it would explain how she ended up a slave in the Rix's court."

"If we were swapped at birth, the Rix was my father."

Roan stared at me, the shadows around him thickening. "It's possible."

The theory *was* possible, and I felt like I'd been punched in the gut, but I tried to focus. "Okay. So if she gets her power from a tree, how would we find this particular tree?"

"You wouldn't. It's impossible to know which one she's using."

Disappointment pressed on my chest. "That's not particularly helpful." I cocked my hip, trying to control my roiling thoughts. "Why are you here, anyway, and how did you know where to find me?"

"Elrine told me where you were, and I've come to collect you. I can explain on the way."

Of course she had. Her tracking ability was quite unnerving. "What do you mean, 'collect me?' On the way to where?"

"To the Cliffs of Albion. It's a long journey, and we have to leave now."

"What?"

"You promised that when Scarlett was safe, you'd come with me. She is safe. And the council is meeting soon."

My head was spinning. I couldn't run off to the fae realm when I still hadn't captured Siofra. "Does it have to be now?" I couldn't leave now. Not with Siofra still slaughtering people across the city, vying for my attention.

He clenched his jaw. "The council only gathers once every few months. They meet in two days by the Cliffs of Albion, outside of Trinovantum."

I blinked. "How long does it take to get there?"

"Nearly two days."

"I don't have time for a two-day journey to and from the Council. You didn't tell me it was so far."

He shrugged. "You never asked. The Council won't meet in the city itself. Too many spies. We must act before the king of Trinovantum tries to move further into the Hawkwood Forests. If he does, many Elder Fae will die, and he'll gain more and more power. The Callach said your presence at the Council is key to stopping him."

My fists tightened. "I can't spare four days. You want to stop the king. And I want to stop Siofra. She killed my parents, Roan. She has a sick vendetta against me, and she's still out there, still killing Londoners right now. She's doing it to get at me. Because of *me*, because I'm probably her changeling, and she wants my attention. Desperately. I *have* to stop her before anyone else gets hurt. Don't you understand?"

Roan narrowed his eyes, and his fingers tightened on the edge of the bed. "An excuse."

My jaw dropped. It was more than just an excuse. Peoples' lives were in the balance. "Listen, Roan. Your whole plan hinges on the fact that a crazy old woman in the woods said I was a 'key,' and no one knows what that means. If she was such a brilliant prophetess, why couldn't she give you more specifics? The bag lady who lives outside my apartment once told me her shopping cart full of cabbages would save the world. Guess what? I ignored her."

Roan's eyes gleamed with dark gold, and I could see the flicker of horns over his head. "I realize the Elder Fae and Trinovantum politics don't matter to you. But they matter to me, and to many other fae. Lives are at stake. And you are the key to saving them."

"I need one more day," I said.

"We don't have one more day."

I crossed my arms. "I can't go."

He stared at me, his jaw tightening. "You can't break your promise."

"I'm not breaking it. I said I'll come once Scarlett is safe. And I will. We defined no timeframe. I can come tomorrow. I'll journey through reflections if I have to." I couldn't, though. Not without burning out my magic and trapping myself between dimensions.

Shadows slid through his eyes, and the air around me cooled. "There aren't many reflective surfaces in the wilderness, and none in the council hall, precisely so people like you can't break in. I hadn't expected you to be so faithless, Cassandra."

"People are *dying* in London. If you saw what I'd seen in the hospitals, you'd understand. Old women, children, dying of exhaustion from the dancing plague."

"Fae will die if you don't come with me. I have a responsibility to protect them, to safeguard our realm from the king's incursions. You are fae, too, Cassandra. These are your people. And before our current king, pixies like you once thrived in Trinovantum. We can revert to our former glory, but I need your help."

I was in an impossible situation, but I had to make a decision and stick with it. "I'm sorry. But you don't know that fae will die, and I can see people dying all over London. It's happening right now. We're talking about a certainty versus a probability. If I don't help London now, it will haunt me forever."

Roan rose from the bed, towering over me. His raw, primal power seemed to fill the room, washing over me in waves, and my stomach dropped. I'd pushed him too far. "Believe me, this will haunt you one way or another. You can't escape your fate."

My throat tightened. *Mother of Death.*

Roan moved swiftly past me, slamming the door behind him. The sound of splintering wood echoed through the room, and the plaster above the door cracked. I sat down on the bed, heart pounding.

* * *

I ASKED the barista in the café to make me a double espresso. The barista—a teen with a staggering number of facial piercings—handed me a cup dark as ink, bitter to the point of undrinkable, and muddy in texture. Exactly what I needed. At the chrome counter, I sipped it and tried to work up enthusiasm for the scone in front of me.

Siofra had been raised in the Rix's household. And that meant I was the Rix's daughter.

I'd killed my father without even realizing, like some kind of tragic Greek hero. The world seemed to tilt beneath my feet, and I took a deep breath, forcing myself to look around me at the coffee shop patrons, drowning the roar in my brain with random noise—the man sighing and tutting over his cell phone. A woman eating a cheesecake while sobbing silently. A blind man smiling at a woman, who caressed his arm lovingly. Slowly, I got my emotions under control.

Focus, Cassandra. Get your shit in order. First, find Siofra. Then have the meltdown you're clearly due for.

I knocked back a long slug of coffee, as another thought began percolating in my mind. If Siofra was human, I could profile her.

What did I know? She'd been stolen from her biological parents, raised by a man with twisted soul who had treated her as a slave. Now, she was following his footsteps. Rhyming poems—just like he'd written. Spreading chaos and fear, killing randomly. Sadism. She looked up to him, wanted to fulfill his legacy. Nurture, not nature.

Now, she was taking it further. She was targeting me, as well. Not only trying to kill me. Trying to hurt me—the Rix's daughter. She'd cleverly managed to isolate me from everyone who could help me. She'd abducted my best friend, letting me take the fall as the main suspect. The CIA had turned on me. She'd sent me on a task to break into the Tower—at the cost of Gabriel's support. She'd pitted me against Roan in a battle to the death. She'd tried to flood me with guilt until I lost my mind.

What else? Oh. She'd slaughtered my parents.

Slowly, she'd been stripping me of the life she thought I'd stolen from her.

I swallowed hard. Now, how could I find this bitch?

I could try and trace the paperwork of the Whitechapel Mansion, where she'd hidden Scarlett. I could find out who rented it, who owned it. But that would probably require the police's cooperation, and I couldn't imagine Gabriel giving me that information at this point.

Maybe there was some sort of magic to find a changeling.

But that would require Roan's assistance, and he was gone too.

I only had myself.

I could do this. I just had to *think*. What was she trying to do? Follow the Rix's footsteps. Cause chaos, death...

But the Rix had been clever about it. He had wormed himself into a place of human power—a high-ranking police officer. And from that position he had fanned the flames, making them grow, making the fire spread.

I sipped my bitter coffee. What if Siofra did the same?

Maybe she'd joined the police as well. But it didn't quite fit for Siofra. The way she'd hammered me with messages, determined to keep herself in my thoughts at all times, she was desperate for attention. As a slave in the Rix's house, she'd probably been starved of attention. She probably always felt the need to prove herself, desperate for love, desperate to get everyone's eyes on her.

The media? Could be. She could definitely fan the flames from there, and get the crowd's adoration. But would the Rix approve? The Rix had believed in raw power.

It was more likely she'd go for a position of authority, try to prove herself to the Rix. But one that came with a lot of media attention.

I closed my eyes, letting a sip of coffee roll over my tongue, and a random memory rolled around the back of my mind. A strange sentence. Something I should have noticed earlier, if I hadn't been so desperate to get away from the CIA agents.

The mayor, telling Gabriel she was going to get her car. The same mayor who, last year, had campaigned on a platform of London congestion, making a big show of riding her bike all around the city—all while slyly blaming immigrants for overcrowding, of course.

Had she changed her mind?

I'm going to get my car.

That hadn't been all she said, was it? I concentrated, trying to remember exactly how she'd phrased it. Typically, language was encoded for meaning, not for precise word choices. Just one of the things that made eyewitness testimony so unreliable, when memories were faulty. And yet, something about the way she'd spoken had been... odd. The phrasing had stuck in my mind. Why? I replayed the conversation in my mind.

The explosions, the floods, the ravens, the plague. They're all connected. It isn't vague. I've seen zero progress so far... I'm going to get my car.

It was a rhyme. She couldn't have said "bike" because it wouldn't have rhymed, and I remembered her idiosyncratic phrasing, because it had sounded almost like a song. Like a nursery rhyme—designed to be memorable.

> *The explosions, the floods, the ravens, the plague*
> *They're all connected, it isn't vague*
> *I've seen zero progress so far*
> *I'm going to get my car*

Rhyming just for the sake of it. In my field, we called that clanging. Usually it was associated with psychosis, which did not fit the mayor's profile. Even though she was a sadist, she was clearly sane. Still, maybe she'd adopted this method of speaking as a way of soothing herself, or just a compulsion borne out of her relationship to the Rix.

What had the abductor said to me when I'd delivered the pelvic bone? "Well, you made it. I'm surprised, I admit." Another rhyme.

I pulled out my laptop, my mind buzzing with excitement. The mayor hadn't done anything to stop the mass hysteria spreading. In fact, she'd encouraged people to take matters into their own hands. She'd linked the floods, the fires, the plague, and the ravens all together, and she'd allowed the hysteria to foment. She'd encouraged the idea that London was under a terrorist attack.

I opened the browser, and searched for the video of her reaction to the first attack. I found it quickly, and listened to her words in amazement.

> *Those people are attacking our homes and*
> *spreading fear*
> *They seek to disrupt our life and endanger what we*
> *hold dear*
> *But I promise you this!*
> *This fire is not something we will dismiss*
> *We will find the people responsible for this*
> *terrorist act*
> *and they'll learn the full force of our impact*
> *I urge the citizens, if you know of anyone who might*
> *consort*
> *with those who harm us, do not hesitate to report*

Bingo. I began searching for articles about the mayor. She looked about fifty. Gray hair, sharp eyes, and a firm mouth, but that meant nothing. It could easily be glamour. I tried to imagine the blurry figure I had seen in Kent. Did it match this woman?

I wasn't sure, but her voice matched the mayor's.

According to the internet, she'd been elected in May 2016. And her previous political experience included…

Absolutely nothing.

There was a lot of talk about her belonging to a covert section of MI6, which both MI6 and the mayor denied. The denial had only fueled the rumors, of course. She'd probably spread them herself, acquiring a past that bestowed her with an aura of authority and ruthlessness. Especially in those times when people were scared, and facts didn't matter as much as before. One of her biggest supporters had been none other than DCI Wood, AKA the Rix.

An obsession with rhymes. A clear link to the Rix. Someone in a position of authority, in the center of the limelight. A person using the recent events to fuel the fire of hatred and fear in the city. Keeping very close tabs on the investigation.

And that's when I found an article that made me pause.

"Mayor Hosts Mirror Exhibition in City Hall."

It was dated six days ago, and featured a photo of the mayor standing amidst dozens of artfully framed mirrors, her own reflection refracted around the glass, and a small, satisfied smile on her face.

CHAPTER 31

L ondon's City Hall jutted out over the Thames like a glass thumb, and gleaming sunlight reflected off its vast array of windows. A building of mirrors—the perfect place for reflective magic. As the breeze from the Thames kissed my skin, I hurried past a young couple in jogging gear, caught in the grips of the dancing plague, eyes terrified, bodies covered in a sheen of sweat. The young woman's blond ponytail flipped and jerked in the wind, mouth strained in a horrified grimace. My stomach turned at the sight of them.

If I could stop Siofra, maybe I'd be able to save them.

I strode up to the front doors, ready to show my bag to the security guard. I'd removed the weapons earlier, strapping the Rix's knife to my ankle.

But when I reached the doors, I found no guard. In fact, the whole building seemed eerily quiet—no one at the front desks, no one walking through the lobby. Slowly, I crossed into the circular hall, glancing up at the modern architecture —a vortex of levels that spiraled up above me like the inside of a seashell.

Siofra knew I was coming for her, and she'd followed my movements through the reflections. She could have stopped me anywhere she wanted.

Maybe this is what she wanted.

And there was only one place she'd be waiting for me. I followed the signs to the exhibition of mirrors, following the spiraling levels down to the exhibition hall. My footfalls echoed off the floor as I slowly descended, already catching glimpses of the hall of mirrors below me. Anticipation prickled over my skin as I reached the bottom floor.

Dozens of mirrors lined the circular hall—some gilt-framed and antique, others modern and sleek, or inscribed with poetry. Some were tilted slightly so that their reflections intersected, infinitely reflecting each other. Another was curved, a half-shell shape. And in the center of the hall stood an enormous shard of mosaic mirrors, pointing up to the vortex like a pillar of light.

Siofra wasn't here, which didn't surprise me. She was watching me through the reflections, and I was a fly walking into her trap. She'd make her dramatic entrance soon enough.

I lifted my arms. "Well? I'm here!"

I waited, my heart pounding, feeling completely exposed. As I tried to form a bond with any of the reflections, I felt them blocked, empty. Siofra was in control of them all.

The mirrored shard shimmered, and slowly, an image appeared on the shard in the center of the hall—an enormous reflection of the mayor I had seen in the newspaper. An aging, formidable woman. Then, one by one, all the mirrors around me filled with the same reflection. She smiled at me, blinking her eyes, her expression oddly girlish.

At the sight of her, rage burned through my veins. I wanted to rip her heart out of her chest and cram it into her stupid, smirking mouth. She'd murdered my parents. She'd tortured my best friend. She'd tried to slaughter half the city of London. Here before me, smiling and batting her eyelashes, was the face of true evil.

She couldn't hear my voice through reflections, but some things needed no sound. As fury ripped through my veins, I snarled at her, baring my teeth—a vicious, primal instinct.

The multitude of faces around me widened their eyes, their mouths opening in feigned surprise. This woman who appeared to be in her fifties was acting like a child, and the sight disturbed me. And yet I had to get her much closer.

And then, to my utter shock, eight of her reflections walked through the mirrors, their identical bodies emerging into the room.

"You came here to play, fortal?" all eight said together, their voices echoing in unison. In sync, the mayors toyed with the edges of their jackets, swinging their shoulders playfully back and forth, their voices singsong. "You want to play with me now?"

She'd surrounded me, and I felt the world tilting beneath my feet at the sight. Frantically, I looked around me, trying to figure out what was happening. This woman was a million times more powerful than I was. Eight mayors, and they all seemed to be regressing into childlike behaviors before my eyes.

I had just one ace in the hole, one crazy-assed plan.

I schooled my features to calmness, trying to mask the fear that lit up my body.

"Afraid to face me alone?" I asked. "Eight of you against one of me?"

"Well, of course," they responded in unison, smiling shyly. "Who wouldn't be afraid of the big, bad Cassandra Liddell? FBI Agent, beloved daughter. Admired and loved by all." The mayors nibbled their lower lips, smiling coyly. "Cassandra Liddell the thief, the life robber, the murderess." The mayors clapped their hands. "What's your plan, dear twin? I can't wait to see what you have in store for me."

"My plan is to stop you."

The mayors raised their eyebrows, eyelashes fluttering. "You want to feel my fear, though, don't you? A monster like you thrives on fear. Feeds on it. Drinks it up when mothers and fathers are dying, because it feels too good to stop."

Hot wrath erupted in my skull, and I lunged for the first mayor, swinging. My fist went right through her, the reflection flickering, and I nearly lost my balance. Immediately, I whirled, kicking the second, meeting only air. A jab to the third got the same result. When I scrambled for the fourth and fifth, my fist hitting only air, she laughed.

"Just reflections," I said. "Smoke and mirrors."

"You should know a lot about that," the eight mayors giggled. "Smoke and mirrors, Siofra's getting nearer."

The closest reflection turned, slamming me in the face with her fist, and I staggered back. It seemed that sometimes, the reflections were tangible. If I could just catch them at the right time, could just sink my fingers into their wretched skin...

As I whirled, another reflection lunged and aimed a kick at my gut. Even as the air left my lungs, I caught her foot and flipped her. But my victory was short lived as pain exploded in the back of my skull, and I stumbled forward. The reflections were strong, their bodies sometimes solid. But every time I tried to hit one, my fist just swung through the air. Siofra was toying with me. *Want to play with me?*

Dizzy, I staggered, and another blow slammed me in the back of the skull, knocking me over.

"Rich man, poor man, beggar man, *thief*," they trilled.

Another one kicked, slamming me in the stomach with her foot and I folded in two.

"A murderer should drown in grief," they sang.

A mayor kicked me in the face, and agony ripped through my jaw.

"Monster." Her voice was still high-pitched and girlish, but there was an edge to it now.

And as she grew angrier, the voices slipped out of sync, the reflections beating me with a rising fury. Curling into a ball, I took the blows, took the pain. The little mob of clones devolved into incomprehensible shouts, kicking and spitting at me.

Just as I felt as if I couldn't take anymore, the attack stopped, the reflections looking down at me.

I coughed, rolling to my back. She'd bruised several of my ribs, and blood filled my mouth.

"Okay," I wheezed, staring up at her. "I get why you call me thief. I stole your life, right? No daddy and mommy for poor Siofra. But I don't recall murdering anybody."

Around the hall, the mirrors flickered, all showing the same place: the stone vaults of a medieval church, shadows dancing around them. Cassandra Liddell lying on the floor, the Rix on top of her. A knife in her hand. With one sharp, brutal slash, she slit the Rix's throat.

"Murderer," said the mayors.

"Well, he was an asshole." I forced myself to sit up. Slowly, clutching my gut, I rose. Pain splintered my left leg. Probably fractured as well. "I'm sorry, do you miss your daddy?"

"Do you miss yours?" They inched in closer, reaching for me, their girlish smiles faltering. "Let's meet him again!"

Two mayors lunged for me, fingers hard as rock. They shoved me, slamming me back into the curved mirror. Then, they swarmed around me, holding me in place, fingers digging into my flesh. Everywhere around me, I could see the mirrors—the half-dome, the shard, the gilt-frame mirrors. Siofra had something she wanted to show me.

"Remember this, Cassandra?" one of them whispered in my ear.

Around the hall, the mirrors shimmered to life, the reflections shifting to show me a blue-walled room, and a sharp pang of longing pierced me to the marrow. A living room. The table where I'd cracked my chin open when I was four years old. The sofa where I used to curl up with a book, drinking hot chocolate with marshmallows that mom made for me. The carpet, with its intricate patterns that I loved to follow with my eyes as my parents watched the news. I froze, staring at it, unable to move, the breath leaving my lungs. Even if the mayors hadn't been pinning me, I didn't think I'd be able to move.

My old house. In my parents' bedroom, portraits hanging on the wall, my mom's red bathrobe tossed across the bed. My parents stood with their backs to the wall, mouths open, expressions confused. A woman stood in front of them, holding a large knife. Not a woman. A girl.

I could see her face clearly—a face like my mother's, but younger. So much younger. She couldn't have been more than thirteen, her hips just slightly curved, her face full. Her vicious smile and dead eyes jarred incongruously with her baby-like features.

I needed to stop watching, needed to tear my gaze away, but I couldn't. Even if I could free myself from the mayors' rigid grasps, I wouldn't be able to stop staring. I had to see what had *really* happened. All these years, I'd been so certain my father had ruthlessly slaughtered my mom, and now I needed the truth. I needed to know.

The girl—Siofra—was talking, pointing the knife. My dad was talking back, looking scared and angry. And then he lunged for the knife.

As he did, my mother screamed. I couldn't hear her voice, but her words had been seared into my soul for a long time, and I could see her lips form the words. *Horace, Don't!*

My heart slammed against my ribs, so hard I was sure Siofra could hear it.

The girl's hand moved fast, so fast. Grabbing my father's wrist, pulling him closer. Their eyes met. For a moment, it almost looked as if she was about to hug him.

I stared as little Siofra lunged past him, plunging the knife into my mother's chest. I let out a sob as my mother's mute face twisted in pain. Blood sprayed from her chest, covering the girl. My father's bulging eyes suggested a heart attack. Aghast, he wrapped his arms around my mother to keep her from falling.

While he gripped onto my mother, gently lowering her to the ground, Siofra reared back the knife again, and thrust it into his neck. He collapsed, my mother's limp body falling along with him. Blood pumped hard from my father's throat, arcing over the floor, the bed. His eyes were wide, shocked. Still alive. My mother clutched her chest, gasping for breath. Siofra had missed her heart, I knew. She had punctured her lung, instead.

The girl crouched down, then grabbed my father's hand, wrapping his fingers around the knife's handle. Just then, the life went out of my dad's eyes, and his head slumped to the side, fingers limp on the knife's hilt.

Monsters aren't real, princess.

They are, Daddy, but you didn't raise one. You simply spawned one.

Grief ripped me apart. Tears were flowing down my cheeks, and my body shook. All these years…

The investigators should have realized that this wasn't a murder suicide. My father's autopsy should have uncovered the bruises on his wrist. A skilled crime scene technician would have observed the traces Siofra had left behind. The angle of the knife thrust was all wrong, too low for a grown man to have done it.

But no one cared enough. My father had been struggling with some mental illness. Depression, perhaps. He didn't sleep well, and had to take pills. I remembered overhearing my parents arguing. He'd nearly lost his job after lashing out at a coworker, the result of weeks of insomnia.

An unstable man, medicated. History of personal problems. The classic scapegoat. Murder-suicide, and a daughter who'd hate him for years to come. An open-and-shut case.

The mayors' fingers tightened on my shoulders, pulling me out of the nightmare. "And where is the great Cassandra Liddell?" Their singsong voices giggled in my ear, eerily high-pitched. "About to storm in and save her parents? Or maybe just call the hospital? Ooooh!" Some of the mayors clapped their hands. "Your mother moved. She's still alive! Maybe if you move fast enough, you can save her! How will it end, Cassandra?" The mayors' eyes flashed with excitement, then they pouted. "But you know how it ends, don't you?"

Sorrow and shame gnawed at my chest, and the reflection changed, shimmering to show me a teenager's room. Messy, a backpack dumped out on the green carpet, a half-finished art project on the floor. And under the bed, a blond girl, shutting her eyes, her hands on her ears, trembling in fear.

I didn't try to save my mother. Didn't get help. I had just lain there, until someone came.

"Awww. Little Cassandra didn't want to help." The mayors pouted. "Maybe she liked all the fear her parents were feeding her. Too good to interrupt that rush, wasn't it? That's when you learned your dark little secret. That you got off on terror, that you'd rather soak it up then save those you love. Because the truth is, Cassandra, monsters can't really love. You know that, don't you?"

The mayors let go of me, and I sank to my knees, the memories of that night swirling through my skull, poisoning my mind like acrid smoke. I tried to block out the memory of that sound my mother had made when that knife had punctured her lung—a wheeze, a gurgle—but the sound hammered in my skull. A sharp tendril of sorrow coiled through me, threatening to break me. *Monsters can't really love.*

Siofra stroked my hair from behind me. "My parents should have known." She spoke in her light, singsong voice. But this time, it was just one voice, not eight. "As soon as they looked at you, they should have known that someone had taken their baby. Their little girl. They left behind a monster. A creature of nightmares. A terror leech."

The fury burning through my blood nearly simmered away the pain of my broken bones. Slowly, I turned to look at her. She didn't look like the mayor anymore, but someone much younger, and almost exactly like my mother. The woman who'd told me bedtime stories and fixed my hair in the mornings, who'd brought me flat ginger ale when I'd been sick and put blankets over me when I'd slept on the sofa, who'd had the most beautiful laugh. Maybe they had the same features, but the expression was pure Siofra: a childish grin that never reached her eyes.

I looked at the mirror again. Siofra was showing me the same image: Little Cassandra, cowering under the bed.

"How does it feel?" Siofra giggled. "To know that you could have saved them, but didn't? That you hid underneath the bed, a coward?"

"I was just thirteen," I said through gritted teeth.

"So was I, and look what I managed to do. I changed everything for them."

I stared at the girl under the bed, her eyes wide, body shaking. For the first time, I had an inkling of how *young* I'd been. I hadn't known what had been happening in the next room, or why I could feel their fear coursing through my veins. I hadn't known anyone was dying. I knew something terrifying was happening: a brutal argument between adults, noises I couldn't explain, and emotions I didn't understand.

Siofra raised her eyebrows, all innocence. "You could have saved them."

"You could have *not killed* them." And in one sharp motion, I pulled my collar to reveal the crystal that Alvin had given me.

CHAPTER 32

*H*er eyes widened as she saw the crystal. "Oh."

I took a step toward her, rage igniting my veins like a volcano.

"Please, Goddess," she fumbled back. "Forgive me. I'll do anything."

I took another step, blazing with fury. "You killed my parents."

She averted her eyes. "I didn't know they were the Goddess's parents."

"Now you do."

"What would you want me to do, Goddess? I can atone for my sins. I'll do anything you want to repent. I'll flay myself."

There was something in her voice that made me hesitate. A certain tone...

Lightning-fast, her hand shot out and she reached for the crystal, snapping the cord around my neck. Grinning, she held it up to her eyes. The breath left my lungs. That had been my plan. My one and only plan.

"Perhaps I should make a sacrifice to you, *Goddess?*" She

295

pivoted, hurling the crystal though the reflection. "Oops. I seem to have lost your trinket."

Shit shit shit. Still, it wasn't over yet. I crouched, grasping for my knife in my boot, but as my fingers curled around the hilt, my own reflection crawled from underneath the bed, out through the glass, moving at the speed of a storm wind. My heart slammed against my ribs as I rose.

But the reflection—Little Cassandra—was already grasping for my hand with frozen fingers. She twisted my wrist until I cried in pain, dropping the knife. In horror, I stared as a second Little Cassandra crawled from the reflection.

"*That* was your plan?" Siofra asked in her childlike voice. "You thought you could control me with a bauble?" Biting her lip, her face all innocence, she crossed to me.

Her expression darkened, and she slapped me hard.

"Is that what you thought? That you could defeat me with a trinket from a gutter fae, you worthless bitch? I will end you." Darkness slid through her eyes.

Pain wracked my body from the beating I'd taken, the broken ribs and the cracked leg bone. The Little Cassandras pressed their icy fingers into my flesh, jabbing at my cracked ribs.

Siofra shook her head. "So disappointing. You stole my life. And you're pathetic." Her features had shifted, now vicious, snarling. "You *wasted* it!"

Reflections shimmered around us: moments from my own life flickering in the mirrors. My pulse raced as I stared at them. All the reflections starred Siofra. Siofra going to the zoo with my parents, squealing excitedly when she saw the giraffes; Siofra at her sixth birthday, clapping her hands glee-fully at the red bike she'd always wanted; Siofra aged eleven, dressed as a vampire, trick or treating, collecting candy; Siofra having her first kiss with Ryan Mahoney in the back of the movie theater, then wiping the drool off on the back of her hand; Siofra and Scarlett, drunk in a Dunkin' Donuts on St. Patrick's day, wearing stupid green hats, with donut jelly on their chins, and Scarlett threatening to pee on their floor if they wouldn't let her use the employee bathroom. Dozens of memories, shimmering over the mirrors.

"I want my life back, Cassandra! That was my life you stole." Her voice was high-pitched, hysterical. She was no longer in control. "I should have been Cassandra Liddell. I *was* Cassandra Liddell until you stole my life, drowned me in grief." Her cheeks were pink, and spittle flew from her mouth as she spoke. "Rich man, poor man, beggar man, thief!"

She was losing it, no longer in control of the images, and yet they played on behind her, taking on a life of their own. As rage consumed her, her mind simply leaked into the mirrors. Her bond with the reflections was so complete, they'd become part of her. When she was emotional, her own thoughts began to spill onto those reflections.

How could I use that?

My body aching, battered, I struggled against the Little Cassandras, desperately trying to think of how I could use Siofra's reflections and emotions against her.

Think Cassandra. Think through the fury. What did I know about her? She felt abandoned, robbed of a life she deserved. Forced to grow up as a slave in the Rix's household, yet strangely loyal to him. What did that mean? She must have been desperate for his attention, for his love. Starved of affection, vying for it even after his death. Still trying to imitate him, to impress him. I'd robbed her of the chance of getting his approval.

"I didn't rob you of a family," I said. "You had the Rix. He raised you. He taught you."

Her body began to shake. "And you took him from me

too. Because of course, Cassandra Liddell had to take everything from me." The visions in the mirrors disappeared as she got her emotions under control.

One of the Little Cassandras grabbed my throat. She squeezed, and I struggled for air.

I elbowed her in the gut, knocking her off. "You can have him back!" I shouted. "The Rix still exists!"

The Cassandras were at my throat again, squeezing, fingers like shards of ice.

Siofra curled her lip in distaste. "I'm done playing, Cassandra. Fun's over. Your time is up."

Frantically, I thrashed, freeing myself from the Cassandras' frigid grasps. "Check it out." I gasped. "His soul... captured in the knife."

Slowly, the Little Cassandras relaxed their icy grips. Siofra frowned at the knife on the floor. "One last game?" she trilled. "You know, the iron won't hurt me. Unlike you, I'm human."

"Not a trick. Not a game." I rubbed my throat, swallowing hard. "Pick up the knife. See for yourself."

One of the Little Cassandras kicked the knife over to Siofra. Narrowing her eyes at me, she crouched and picked it up.

The effect was immediate. Her face softened, and she stared at the blade in amazement. A girlish smile brightened her features. "It *is* him," she whispered. "He's alive!"

Around us, the mirrors flickered to life again. Memories of Siofra and the Rix materialized everywhere. The two of them, eating dinner at a round table beneath a willow tree. Siofra walking behind him on a gleaming Trinovantum Street, as other fae cowered before him, bowing low. The Rix, seen from below, staring up at the stars,

Tears shimmered in her eyes as she stared at the knife. "My King."

I searched at the visions, searching for something I could use.

The Rix sitting in a throne-like chair by a hearth, and Siofra handing him a goblet. The Rix whipping a woman in a cellar, while Siofra looked on with fascination. The Rix walking briskly down a hallway, and Siofra hurrying after him.

Those were her fondest memories of him, and he didn't show the tiniest spark of warmth in any of them.

I stared at her, taking in her reverence for the knife. "He didn't really care about you, did he?"

Her gaze darted to me, anger burning through the tears. *"He cared."*

"Really? *My* parents kissed me before I went to bed. They hugged me in the morning. They bought me presents—"

"He bought me..." She heaved a sob. "You have no right... he gave me..." She could hardly talk, her entire body tense, her face crumbling. The mirrors flared to life, showing me her grief.

Burning into the mirrors was an image of the Rix, handing her a doll.

She was crying, a little mop-haired three-year-old, desperate for attention. Hiccupping, her chest heaving in irregular breaths, dirt or food smeared around her mouth. She sat on a stone floor, and he turned to shout at her, his voice mute in the reflection. And then, as an afterthought, he grabbed a wooden toy that lay discarded on his desk, some sort of carved doll with hollow eyes, and threw it at her.

He missed, or maybe he didn't really mean to hit her, and the doll landed by her side. She wiped her tears off on the back of her hand, smeared the mucus from her nose with her tiny fingers, and picked it up.

All around the hall, the mirrors shimmered with different memories. Siofra going to sleep, curled up and clutching the wooden doll. Siofra in a garden, whispering in the doll's ear. Siofra pretending to spoon-feed her doll. Siofra crying in the corner of her room, hugging her doll hard.

And in the corner of the hall, a mirror reflected a memory that snagged my attention. The Rix, towering over her by a blazing hearth, shouting. A young Siofra, maybe seven years old, still clutching that wooden doll. The Rix snatched it from her hands and tossed it into the burning fireplace. Siofra ran for the fireplace, trying to grab for it in the flames, screaming as her hands burned. She couldn't get the doll. It was too late, and she fell back onto the stone floor, sobbing.

My heart tightened, ached for the little girl. I know what she'd become. And this was why. Tears streamed down Siofra's cheeks, and mine too.

But if I wanted to survive this, I had to be ruthless. I had to be a monster, just for now.

I felt for the reflections around me, no longer blocked. Siofra's attention was too intent on the knife, too subsumed by her own memories. Closing my eyes, I forced the mirrors to all display the same memory.

The Rix shouting, snatching the doll, tossing it into the fire. Siofra, reaching for her beloved toy the one thing she cared for, not able to save it. Fingers burning. Battling between love and self-preservation. All around the hall, the mirrors replayed her memory. Her failure. Her torment.

"What did he give you, Siofra?" I asked, wiping a tear from my cheek. "A doll? You mean the one he threw at you? The one he *burned*? Did he really even like you? Did he ever show you a single moment of genuine warmth?"

"Shut up!" she shrieked. "He... he did love me! He was very strict, but he... he..."

The memories poured over the mirrors.

The Rix turning his back in the midst of Siofra talking. The Rix, slamming the door to his study as she was approaching it. The Rix leaving his castle, while Siofra watched him leave from her window.

In every memory, he turned away from her, left her behind.

She was sobbing now, still looking at the knife, muttering. "He *did* love me. He *did*."

The images flickered again, showing the Rix smiling at a young woman, ignoring Siofra. Crumpling up a drawing she'd made, his lip curled in a sneer. More memories, dozens of Siofra sitting alone, in large, empty castle rooms, eyes increasingly hollow, the life slowly dimming from them.

A flicker caught my attention outside the windows, and I turned my gaze, the breath leaving my lungs. Her memories were flickering outside, dancing in puddles, shimmering over the Thames. Across the river, I could see glimmers of color, dancing over the buildings' windowpanes

How many mirrors and windows displayed Siofra's memories out there?

Siofra held the knife to her cheek. "Say something," she whispered. "Talk to me."

Outside, the visions were disappearing from the windows and river, shimmering away, one by one. Siofra's magic was draining, the effort of manipulating so many reflections taxing even her.

One of the Little Cassandras holding me disappeared into thin air, while the other's grip wavered. Outside, the river reflected only the sky, and the mirror in the hall shimmered returned to normal in the street. And all around the hall, the mirrors began to reflect the world, and not Siofra's mind.

The icy fingers gripping me dissipated, and only one mirror still displayed a memory. The Rix, sneering at something Siofra was saying. And then it shimmered away, and showed only her. Burnt out. Her own magic was completely spent.

The images of her life had sickened me, and grief welled in my chest. "I'm sorry," I whispered.

She raised her glistening eyes. "You stole my life! Of course you did. Took my place after you were born twisted. A monster."

Slowly, I shook my head. "Monsters aren't born, Siofra. They're created."

As quickly as I could, I bonded with the half-dome reflection, feeling it click with my mind. Siofra charged at me, and I moved aside, grabbing her arm. I threw my weight onto her, using her own momentum to fling her at one of the mirrors. Along with her, I plunged through, feeling the reflection slide over my skin, ice cold.

For a fraction of a second, we lingered in the world between reflections, everything sluggish, my own powers still drained.

I let go of Siofra's hand and moved through the other mirror, slipping out through City Hall's reflective windows, leaving her behind.

As I slid through the chilling reflection, I turned my head to look back, and saw her. Frozen between reflections, her power drained, unable to push through. Her eyes were wide open, terrified, and my throat tightened.

The mirror shimmered, and she disappeared from view. I'd survived—I'd stopped the monster. And yet, at the thought of her trapped there, like an insect in a drop of amber, a hollow had opened in the pit of my stomach.

I glanced at the two joggers—the couple who'd been trapped by the dancing plague. They lay, on the ground, moaning, catching their breath, rubbing their muscles.

Siofra was gone, and the plague was over.

CHAPTER 33

I paused outside Gabriel's flat near Brick Lane, staring at the bright blue door by the gardening shop. I'd lived just upstairs in his home for over a week, walking freely in and out. But I couldn't just stride in now, even if I still had a key. After a moment's hesitation, I pushed his buzzer.

The intercom crackled to life. "Hello?"

Gabriel's voice was cut off by a squawking behind him. "My nipples are pulsing with delight! Squawk!"

I bit down on the urge to laugh, and said. "It's Cassandra."

"One minute."

I heard the stairs creak on the other side of the door as Gabriel descended—along with high-pitched squawks. A few moments later, a flustered Gabriel opened the door.

From Gabriel's shoulder, Odin fluttered his wings. "Betraying wetness! Nevermore."

I quirked an eyebrow. "Is it a bad time? Seems like you have company."

He frowned at me. "It's all your fault. The Ravenmaster at the Tower refused to take him back."

"Sorry."

"He was also under the impression that he was acting at the will of a divine Goddess of Dread. Do you know anything about that?"

I blinked innocently. "Sounds like a nut job."

"Is that your official diagnosis?"

"Absolutely. My professional opinion."

"The spooks stopped asking about you. How'd you manage that?" The late afternoon light washed his skin in gold, glinting off his hazel eyes.

"Scarlett convinced them I was working for her as a fae informant. A spy from the dark side. They took my clearance away, though, of course."

"I see. And to what do I owe the pleasure of this visit? I wasn't expecting to see you."

I shrugged. "I just came to say thanks. And goodbye."

He frowned, taking a deep breath. "You're going back to the states?"

"Not exactly." He'd flip if I told him I was going to Trino-vantum to honor my promise to Roan. "But I'll be gone for a while, I think."

"I see. Well, check in with me again soon, let me know you're all right. You're a magnet for chaos, you know that? I don't want to have to worry about you."

I blinked away the tears of gratitude. "Sure. Thanks."

"The attacks stopped, completely. And the deputy mayor is really doing a good job so far. But if I had to guess, you probably knew all that."

"I had a hunch."

"You wouldn't happen to know where the actual mayor is?"

"Are you asking as DCI Stewart, or just as Gabriel?"

He stared at me. "Which of them would get a straight answer?"

I quirked a smile. "The mayor was colluding with the fae, Gabriel. She was behind the attacks. I've dealt with her."

His eyes widened. "You killed her?"

"No. But she can't hurt anyone else."

"Colluding… was she human?"

"Yes, but she could use magic. It's complicated."

"Right." He sighed. "Everything is."

The sad glint in his eyes killed me. I took a step closer and wrapped my arms around him, hugging him tightly. "Thanks for being so amazing," I whispered.

He wrapped his arms around me, and I breathed in his clean, soapy scent. From his shoulder, Odin puffed his wings, and Gabriel pulled away from the hug.

I nodded. "Right. So… I'll be in touch."

"Wait." He hurried after me, pulling Odin from his shoulder. "Take him. He's yours."

"I can't take care of a bird."

He smiled. "I guess you shouldn't have broken into the Tower of London and stolen him, then."

Sighing, I gently pulled the raven from his hand. Odin flapped his clipped wings angrily and I let go. He jumped up, settling on my shoulder.

Gabriel looked at the bird with regret, his brow furrowed. "Well, if you really can't take care of him—"

"Thrust your manhood into me! Squawk! Nevermore!"

Gabriel shook his head. "Nope. Get him out of my sight."

I grinned and turned away, as Odin squawked sweet nothings into my ear.

* * *

My second stop was the hospital, and I walked through the white-walled trauma ward on my way to find Scarlett. When I'd arrived downstairs at the hospital, I'd been relieved to find that no one else danced outside the hospital entrance. Even so, the raven on my shoulder had posed an instant problem. I'd had to leave him with an old man in a wheel-chair who sat outside, smoking, muttering about turnips. Fifty pounds to look after the raven, and another fifty when I returned. This damned raven was already more expensive than I'd anticipated.

When I reached the room labeled 324, I crossed through the door. Scarlett lay on a bed in a room divided by a blue curtain, her auburn hair spread out over the pillow, her face wan.

"Hey, you," she said, her words slurring a bit. "Nice of you to drop by."

"Are you okay?" I asked.

"I'm super." She gave me a thumbs-up. "They're pumping me full of painkillers. It's the best. Right, Jeeves?"

A London-accented voice from the other side of the curtain called out, "My name's not Jeeves."

I leaned over, hugging her as gently as I could. Then, I pulled out a small bottle of Glenlivet from my handbag, leaving it on the table next to her. "For when you're feeling better. Don't mix it with the pain meds."

"You bring the best get-well presents," she said.

I smiled. Then I mouthed, *are we listened to?*

She shrugged, wincing in pain as she did. "Probably."

I glanced around the room. The CIA didn't even have to hide a bug here. They could be tapping Scarlett's phone. I definitely didn't trust them enough to speak candidly about anything. "Well... you'll never guess who I ran into. Remember that girl from our college, who looked just like my mother?"

"Oh, yeah, you met her here? How is she doing?"

"Not so hot, really. Got fired from her job, and is currently kind of stuck. In limbo, you know?"

Scarlett smiled. "Never liked her anyway. And Elrine?"

"She's fine."

"Oh, good. I was worried about her. She seemed so fragile."

"Stronger than you'd think. So, what's next for you?"

"I'll be staying here for a week or two, I think. There have been some interesting developments."

I raised my eyebrow. "Anything you can tell me about?"

She shook her head. "Sorry. Highly confidential. And you don't have clearance anymore. Fulton is completely against working with you. You really managed to piss him off."

I huffed a laugh at the thought of Fulton pissing in the chief's plant.

"What?" Scarlett asked.

"Oh, nothing. I'll tell you some other time." I heaved a sigh. "Look, Scarlett, I'm going for a while. But I'll be in contact, okay?"

"Sure, Cass. Do what you gotta do."

"Love you."

"Love you. And be careful." She mouthed something, but I couldn't quite make out what she was saying.

I frowned, leaning closer. With her eyes locked on mine, she mouthed it again, her lips moving slowly. It took me a moment to take in what she was saying to me, and I when I did, a shiver inched up my spine.

A war is coming.

* * *

I FALTERED in the snowy forest, clinging tightly to my damp jacket, my fingers numb. I'd come prepared for my trip to Trinovantum, but I'd still ended up soaked and freezing. It had taken two days to find Roan's cabin in Trinovantum, and

I could now see it between the oaks, candlelight flickering through the round windows.

Two days, and fatigue sapped my body, cut me to the bone. I'd needed to move at night, to slip out of the city walls, circumventing the populated areas. If I hadn't, my pixie aura would have brought fae mobbing me like a swarm of locusts.

Even as I'd moved through the Hawkwood Forest, I'd needed to escape inquisitive fae twice by leaping into the reflections in my dwindling supply of hand mirrors. As a result, my wool winter coat was now frigid and damp from the icy ponds I'd crawled out of. And as I'd moved deeper into the Hawkwood Forest, icicles had formed around my collar, my breath misting in clouds around my face. My teeth chattered uncontrollably. Even through the snow, hemlock grew wildly from the forest floor, the white blossoms beautiful, delicate, and poisonous. They sent a shiver up my spine.

But I was almost there, almost to the delicious promise of warmth. Candlelight dancing in the windows. A hint of smoke coming from the chimney. God, I just wanted to peel off my icy clothes and warm myself on the hearth. I just had no idea what Roan was going to say when I got there, and I could only pray he wasn't going to turn me out again into the frozen forest.

I crossed to the door, my body shivering, and knocked twice, pressing my ear to it to listen for sounds of movement.

Nothing.

I knocked again, hugging myself tightly, and listened.

Nothing.

My fingertips had turned red, with white circles around the tips. The first signs of frostbite. I couldn't stay out here a moment longer.

I pushed through the door, finding the hall empty—just the tree growing in the center of the room, its boughs arched around the walls, twinkling with lights.

Embers in the fireplace glowed orange. I threw my backpack on the floor, and pulled off my coat, laying it on the hearth. A soft blanket lay on Roan's sofa—that would do. I'd come prepared with changes of clothes, but of course, they'd come through the water with me, too. I was too cold and exhausted to care about modesty at this point, anyway. I pulled off my boots, then slipped out of my icy, damp black shirt and jeans, hanging them on hooks just over the fireplace. When I continued to shiver, I stripped off my bra and panties and hung them up, too, then quickly pulled the blanket around me, teeth chattering. The soft, green blanket felt amazing against my skin. With the blanket around my shoulders, I managed to get the fire going again, using some pieces of paper by the fireplace to ignite the flames again from the embers. When it roared to life again, I sat in front of it for a few minutes, letting my body thaw.

Before leaving to find Roan, I'd entrusted Odin to a bird sanctuary just outside London, and I couldn't help but wonder how he was faring, or how many people he was shocking with his filthy romance quotes. I kind of missed the bastard and wanted to get him back as soon as I was done here.

As I stared into the fire, my stomach rumbled. When was the last time I'd eaten? All the cereal in my bag had become completely waterlogged and inedible.

Clutching the blanket around me, I crossed to the pantry through a set of leafy, arched boughs.

When I pushed through the door into the pantry, I found a basket with six eggs, a large slab of meat, some dried mushrooms, and a glass jar of flour. I took the supplies inside a metal kettle to the main room. My gaze landed on the eggs, and I stared, an idea percolating in the back of my mind.

Over the past few days, I'd had time to think. I'd gotten used to the idea that my father, whom I had loathed for years, was innocent. On the two-day journey, I'd spent half the time crying for him, and for my mother, their lives cut short in the most brutal way. I'd also had time to think about the fact that my parents' killer was a girl who had been taken from her home and abused until she'd grown into a monster. I wasn't sure if she might have died there, trapped in the mirror world, but if she lived, she was now trapped in Hell.

But I still struggled with the idea that the Liddells weren't my biological parents. Why did it matter? I didn't know. What mattered was who raised you, not who spawned you. Surely Siofra and I were proof of that. I was born a terror leech, and the parents who'd raised me had taught me to love. Siofra was born human, but had twisted into a monster over time.

And yet, I had to know for sure. Despite everything I told myself, the idea of being the Rix's biological daughter sickened me. And now, I had no idea who my biological mother was—but what if Siofra had gotten it wrong?

As I stared at the eggs, I formed a plan. Maybe there was a chance...

I dropped the blanket for this.

I cracked an egg into a bowl, and put water in the metal kettle. I filled the two eggshell halves with some water, flour and a piece of meat in each. Then, I placed them in the water. One sunk immediately, but the other one floated daintily on the water's surface.

Before crossing back into the main room, I pulled the blanket around me, and grabbed the kettle. Careful not to disrupt my broth, I hung the kettle from a hook in the top of the fireplace, wrapped myself back in the blanket, and waited for my stew to boil.

Alvin's cheerful voice laughed in my mind. *Did you ever try to boil stew in a couple of eggshells? You should try it. It's fucking hilarious.*

In the presence of eggshell stew, a changeling will burst out laughing, or shed her glamour. Thus said the internet, and the internet is never wrong.

Holding tight to my blanket, I watched the water start bubbling in the kettle, the eggshell bobbing in the small eddies of the water. Its contents began to sizzle as well.

I felt nothing. And that proved—nothing. It was a ridiculous test. Absolutely stupid. Boiling stew in an eggshell? What sort of insane nonsense was this? I laughed to myself.

And kept laughing. The laughter bubbled from me uncontrollably, and there was nothing I could do to stop it. I fell to the floor, convulsing with laughter, the blanket falling from my body. Tears streamed from my eyes, and my stomach hurt from the endless laughter. The tears just kept spilling down my cheeks, staining the floor, and I couldn't be sure if they were tears of laughter… or tears of grief.

I was the Rix's daughter. My father was a monster, and I'd killed him. I was the reason my real parents had died—the people who'd raised me, the Liddells. When they'd given birth to a perfectly normal human baby, the fae had stolen in, snatched her, and replaced her with an unwanted baby, an abomination, a pixie. And that abomination was me. The tears, the gasps of laughter—it just wouldn't stop.

I finally stopped laughing, and then just lay there, feeling empty and drained. Exhausted, I pulled the blanket back around me, wiping the tears from my eyes.

The floor creaked, and I opened my eyes. Roan was there, staring down at me, his expression a mixture of shock and irritation.

"Something funny?"

"No." I sat up. "Nothing is, really."

He crouched down, meeting my gaze. "The king attacked the Sluagh. Dozens died. The rest are in hiding. With every incursion into the Hawkwood Forest, he grows in strength."

"I'm sorry. I had responsibilities here."

Warm firelight danced over his skin. "You could have stopped it."

I shook my head. "No, I couldn't. I had another battle to fight, Roan. I stopped Siofra from hurting a lot of people."

He traced his fingertips over the edge of the blanket. "Are you going to explain why I found you in here, laughing and naked?"

My cheeks burned. "My clothes were frozen." Tears welled in my eyes. "And as it turns out, I'm a changeling."

He wiped one of the tears from my cheeks, then pulled his hand away, standing up. "You broke your promise."

"No, I didn't. I'm here. I'm willing to do what I can to help."

"Good. Because soon, we'll need all the help we can get."

"Why?"

"War is coming." For a moment, Roan's eyes flickered to gold.

Even as I stared at the roaring fire, its flames gilding the hearth, a chill ran up my spine. It was the same thing Scarlett had said to me, and dread bloomed in my chest like the flowering hemlock.

ACKNOWLEDGMENTS

We'd like to thank Alex's lovely wife Liora for her amazing notes and for being a superhero.

Our cover designer, Clarissa did another fantastic job.

And finally, we'd like to thank our wonderful editors, Elayne and Izzy.

ABOUT

Alex Rivers is the co-author of the Dark Fae FBI Series. In the past, he's been a journalist, a game developer, and the CEO of the company Loadingames. He is married to a woman who diligently forces him to live his dream, and is the father of an angel, a pixie, and a gremlin. He has two voracious hounds that wag their tail quite menacingly at anyone who comes near his home.

Alex has been imagining himself fighting demons and vampires since forever. Writing about it is even better, because he doesn't get bitten, or tormented in hell, or even just muddy. In fact, he does it in his slippers.

Alex also writes crime thrillers under the pen name Mike Omer.

You can contact Alex by sending him an email to alex@strangerealm.com.

C. N. Crawford is sometimes two people—a married couple named Christine and Nick. But for the Dark Fae FBI series, it's just Christine. Christine grew up in New England and has a lifelong interest in local folklore—with a particular fondness for creepy old cemeteries. She is a psychologist who spent eight years in London obsessively learning about its history, and misses it every day.

Please join us here to talk about books, fantasy, and writing   updates!
https://www.facebook.com/groups/cncrawford/

https://www.facebook.com/groups/cncrawford/
riverscrawford@strangerealm.com